PAPER CUT HEARTS

A collection of short stories

PAPER CUT HEARTS

A.M. KHALIFA

MAVENHILL

SYDNEY•LOS ANGELES•ROME

For every soul in perpetual forward motion,
for every butterfly and for every phoenix.

Mulier. Corpus. Vita.

THE EGYPTIAN AFFAIR

When you pay a man to commit a crime on your behalf, the only thing you're possibly avoiding is getting caught. Feelings of guilt and ineptitude will ravage you from the inside just as if you had done it yourself. Even before you get the confirmation call, your hands will feel tainted with blood, your eyes dry and gritty, your bowels rotting on the inside, and the weight of a massive boulder crushing down your chest. With your moral compass vaporized, sleep will elude you and that alone can drive a man off the edge. Peace of mind becomes a distant memory of another life lost forever.

I should know—I paid a man to kill on my behalf.

I had no other option. Cornered like a wounded bull, I charged back in self-defense to avoid a fatal thrust to my heart. Levelheadedness and rational choice were the extravagances of the men yet to walk in the shoes of a betrayed husband.

But things weren't always this bleak for me. I used to sleep like a baby on his mother's bosom every night. I too remember when I could judge the despicable actions of other men from an elevated moral ground.

Once-upon-a-lifetime ago I felt like the luckiest man alive.

Long before I was married, I thought I had it all figured out. I held strong opinions and theories on love and relationships, including how a man should react if he discovers his wife is cheating on him. You must confront her quick to suck out the air that fuels illicit sex. The longer you wait in the background plotting, rotting or doing whatever it is betrayed husbands inevitably do, the more you'll suffer.

Just look the cheating cow in the eye and declare your marriage over in cold, calculated words. Then bolt as far away as possible from her and restart your life. Forget drama—only cowards extort retribution for infidelity.

Real men move on.

When I was young and stupid, these were my simplistic views on how infidelity must be dealt with.

All that changed, however, two months ago when I discovered my wife Molly was cheating on me. Whatever foolish idealism I had been clasping on to for pure comfort fizzled out, leaving behind a single, terrifying desire to kill the bitch and her wretched lover, and, above all, to get away with it.

My father, Baba, was a crusty old bastard. He had no shortage of jaded wisdom to impart on me and my three younger brothers. While normal fathers may have counseled their sons on how to be good husbands, or even future fathers, the only piece of advice Baba cared to dole out on my wedding night was how to protect my honor at any cost and make sure my wife never made a cuckold out of me.

Contrary to common wisdom, he'd told me, the first sign your wife is sleeping around is not when she stops wanting to make love to you, but quite the opposite. Cheating women bring back new tricks to the bedroom either out of guilt or for the thrill of finding out exactly how half-witted their husbands are. Maybe even both, he said.

"As for you, son, it's entirely normal to lust for new flesh after many years with the same woman. You'll become like siblings, stripped of the sweetens of physical desire and the animalistic hunger and yearning of fresh love."

My eyes widened as I considered what he was about to sanction.

"It's natural!" he boomed in my face laughing. "We're built like that. Us men, we need to have a little on the side, as long as it doesn't destroy our marriage."

"You're telling me it's okay to cheat on my wife? On my wedding night?"

"Cheating, bleating—what a loaded word! Remember this son, the only real sin would be if you slept with another married woman."

"How's that any different? How's that any more wrong?"

"Because you'd be backstabbing another man, that's how. It goes against the code of honor."

Baba explained everything with sardonic conviction while he fixed my tie. He could have been instructing an inexperienced farmhand on how to train a sheep dog or breaking a work-horse.

"That being said, if your desire for more than one woman is persistent, the right thing to do is to marry another one. And provided you can afford it, you can marry up to four women."

With a pat on my face and a kiss on my forehead, as if to enshrine his main hypothesis, he looked me straight in the eye and said, "Show me a modest or frigid woman in bed who starts to behave like a whore with her husband, and I'll show you a cheating wife. Never forget that, son."

After nine years of a blissful marriage, I had shelved Baba's advice to the deepest recesses of my mind. That is, until Molly gave me an unexpected gift and everything changed forever.

It all started last May during one of the hottest summers on record. Desperate to escape the heat wave engulfing Cairo, we left work well before midday on a Thursday to drive up for a long weekend at our gated beach home on the north coast of Egypt. *Our little slice of heaven,* as we called it, was perched on the golden sands facing the crystal waters between Alexandria and El Alamein.

Schools hadn't let out for vacation yet, so we owned the road up north, singing along to old Om Kalthoum love songs playing on the radio, while we nibbled on Bulgarian feta cheese sandwiches and slices of cold watermelon Molly had prepared.

Only the occasional trucks crossing over to the wrong lane to cut illegal U-turns sullied what would have been an otherwise perfect road trip. Damned truckers stoned out of their heads on cheap hashish.

At around midday we reached our destination, welcomed by the guards at the gate baking under the blazing sun, waving with mechanical courtesy, deprived of even a perfunctory canopy for protection.

We dropped our bags at the staircase of our beachfront villa and opened the windows to allow the crisp Mediterranean air to circulate inside. Molly prepared some towels and I grabbed a few cold beers from the fridge.

Hands entwined, we raced to the beach to see who was brave enough to take the first plunge. Molly won, of course. The cyan water dissolved the week-long stress in our bodies like effervescent tablets, with hardly the need to acclimatize to the near-perfect temperature of the sea.

Never did an awkward silence dampen the mood between us. Nine years of marriage, and Molly and I were still best friends, even soul mates.

She relished my office gossip, especially the drama of the social tension bubbling between our overpaid engineers who leached on the company, and the underpaid blue collars who actually did the work. Not to mention the religious animosity between the crescents and the crosses. Our workplace was no different from the country. A tenacious patriarchy that still unfairly rewarded older men and took advantage of young women. Lurking in the shadows, a thriving underground ecosystem of extramarital affairs and sexual conquests was—and perhaps counterintuitively—blind to class, religion, gender and ages.

I never disappointed her, always delivering a salacious anecdote or two.

"Do you remember Samira?" I asked her of Baba's attractive secretary with ample curves and suggestive eyes whose husband had been paraplegic for years.

Molly nodded. "Of course. What's up with her?"

"There's a rumor she's sleeping with Zeyad."

"The baby-face your dad hired last year?"

I found it interesting how Molly remembered our good-looking Coptic accountant so effortlessly.

"Easy on the eyes, isn't he?"

"If you're a cradle snatcher, yeah. That kid's like twenty if I am stretching it. Samira has to be forty-nine, fifty, give or take?"

"I guess..."

She raised her eyes to the heavens, then down to the sparkling Mediterranean before a meaningful silence engulfed us. Something was revving up in that beautiful skull of hers, which I, of course, would never figure out on my own.

"Despite the age difference, she's an attractive, sensual woman with needs," she finally said.

7

Where the hell did that come from?

"Needs her disabled husband can't fulfill, is what you mean to say?"

She smiled as if I had saved her the trouble of explaining a complex algorithm.

"Why not divorce him on the grounds he can't satisfy her sexually? It's more honorable and sanctioned by the Koran."

Molly didn't seem swayed by my logic. "What if she still loves her husband but just craves the lovemaking? Have you considered that?"

"Come on, Molly—cheating? That's just low. If she divorces the wretched bastard, she'd be free to sleep around with every chap who fancied getting into her pants."

She pursed her lips into a perfectly straight line and knit her brow, but was a galaxy away from seeing things my way.

"Easy for us to say. Who knows what she's up against? Divorce comes at a price in our society, especially for a woman. With kids involved, it's even worse."

Her eyes shied away from mine, as if knowing I would never approve of what she was about to say.

"Maybe she's doing it with her husband's blessings?"

Her eyes were right.

There's never much to be won when a perfectly innocent discussion sours on differences in opinion. The whole point of this break was for us to relax, not argue deep moral issues.

"So how's your family?"

Molly smiled ruefully at my lame attempt to reroute the discussion away from a major collision. Still, her eyes suggested my question had stirred a different bitterness in her.

She bit her lips again then came clean. Her sister Lana and

her husband Ragi were forced to bring Ragi's father, Uncle Emad, to live with them. A widower of ten years, Uncle Emad's health had deteriorated rapidly over the past six months. Dementia was just one of his many ailments. He could no longer live alone, and Ragi didn't trust to leave his father in the care of a paid nurse. Because Lana was a copy writer who worked mostly from home, she volunteered to baby-sit him.

Ragi was a decent fellow. I respected the way he took care of his old man in his twilight years. A lesser soul would have dumped the old man in a nursing home.

"I don't think it's fair for Lana to take on this responsibility."

"Lana is a good kid. She's standing by her man," I said, thinking of how very unlikely it would be for Molly to make the same sacrifice for my own father. Not because she loved me any less than Lana loved Ragi, but because how little regard she had for my old man.

"I suppose you are right, though, but the deeper issue is..." Molly launched into a long missive about our patriarchal society and women's rights that didn't quite capture my attention.

Instead, my thoughts were severely distracted by the image of Molly's perfect body cutting lithely through the water. She had her mother's lush green eyes and abundant caramel hair now tied in a ponytail. Her peach bikini bottom was skimpy but she might as well not have worn it. It would have to take far more than a tiny piece of cloth to render Molly's perfectly rounded behind modest or irresistible.

As we spoke, she would come up to me to twiddle the hairs on my chest. The contrast of her milky body against my olive skin spurred a frenzy in me, and the way she bit her lips and smiled confirmed we were reading from the same dirty page.

She would swim away pretending to do laps, then circle back like a mermaid to plant salty kisses on my lips and nipples. I nibbled on her ears. And other places...

This went on for a while.

As far wide as we could see, the shoreline was empty, except for a lone security guard glued to a flimsy plastic chair at the other end of the beach. Now, if we were so inclined, we could have acted upon the fire she had started there and then, but I knew Molly would never take such a risk while we remained in the scope of vision of the sphinx-like security guard.

Eventually, the scorching sun or God almighty tipped the odds in our favor. The guard stood up and shuffled back to the compound to cool down or maybe to answer the call to prayer.

When he had faded to a tiny dot in the horizon, I made my move. I pulled my trunks down to my ankles and grabbed her towards me.

With a flick of a finger, I slid the tip of her bikini briefs to the edge and pushed hard inside of her as she wrapped her soft thighs tight around my body. She gasped and looked reflexively up to our maker with closed eyes.

Then she came fast.

Faster than I had ever known her to be able to.

She screamed louder than I'd ever heard her before.

Even the texture of her voice was unexpected, more carnal, more needy, more arousing.

I remained fused in her, hard as a rock, still caught off-guard by the quick turn of events. When she opened her eyes, I witnessed a sexual madness in them I had never known before.

A few seconds shy from putting out my own fire of

unfinished business burning in my loins, she withdrew quickly and unexpectedly.

Molly took me by the hand and pulled me out to the water's edge. With a swift move that left no margin for uncertainty, she slid down against my body and took me in her mouth.

Ever since we first got in a bed naked, Molly had drawn a big line when it came to what her mouth would or wouldn't do. Not that she was a prude. She had no qualms about sleeping with me just a few days after we met. Our life in the bedroom had never been short of tantalizing. We did it all. Except that. Not that I ever stopped trying. Or that she ever gave in.

I first met Molly at a pretentious conference on the 'social costs of economic growth,' held in the glitzy Red Sea town of Sharm El Sheikh. Like many emerging economies at the time, the Egyptian government was shamelessly in the market to ensnare wealthy bilateral donors and foreign investors. One could hardly keep count of all the mind-numbing events popping up across the country in the name of fuzzily termed panaceas such as 'synergy' and 'capacity-building.'

Molly was a socially conscious, American-trained pediatrician, invited by the organizers to probe the health impacts of mobile phone towers in urban centers. I, on the other hand, worked for our family-owned building materials conglomerate.

Just like the other young participants, Molly and I were on display to showcase the progressive face of the new Egypt. We were the young leaders of the country who spoke English without an accent, embraced technology and shunned radical ideology. We wore expensive Italian suits and drove reliable German cars.

Our political ambitions were nonexistent and we pleaded blind allegiance to our powerful patriarchs. When required, we could invoke fashionable intellectual concepts such as 'globalization' and 'good governance,' as if they were part of our genetic constitution. We could do what we wanted and get away with murder, so long as our actions were kept hidden from the public eye and that we didn't trample on the feet of our political masters.

Molly was eating lunch alone when I first noticed her.

I use 'beautiful' now to describe her, but that's owing to my limited vocabulary. She was far more than that. A vision. Not just of beauty, but of a future I instantly wanted to live.

Unable to conceive how a woman with her looks wasn't being hounded by anyone of the other red-blooded men in attendance, I jumped in hard without thinking of the odds. Mustering every ounce of confidence, I strode to her table.

"May I?" I asked in English as I pulled out a chair, certain she was foreign.

She studied me briefly then smiled like her creep-o-meter hadn't been triggered.

"Sure, but promise me something, champion," she responded in colloquial Arabic.

"Champion?" I smirked. "Sure, I promise, but what exactly am I promising?"

"On your life, not to mention the word 'synergy' while we're eating. I have a weak stomach as it is." She took the plate of smoked tuna and swordfish from my hand and placed it on the table.

By the end of the conference, we had become inseparable.

On the last night, she sneaked into my bed against the very

punishable offense in the land of unmarried locals sleeping in the same hotel room. We made love that wasn't even tempered by the morning call to prayer booming from a nearby mosque, or that just five hundred miles southeast of us in the Saudi city of Jeddah, the punishment for two unmarried people making love was one hundred lashes.

Within less than two business quarters, we were planning a wedding by the Nile.

Looking back at us now, marrying me must have been a huge leap of faith on her part. A sea of social chasms separated us. Molly's family was old money and traced its roots to the landed aristocrats who ruled Egypt in the early part of the twentieth century. She had Welsh, French and Turkish blood running proudly through her veins.

Our family, on the other hand, was new money and by God did it show. We hailed from the stock of peasants who'd moved to Cairo from the countryside in the fifties. One hundred years ago, my ancestors could have very well been the servants and peasants who worked for Molly's family.

My grandfather, or Geddo as we called him, was one of the farmers who'd reaped the benefits of Nasser's popular revolution. The charismatic president had promised Egyptians social, political and economic equality and we were a testament to his making good on that vow. Geddo worked hard as a farm attendant, and saved enough to buy a tiny haberdashery shop in a working-class neighborhood of Cairo. It wasn't much, but it allowed him to move the family from rural Egypt to the big city. It was a stroke of genius or blind luck, because by the time the seventies had rolled over, Geddo was there to capitalize on President Sadat's open-door socioeconomic policies, skyrocketing our family's destiny forever.

Geddo sold the shop and used the money to buy a medium-sized ceramics workshop up for sale. By the early nineties, my grandfather's gamble had paid off by leaps and bounds. The workshop had blossomed into a proper factory, and the factory eventually transformed into one of the country's biggest industrial complexes.

Whatever I lacked in breeding, I hoped would be offset by my family's untold wealth. When you lack quantifiable heritage, the best you can do to start diminishing the odds is a quality education and exquisite grooming for every successive generation. My own father barely made it through high school, but because he possessed the means and the will, he insisted my brothers and I earned degrees from top schools like Princeton, Oxford, Cambridge and Yale.

Maybe that's why Molly's parents finally caved in and agreed to have me as their son-in-law. I was certain it wasn't the money that dazzled them, but the faint hope my exterior veneer of a Westernized, educated young man, despite my under-refined family, would make me a somewhat less bitter prospect for Molly, who made no secret of how intent she was to fight for us.

As we lay naked on the beach under the amber hue of the afternoon sun, Molly licked me voraciously with her upper-class lips.

Peering down at her shimmering body, I glimpsed her face entranced, and that same insanity exuding from her eyes when we had started kissing in the water was now even more palpable.

Her lips were warm against my skin as she maintained a steady rhythm at first that escalated to a deep, animalistic crescendo. I tried hard to resist at first but finally gave up and erupted.

We drifted into a spiritual oblivion. Our sense of time and space was pulverized. We could have remained there for an eternity if it wasn't for the smoldering rays of the sun, the waves finally reaching our feet, and the ever-increasing hysterical cries of the seagulls.

When we finally woke up from our delicious slumber, I noticed the security guard shuffling back to his station with a parasol in one hand and a bottle of water in the other.

Giggling like a couple of reckless teens, we grabbed our swimming suits and jumped naked in the sea for one last dip.

My eyes must have betrayed my intention to ask her, "Why, after all those years?" Molly was quick to read my mind and put her finger on my lips to leave it unspoken, like she feared I'd ruin the spontaneity of what we had shared.

Back at home, as she prepared spaghetti with a *pesto* sauce and a baby spinach salad for dinner, I showered to wash away the salty water and tenacious sand granules, with nothing on my mind but the improbable events that had just transpired. At first, the predictable exhilaration of a man whose sex life had just taken on a more interesting turn kept me smiling. Before long, and like a derailed freight train of terrible demons, the dreadful thoughts about infidelity my father had poisoned me with came crashing in my mind.

From that day onwards, *nothing* I tried could exorcise them.

The first speck of doubt was borne of my intimate knowledge of how Molly operated. Being spontaneous simply wasn't her thing, not now, not ever. All my past requests for her mouth to do more than kiss me had been snubbed. The inexplicable motivation behind her changed imperative was an ever-deepening thorn in my side, slowly festering with the mental puss of insecurity.

While I had enjoyed every last lick of her unexpected gift, it was the unsolicited nature of her actions that kept flaming the doubt raging in my soul.

Then there was the discussion we had about Samira, my father's secretary, right before the events on the beach. Molly had seemed to morally justify as acceptable for a wife with unsatisfied needs to cheat on her husband, even strike a deal with the wretched bastard to grant this unholy arrangement his 'blessings.' I couldn't help but wonder if Molly's guilty subconscious was betraying her own dark secrets.

Weeks passed and I failed to suppress my doubts. I tried meditation, booze and long hours at the gym but failed miserably to extricate the seeds of sedition from my mind. The image of Molly lying naked, pinned under the body of a man other than me had been firmly planted in my head, sprouting tough roots.

When a husband starts suspecting his wife of cheating, it's nothing but a downward spiral from there, and I was not immune from plummeting into that abyss. Did I ever consider confronting Molly, hoping she'd laugh about it and provide some plausible explanation? Of course I did, but I never had the courage to follow through on it.

Instead, I chose to spy on her, although I found nothing. Her e-mails were all work-related, in other words as mundane as they were private. Her Facebook account was sterile and devoid of unfamiliar males in her network. Her computer history logs hadn't been deleted in over a year. Her mobile phone was free of suggestive texts or unrecognized numbers calling at awkward times of the day.

Failing to dredge up a single shred of proof against Molly hardly laid my mind to rest, though, but in fact catapulted it towards even more tenacious doubts.

What if she was always a step ahead of me, shrewdly covering her tracks like a street-smart hooker?

What if she had been doing it for even longer than the history of that beach encounter?

As I sunk deeper in the quicksand of insecurity, eventually I came to believe a plan of action was required if I was to remain sane. Rather than scour for evidence of infidelity, I needed to catch Molly red-handed. I needed irrefutable evidence.

But how?

Molly had little time to breathe, let alone nurture an affair. At work, her schedule was cutthroat, and every minute of her life after she left the hospital was scrupulously accounted for. We had the same friends, did the same things and frequented the same places. Whichever way I mulled it over, I reached the same conclusion. If she was having an affair, it must have been in the mornings at the hospital.

First, I started with the random calls at work, but she was always available. I found that only mildly reassuring, but not quite the conclusive proof of innocence I needed.

What if she was sneaking out of the hospital during work hours for quick rendezvous?

It would be impossible to spend all day stalking her.

A different kind of plan was in order: A trip-wire that would alert me whenever she left the hospital during work hours.

I got out of my car and walked towards the parking attendant at the New Cairo Clinic. The hospital was riddled with Molly's colleagues who could recognize me, so I had to do this quick.

I patted him on the back with a hearty laugh and pointed to his tag. "Aboud—that's your name, right?"

"Yes, your servant, Aboud."

His eyes glistened and he smiled. I must have stunk of money. Not wanting to refute that impression, I slipped a twenty-pound note in the pocket of his grimy, blue overalls and offered him some smokes to jump-start our camaraderie.

After a few deep drags, I cocked my head in the direction of my shiny Mercedes CLS.

"Do you know what brand of car this is?"

He turned to observe it, rattled it over and then glanced back with concerned eyes, as if he was about to fail a most profound test, upon which his life could have depended on. Then a huge smile erupted on his face.

"It's the queen of all cars, Doctor! Mercedes CLS, of course. Right?"

I nodded.

"Leave it to me. I'll take care of this princess and park her in the shade. Giver her a nice wash as well?"

"Thanks, Aboud, but I am not staying."

I peeled off my sunglasses and bit the tip of the frame to scrutinize him for competence. Something gleamed in his eyes, but I wasn't sure if it was intelligence or cunning. Not that it mattered, because for what I wanted from him, either one would do.

"Would you like to earn some honest money on the side?"

"I am a servant under your feet! Command me, *basha*."

"Ask God for repentance immediately. We are all servants to the Lord and equal before his eyes. We are—brothers."

"Thank you, sir."

I extended my hand to him and invented a name to match the well-crafted bullshit story I was about to shovel.

"My name is Taha. I work for Mercedes Benz. We're conducting some market research. Do you know what 'market research' means, Aboud?"

"Of course—I have a high school degree and know about these complicated matters, *basha*."

"Good. So here's the thing. We're doing a study to see how visible our cars are during peak hours of the day. We've chosen this hospital as our case study."

Aboud stood silent like a cheap alabaster statue. I may have overestimated what this chump could grasp, but now that I had started, I had no option but to push on.

"Let me put it this way. Mercedes is a luxury brand, as you know, and we don't want to be oversaturated in the market. If our research shows we have too many cars on the streets of Cairo, we'll need to curb our sales accordingly to maintain the impression that not everyone can afford a Mercedes. See what I mean?"

He nodded, his eyes sparkled and focused on my mouth, as if he had indeed understood, or had decided to pretend he did just so I could get to the part of the story where he makes a lot of money on my account.

"One million percent, Doctor Taha."

The idiot still thinks I am a doctor at the hospital.

"Aboud, I am not a doctor—"

"I know, I know, boss, but you really look like one. You even smell like one."

Smell like one? Medicine? Vomit? Bad cologne?

He moved close enough for me to inhale the nauseating fumes of fermenting onions and fava beans on his breath, probably lingering from breakfast. There was certainly no risk of mistaking him for a medical professional.

"Your task would be very simple."

He panted in the heat, eyes wide and mouth almost salivating.

"Every day between ten and three, if you see a Mercedes owned by a staff member exiting the hospital, call me and let me know. If that particular car returns to the hospital during the day, I also need to know. Not any car, Aboud, just Mercedes."

He was silent for a beat as he played around with his lips.

"Does that include Smart cars, boss?" he finally said. "Those tiny ones that look like toys? They're also produced by Mercedes, aren't they?"

For a brief second, his knowledge of the global auto industry elevated him in my eyes. I smiled and patted him on the back.

"No Smart cars, Aboud. Just Mercedes."

Like an eager dog he nodded repeatedly, now that the mission was becoming more vivid in his mind.

"For your trouble, I'll give you five hundred pounds at the end of our study."

His eyes popped out of their sockets.

"Five hundred pounds?" He repeated the words, as if he had never uttered that amount, let alone considered receiving it in one payment.

"That's right. You'll get them in four weeks, at the end of the study. Here's an extra bonus of one hundred pounds to start our new venture and friendship."

The smile on his face suddenly dried, like an etching on the sand washed away by persistent waves. Aboud's eyes drifted to a darker place and his tail stopped wagging. The weight of his head dropped and he stared aimlessly at his feet as if they had just materialized.

"What's wrong?"

"A huge problem, *basha*. I can't help you."

Even his voice had dropped a few decibels.

My heart skipped a beat.

Had he recognized me? Was he on to me?

"What's the problem?"

"The closest public phone is inside the hospital. People like me are not allowed in the main building, by order of the director. There's no way for me to call you, is what I am trying to say."

I sighed with relief and pulled out a brand new, feature-rich Nokia phone, and passed it to him.

"That's not a problem, Aboud. At Mercedes, we think of everything. This phone is yours to keep. A gift. It has a prepaid SIM card with a balance of two hundred pounds."

I scribbled my number on a piece of paper and put it in his other hand.

"Do we have a deal, Aboud?"

He observed the phone, then glanced at me, then back at the phone, then me again, and finally pranced on me with an impulsive hug.

"With the grace of Allah and his prophet Mohammad, we have a deal! I will not disappoint you, *basha*. I swear on my mother's life and my virgin sister's honor."

Back in my car, a dark membrane had grown around my heart as I drove past Molly's silver S-Class. Parked at the east end of the hospital garage, my wife's delicate features were engraved all over it, staring at me with disappointed eyes.

A few days went by and I had yet to hear from Aboud. I revisited the possibility Molly was having her affair at the hospital after all. Perhaps a young resident with a hard body would corner her daily in the supplies room, his pants down to his knees as he rammed her hard while covering her mouth to drown out her involuntary screams of pleasure. Other times I pictured her spreadeagle on an expensive mahogany desk, her hair loose and sprawled in a big mess as an older mentor who'd seduced her intellectually would make love to her slowly, tenderly, with the renewed confidence of a mature gentleman spiked high on Viagra.

One day while I was on a conference call kissing the derrière of a Japanese client, I saw Aboud's name flashing on my cellphone. I hung up abruptly with Tokyo to speak to him.

"Good morning, Doctor. I bet you thought I ran away with your money and the nice phone you gave me, forgetting our arrangement?"

The little shit was in a particularly good mood. It was the first time I heard him laugh and he sounded like a deranged donkey getting a prostate check, all the while enjoying it.

My heart pounded like a tribal drum before a sacrificial ritual, and I had to mechanically affect a casual tone.

"Not at all, Aboud. I have blind faith in you," I lied.

"It is a nice phone by the way. All the people in my neighborhood think I stole it. But I just tell them what you told me and they shut up."

"What did I tell you?"

"You don't remember?"

Say what you have to say and quit with the small talk, you little turd.

"*At Mercedes, we think of everything.* I am telling everyone I work for Mercedes now."

"In a manner of speaking, you do. Talking of which, anything interesting to report?"

"A Mercedes pulled out of the garage a few minutes ago," he whispered.

His unwarranted cautious tone perturbed me, like he had figured out exactly what I was up to and was playing along. I wasn't comfortable one bit with a lowlife like Aboud thinking he and I were in cahoots.

"What model and color was it?" I said, pretending to be typing.

"The nicest one in the hospital. A silver S-Class. It belongs to a sexy lady doctor who works with children. She has a foreign name—Molly, I think."

"Thanks, Aboud." I raised my voice to sound casual and therefore remind him this was still a legitimate affair, but mostly to douse the fire that had erupted in my chest when I had heard him utter her name.

The bastard kept burrowing.

"I swear to Allah if you saw her, Doctor Taha, you too would want to devour her. She's like a piece of soft Turkish delight that would melt in your mouth. I eat her every day with my hungry eyes, and then when I go back home I think of her and—"

"That's enough, Aboud! There's no need to speak in those terms about a respectable woman. I am not interested in the people—just the cars."

Every part of me wanted to reach into the phone and strangle the little shit. Instead, I hung up with him, cancelled my appointments for the day and raced back home.

Somewhere in the reams of research on infidelity I had ploughed through online, a few experts suggested that disloyal wives preferred to cheat on their marital beds. Apparently the thrill value is higher, making for more intoxicating sex.

I drove by our building but Molly's car wasn't there. I parked a block away on the other side to avoid running into one of our nosey neighbors, and waited. The image of a man staking out the entrance of his building can only mean one thing.

Even while acting like a two-bit private eye shadowing my wife, a part of me wanted to give her the benefit of the doubt. She could have left the hospital for a most innocuous reason. A reason she would no doubt disclose later tonight over dinner.

Our marriage had been the envy of our friends. We had delayed having children to enjoy our lives and build successful careers. Other couples who had inundated themselves with a litter of kids early were now either locked in loveless relationships or long-divorced. But we were different.

Molly had never behaved inappropriately. Her only sin was to do something that I had in the past begged her for. What was the big crime in that? Any other man would have been grateful, but here I was spying on her, presuming her guilt, condemning her as unfaithful without any proof.

After an hour cooped up in my car like a hapless chicken waiting to be slaughtered, I had gone through our marriage with a fine-toothed comb and found no evidence of infidelity, other than my own unsubstantiated and likely exaggerated fears.

There was still no sign of Molly.

That's it, dammit! Enough of this insanity. My wife is not cheating on me. I have to get that through my thick skull.

Click-clack, my seat belt latched and I was ready to pull away.

And that's when I saw it, staring me in the face all along.

My obsession with a silver Mercedes had stymied my perception of anything else. There in blatant view was my brother-in-law Ragi's 2005 black Toyota Corolla.

I recognized the license plate number and the bright red stickers on the windscreen declaring his lifelong loyalty for Al Ahly, his favorite soccer team.

When I had decided to investigate Molly's infidelity, I always accounted for the possibility I would walk in on her with another man lying on top, screwing her on my bed. In my mind, I possessed the courage and moral authority to have that confrontation.

Now staring at Ragi's sin wagon parked on my street, I realized I patently lacked the balls to have that showdown. Now even less so that her cheating partner was someone I knew. My own brother-in-law.

I do not know how long I stood frozen in my seat, staring at Ragi's car, only to have it stare back at me. Taunting me, even hurling insults at my manhood.

Whatever trance-state I was in was broken when Ragi traipsed out of our building with the smile of a man who'd just sunk his teeth into a sweet, forbidden fruit. A brother who had just stabbed another. Whistling. Running his hands through his messy hair. Floating, not walking towards his car.

The sight of Ragi driving off and turning at the corner left a nuclear pressure in my head and pure heat drenched in sweat radiating from my body. Confusion and disbelief wrought havoc in my belly then quickly mutated from sickening to intolerable. Lucky I had a plastic bag in the car.

Molly never followed him out, so I could only guess she had probably used the rear exit of the building and had parked on the parallel street. Smart little bitch.

With no direction or purpose, I drove off. I hadn't even realized I had been crying until I tasted the saltiness on my lips. *People are cruel. I gave her everything I had to give. I don't deserve this. And Ragi—that human scum. I loved him like family.*

Not long ago, Ragi and I had raised our wine glasses over dinner to declare each other brothers from different mothers. What a despicable lie. Every time he'd stepped into my house he had been lusting after my wife, at the expense of Lana, the other innocent victim in this heartless web of deceit. Suddenly the gravity of it all dawned on me—Molly wasn't just cheating on me, she was also backstabbing her baby sister. What kind of woman does that?

When there was nowhere else to go, and no more tears left to cry, I drove back home to survey the scene of the crime.

Inside my apartment, the treacherous smell of Ragi's Gucci perfume struck me hard in the face. My bedroom stunk of lingering sex pheromones and deceit.

I sized up the bed, now neatly made up, which only a few hours ago had cradled my wife and my brother-in-law while they shagged like bunnies. Ours was a most expensive Italian Flu bed that Molly and I had hand-picked at a showroom in Milan, while the owner plied us with robust espressos and moreish mini pastries.

What the hell am I supposed to do now?

I spotted an empty packet of condoms in the rubbish bin, maybe even from my own stash. Underneath the pillow on Molly's side of the bed, a pair of black lace panties were crumpled, no doubt a careless error of an overconfident woman who had grown giddy in her own disloyalty.

The pressure in my head had not relented one bit. I thought of men my age who have premature strokes and heart attacks, and you wonder how it happened. Now I knew.

That night, I employed the most control I had ever mustered in my life to remain composed and not raise her suspicion.

She had cooked a vegetarian lasagna and we popped open a Tuscan red from the Maremma area where we spend a few weeks each spring.

I gave her the requisite roundup of my day, never once sulking or betraying any signs of the stabbing knives bludgeoning my heart. It took tremendous effort to maintain eye contact with her. When I could, I preferred to stare at the emblem of the wine bottle. A mythical creature of sorts.

Part man, part lion.

A chimera, I decided.

As painful as it was, I too had become less of a full man, that sucker husband who loved and cherished his wife while she did her business with other men.

On my bed.

In my house.

Using my fucking condoms.

When a man discovers his wife is having an affair, self-restraint and reason fly out of the window. Humiliation rests on his shoulders like a burden too heavy to bear, with the onus of doing something about it lying squarely on him. The universe will not permit him to rest or have his peace until he acts to set the balance straight. Even if he wanted to look the other way and take one for the team, he'd still wind up facing his demons with no option but to react.

To do something.

Anything.

The years I invested in my marriage were as good as flushed down the toilet. I was not an abusive or distant husband. I didn't spend my life at the bar with the boys, chasing younger women like most men of my age and financial firepower.

I could have had anyone if I had wanted to. I hadn't even desired another woman in my mind, let alone acted upon it. I never needed to, because I was convinced I was already married to the woman of my dreams. I had loved her in every possible way a woman deserves to be loved. I gave that slut my beating heart and fluttering soul, only to have her squat down and take a long, hard piss on them.

What quality was so deficient in me that Ragi was satisfying?

Whichever way I dissected it, everything came down to our fundamental social differences. Ragi had known Molly and Lana since they were children and shared a history with them. They were cut from the same fabric. Upper-class Egyptians with an impressive legacy of social superiority, regardless of how much money they didn't have.

I was certain that even though they had never said it to my face, Molly's parents preferred Ragi as their golden son-in-law. They had known his parents forever and his upbringing and roots were identical to that of Molly and Lana. I, on the other hand, was merely a rich oaf their daughter had married who makes things a little more comfortable for everyone. The ATM machine.

Most women are attracted to men who remind them of their fathers. Between the two of us, Ragi was the one who most resembled Molly's dad. She may have always been in love with him, only to be devastated when he chose to marry Lana instead. Then along I came. She settled for me. I was her plan B.

For the next three weeks, I received two calls from Aboud every Wednesday to tell me when Molly left the hospital and when she returned. She would pull out around ten twenty and was back by one thirty at the latest.

Wednesday, as it turned out, was her fuck day. Nicely cushioned in the middle of the week, far enough from Monday and close enough to the weekend. A harmless, unassuming day. Unless your wife happened to be cheating on you.

I would borrow a small office car neither Molly nor Ragi had seen before and park it on the other side of our building with a clear view of the entrance.

Without fail, Ragi always skipped out of the building smug and whistling that same irritating tune from Hawaii Five-0. I was certain Molly was leaving from the rear of the building through the courtyard, but there was no way for me to scan the back without running into her.

Despite all the evidence piling before my eyes, deep inside I knew I had to see her walking out of the building if I was to be certain beyond any possible doubt.

Good thing I didn't have to wait too long for that to happen.

On the fifth week after I had started shadowing them, I finally saw Molly's car parked in front of our building. On cue, but a whole thirty minutes earlier than when Ragi usually skips out, I saw Molly herself dashing out of the front entrance.

Perhaps Ragi had taken the rear exit this time. They were mixing it up to play it safe. Changing the routine to avoid getting busted or raising the neighbors' suspicions.

I fumbled for my phone to dial the hospital and asked to speak to Molly. They put me on hold at first then transferred me to her cellphone.

I heard her voice on the other end and looked at her in the car as she fixed her hair in the mirror with one hand, and held the phone with the other.

"Alo?"

"It's me, honey."

"Baby, can I call you back later? I'm in the middle of something now," she said.

In the middle of taking a dump on your husband's honor.

If Molly and Ragi were despicable, I had also learned some disturbing truths about myself.

I'm spineless.

Any man worthy of his Y-chromosome would have confronted his wife and her lover the moment his suspicions were confirmed. I, on the other hand, had opted to watch from the sidelines like a weasel while I turned ash-black and bitter-blue on the inside.

What terrified me most, however, was the speed and conviction by which I had reached my decision to kill Molly.

My youthful, naive theories on how a man should behave

if he discovers his wife was cheating on him hadn't stood the test of anything.

How disappointed the younger version of me would have been to see how I didn't amount to much of anything more than the pathetic, average man. Plotting, rotting, and doing exactly what a cuckold husband was expected to do.

Where was my dignity? My semblance of masculinity and courage to confront my wife and declare our rotten marriage over.

Something else my younger, inexperienced self was not aware of was feeding my desire to kill her and it had nothing to do with retribution. The powerful need—obsession even— to have eternal ownership of her body and soul. My life with Molly was as good as it was ever going to get for me. I could never find a better woman. If I didn't kill her, she would end up leaving me anyway, only to be with Ragi or find another man who could fill in her whatever I wasn't able to.

If I was going to lose Molly either way, no other man could ever have her. Killing her was the only way to make sure of that.

Finding a hired assassin is not as daunting of a task as one might think before developing this need in the first place. The same six degrees of separation connecting you to upstanding citizens like the Pope or Oprah Winfrey can also put you in touch with murderers, terrorists and drug dealers. In my case, however, I wasn't fishing for a seasoned criminal. I had something quite the opposite in mind.

I slipped Aboud a small envelope with five crisp one hundred pound notes as I had promised.

"God bless you, *basha*," he said, unable to keep his eyes off the money in his hands,

"You did a fine job with the market research, Aboud. Now how about some more work for me, this time of a more personal nature?"

"I am your genie in the bottle, master Taha. Just tell me what you need, and I am on it," he said, finally looking up, his face closely resembling sunshine.

"It's really quite simple. A wealthy businessman I know is faced with a difficult test from Allah almighty."

Aboud's beady eyes sharpened their focus on me as he listened intently.

"His father was diagnosed with the 'sinister' disease a few years ago."

"May God have mercy on him, poor man. His testicles? Older men usually get it there and they need to chop them off."

"You mean the prostate, but no, somewhere else. More deadly."

"Oh, God, not his penis?"

"No, Aboud, not his penis. That's besides the point. My friend has vowed to God if he answered his prayers and cured his father's tumor, he would return the favor by helping someone else to claw themselves out of a desperate situation. Guess what?"

Aboud shrugged but kept his eyes fixed on my mouth.

"Praise to Allah, his father made a full recovery a few weeks ago. A miracle, the doctors are saying."

"I understand what you are saying, master Taha."

"And I like that about you, Aboud. You read my thoughts before they fly out of my mouth."

"You're looking for someone who is in a desperate situation

and needs a miracle from God."

"A miracle from God, yes. Think of my friend as an angel of mercy who wants to extend his wings in gratitude. I want to be part of it so I too can taste some of God's grace that will surely touch whoever enables this virtue."

Aboud looked up to the sky briefly then grinned. "I know just the man, Doctor Taha. He'll do whatever is asked of him. He is very desperate."

Maybe Aboud was not nearly as stupid as I had pinned him to be.

"So I can count on you? For your efforts, my friend will compensate you another five hundred pounds."

"Absolutely, Doctor Taha. Remember, at Mercedes, we think of everything." He smiled like a fox.

Days later, Aboud introduced me to Faisal, a bus driver and father of three from the impoverished and crime-infested shanty town of Mansheyet Nasser.

Faisal's twelve-year-old daughter, Munira, needed a life-saving and expensive operation to fix the damage inflicted on her during a forced kidney removal. The organ mafia had abducted her from a summer camp organized by the ministry of social welfare, cut out her left kidney and left her for dead.

I wanted to feel sorry for Faisal. His was a truly miserable existence. As if the poor and marginalized were not suffering enough, their bodies were also coveted. Spare parts to be plucked out when required to replace the rotten organs of the rich and powerful. Whatever empathy I could dispense or ability to connect with anyone else's misery had been chastened by what Molly had done to me.

I peered into his sad, empty brown eyes and asked him flatly if he knew what God had said we should do to a man and a woman who commit adultery.

He shrugged his shoulders, not sure what my question had to do with his sick child.

"One hundred lashes?"

I shook my head solemnly, and paraphrased a fictitious verse from the Koran I had only just made up.

"*It is not only lawful, but imperative on Ye Believers to shed the blood of a Muslim if he or she fornicates outside of wedlock.*"

He nodded with half-certainty, probably unsure whether to pretend he recognized the fabricated verses, or to confess ignorance.

I looked away in feigned humiliation. "Faisal?"

"Yes, sir?"

"My wife—no, let's call her the whore I married—is sleeping with my brother-in-law. On my bed. Every Wednesday."

When I turned to face him, his eyes were wide with fear. He had already guessed what I was about to task him with.

It took the better part of a week and all the religious and moral manipulation I could come up with to convince Faisal of the divinity and providence of our proposed pact.

God had intended for us to cross paths to mete out his justice, I told him. Together, we would sacrifice the life of a cheating slut and her heathen lover to save an innocent, suffering child, his daughter, Munira.

There was no shame in taking the life of a sinner, I told him with the conviction of a passionate cleric giving a fiery Friday sermon. In return for killing Molly and Ragi as punishment for their adulterous infractions, I would front all the medical bills for the life-saving operation Munira required.

The plan was sublime in its simplicity. I would travel to London for a business trip from Tuesday until Friday. Faisal would kill Molly and Ragi on Wednesday, and make it look like a botched burglary.

Our kitchen window was always left open. Our duplex is on the second floor, so it would be easy for Faisal to climb the water pipes and enter as a burglar. We live in Zamalek, one of the fanciest parts of town. Although breaking and entering is rather uncommon in Cairo, if it did happen, it was always in the affluent suburbs.

I instructed him to reveal before shooting them that he was acting on my behalf. I wanted the last thought to travel through their minds to be of me, so Molly and Ragi would die knowing I wasn't the fool they had taken me for.

Once I received confirmation Faisal had killed them, I would call her sister Lana later in the evening to ask if she had heard from Molly, while expressing contrived concern for her well-being. In time, she too would start worrying about Ragi, who would also be missing.

Sooner or later, all the roads would lead back to our place, where they would discover the dead bodies of the two lovers and the traces of the fumbled burglary.

I would have a pristine alibi, but in the unlikely event the police decide to conduct a thorough investigation that includes my possible involvement, our overpaid company lawyers and my father's political connections would ensure no public prosecutor would dare touch me. Not a word would be leaked to the press. If a maverick journalist so much as suggests the story to their editor, they would be dissuaded under the threat of their career taking the most unsavory detour.

The real events would remain as dead as Molly and Ragi. The rest of the world would be fed a different story: While driving to our beach house in the north coast, Molly, Ragi and Lana's car collided with an oncoming truck driving in the wrong direction. The truck driver had been stoned out of his head on cheap hashish. Only Lana survived.

I don't know why, but whenever I worried there were gaping holes in my plan, I kept telling myself, "At Mercedes, we think of everything." It didn't make sense. It wasn't even the company's official slogan. I had invented it for Aboud's benefit, but it had become my own mantra. My impulse to believe that I carried the moral baton and deserved to emerge victorious.

I was lying on a bed in my room at the Park Hotel in London with an ever-widening crevice in my heart, wondering how it all came to this.

Would it have been better to live with Molly's infidelity, and hope her affair with Ragi was just a transient indiscretion? Like a bad flu for which I just needed to bide my time until it tided over. What if the onus of fixing whatever was broken, that had forced her to stray in the first place, was on me? Or maybe the simplest reaction would have been the most apposite: To confront her, then let her go.

I knew even while delving deep into the cesspool of regret that the time for all these retroactive thoughts and alternative scenarios had long gone. I was knee-deep in it, and even if I wanted to, I could hardly call it off. Of course, not the tiniest part of me wanted to call it off. I had played detective, judge and now executor by proxy.

By two p.m. I had yet to hear from Faisal. I had instructed

him to call me from a pay phone on a prepaid anonymous number that couldn't be traced back to me.

We had agreed he would kill them with a silenced nine-millimeter Beretta he had purchased in the black market with cash I had advanced him. After executing Molly and Ragi, Faisal would ransack the house and help himself to whatever valuables he wanted. I told him where her jewelry was, and promised to leave him an extra thousand pounds in cash on the nightstand. Upon my return to Cairo, I would take care of his daughter's operation.

I must have fallen asleep on the couch only to be startled awake by the ominous buzzing of a silenced mobile phone. The digital clock on the nightstand said it was a few minutes after six. I was certain this was Faisal calling, but wondered why it had taken him so long to report back.

When I reached for the second-hand phone I had purchased for Faisal to call me with confirmation, it was inexplicably silent. My real phone was the one trying to get my attention.

The words "Molly's Cell" were flashing on the screen.

What the hell is going on here?

Whatever oxygen remaining in my lungs was fast escaping, leaving behind an asphyxiating vacuum.

Trembling fingers, burning belly, and a light head ready to black out.

If Molly was dead, how could she be calling me?

I reached out to other reasonable explanations to avoid hyperventilating. It was most likely someone else who had found the phone near her dead body. Molly had listed my name as her ICE contact in her address book, *in case of emergency.*

My heart was actively trying everything it could to break out of my rib cage and get as far away as possible from me and my deplorable actions.

I latched at the last molecule of courage before it too exited my body, and answered the phone.

Molly's voice, screaming hysterically.

Faisal must have double-crossed me.

Wailing like a crow in mourning, nothing she was uttering sounded intelligible. The strength to talk back was entirely bereft of me. I waited until she was finally able to say something meaningful through her tears.

"Lana and Ragi were murdered! In our house! On our bed! Shot in the head like stray dogs."

The words thundered through my brain but failed to find any region they could register on.

I am hallucinating. It's a bad dream. This is not me, I am just watching this transpire.

"Someone broke into our apartment and murdered them this morning."

I am still hallucinating.

"What were they doing at our apartment?" a voice that vaguely sounded like mine whispered involuntarily.

"They were having problems being intimate at home after Ragi's father had moved in. Lana asked me to give them our place once a week."

"Who watched over Uncle Emad?"

A desperate attempt to trace any reason in the madness unfolding before me. I still did not recognize my voice, any more than being able to accept the gravity of the unspeakable crime I had apparently committed.

"I did."

Two words that meant nothing and everything at the same time.

"How?"

"I have two free hours on Wednesdays. I used to volunteer at the pediatric clinic in Mansheyet Nasser until Lana asked for this favor."

Damn you, Molly, you never told me. You never told me you had two free hours on Wednesday!

Right on cue, like she had heard my thoughts, she gave me the answer to my unspoken question.

"I didn't tell you about Lana and Ragi using our place on Wednesdays because they were too embarrassed and didn't want anyone to know. They were trying for a baby."

With my head burning hotter than the mobile phone against it, a most incredulous thought occurred to me. One I would have never thought possible. For the first time since this nightmare had started, I would have preferred it if Molly was really cheating on me.

She stopped crying now. "The man who did it called the police and gave himself in. It's someone I know." An unexpected coldness had crept in her voice.

"What do you mean, someone you know?"

Molly didn't say anything, but the lump of silence at the other end of the line was incrementally unsettling.

I erupted in a loud roar. "What the hell does that mean, Molly?"

"His name is Faisal. He's the father of a girl I was treating at the pediatric clinic where I used to volunteer on Wednesdays, and he's come to the hospital with her a few times."

Faisal used to go to Molly's hospital?

That explains how Aboud knew him. Everything fell in place with a terrifying whump.

"She needed surgery and I tried to get our hospital to do it pro bono, on a humane basis. They refused. He must have followed me around and found out where I lived. Maybe when the hospital denied the request, he thought it was my fault or that I had not done enough."

The pressure in the room dropped. The only thing I could hear was my charred, guilty heart pounding in my mouth.

"Where's he now?"

"At a police station in Zamalek. Where else could he be?"

"What else has he told the cops?"

An ice storm engulfed her voice now.

"We'll find out soon enough. Right now, what I really need, is for you to get back here. Immediately."

THE ITALIAN LAUNDROMAT

Donatella considered what the repulsive man sitting at her dining table had blurted, while stuffing his face with chunks of her homemade lasagna.

"I have a surprise for you."

Come again? A surprise?

He spoke no more and continued eating, like he had wanted to plant a seed in her mind then tend to whatever it sprouted after filling his belly. With his mouth open and chewing loudly, his nicotine-stained teeth were visible in a vile tint of sulfur-yellow.

Twenty-four years ago he had melted her heart like soft butter left out on a hot summer night. *What happened to the Neapolitan heartthrob who had stormed into papa's gelateria and made a woman out of me? Look at him now.* His hair had thinned where it mattered and grown where it repulsed her most—on his back, out of his ears and in his nostrils. Her husband Mauro had aged with little grace and had let himself go.

Mauro was the first man to lust after her when she was a homely teenager, with an ironing-board chest and androgynous features. The other girls ridiculed her, and the young men skipped over her like the steamed veggies on the menu.

But Mauro, he was…different. He'd seen something in her. His powder-blue eyes had pried her out of her shy, insecure clam. His strong, ripped body bursting out of his tight shirts had tugged at her heartstrings. Something about the way he stared at her with one dirty thing on his mind had unleashed a flutter of emotions in her heart. A yearning of the flesh in her body and soul the likes of which she had never known.

Every Tuesday when it was her shift at the *gelateria*, Mauro would come by for a *zabaione cornetto* during the lunch-break lull. Idle chitchat was followed by light flirting until she gave in and granted him a first kiss.

Like an early-brewing storm, he started to undo her with deliberate restraint. Slow-burning embraces behind the counter, and an expert tongue that left no stretch of her virginal body unexplored.

Before long they were taking bolder risks and started locking up the *gelateria* and shacking up in the back. In time he excavated straight to her core, and she surrendered—in the name of love, desire or some other madness that had taken over her but which her mind had yet to comprehend.

He pummeled through her inexperienced, hungry body, like a hurricane of desire. On the floor between large sacks of white sugar, two naked, sweaty bodies were fused. Mauro's pelvis pounded her with no mercy as her lustful screams were drowned by the protective sound of whole milk churning in steel drums.

She blossomed after that, like a curse had been lifted.

The angular lines and plain contours of her teenage years morphed into soft curves and womanly swells in all the right places. Donatella grew her hair and started living up to her destiny as a woman, eradicating any doubt in the eyes of onlookers trying to figure out 'what' she was.

Against her family's will, Mauro convinced Donatella to elope with him to Rome in the dead of the night to start a family together. A distant uncle had promised him a job as a mechanic at his auto repair shop. He'd work there until he saved enough money to run his own show. Donatella would stay at home to raise the children, one of whom was already growing inside her. A boy.

The promise of material comfort and a soft life in the eternal city was seductive. Who in their right mind wouldn't want to give up the violence and shattered dreams of Napoli for that?

Now, a whole quarter of a century later, the man she had fallen madly in love with had become a stranger living under a common roof.

What surprise could you possibly have in store for me now, Mauro?

She'd seen all of his 'surprises' and they were always the sort that left her cut open. In their twenty-four years together, he never remembered her birthday or their anniversary. Never once did Mauro bring home some flowers or perform any gesture of unconditional gratitude.

Donatella was married to a pig whose ability to take was bottomless, but gave nothing in return but pain.

The last time he touched her was a whole decade ago. It had been more than fifteen years since she had found any pleasure in being intimate with him. Her eighteen-year-old daughter Sofia, their second child, was probably getting more action over the summer than Donatella's entire pathetic marriage.

Things first started to sour with Mauro when Sofia was

born. He was almost invisible during Donatella's complicated pregnancy. Sofia arrived prematurely. Conveniently, Mauro claimed he couldn't handle the pressure and had a meltdown. The burden of caring for a sickly child for the first seven years of her life fell on Donatella's tiny shoulders.

And this set the tone for the rest of their marriage.

With no family support, she raised their two children on her own, bearing the brunt of the tough, grinding life of the Roman middle class. Before long, Mauro's selfish indifference evolved into blatant cheating, mental abuse and a slow but ruthless campaign to erode Donatella's self-esteem.

The fairy tale life she had sacrificed everything for had fizzled to nothing more but a cruel mirage. Donatella had been reduced to an unpaid maid and a *de facto* single mother. A miserable bundle of bitterness and unfulfilled potential. Mauro alone was responsible for that. She had no practical skills or work experience because he never allowed her to train or gain a degree. Who else would look after the kids and the house?

Her only passion was for drawing and painting, but Mauro nipped in the bud any ambition she had to pursue art as a hobby, let alone a career. Whenever she spoke of it, he would roll his eyes and descend on her like a wet blanket.

"Don't lie to yourself, *amo'*," he would shoot her down. "You'll never amount to anything with those scribbles. A chicken can etch something more captivating with its feet."

Mauro had cast her away from any meaningful human connections until she had become entirely dependent on him. The few girlfriends she had collected in Rome were superficial and only good for air kissing and bitchy gossiping over a coffee at the bar on Sunday mornings.

Other than her children, there was little pleasure in life. Nothing in the future to look forward to, and scant anything in her past to be proud of.

Eventually the children grew up and drifted away from the domestic toxicity of her relationship with Mauro. Donatella could hardly blame them. In fact, if she had the luxury, she would have done the same thing herself.

As one wretched year became yet another, Donatella found herself alone, destitute and desperate for a way out. But Mauro had made her beholden to him without a cent to her name. She couldn't just pack her bags and move out.

Even the lowliest profession, which Donatella had considered, wasn't even a viable option. The life of a hooker on the main thoroughfare of Cristoforo Colombo couldn't be much worse than her current sham of a life. But at forty-one, the competition from younger eastern European and Moroccan imports with long legs and perky, un-milked boobs was unbeatable.

Hooker or not, it had been a long time since she felt like a woman, let alone a seductive one. She never went to the hair dresser and her uniform was monochromatic baggy clothes like her life was a perpetual home renovation project.

"I have a surprise for you," he repeated, as he scrapped the last patch of béchamel sauce with a piece of fresh focaccia she had baked this morning. He smacked his lips and reached out for a sharp knife to carve out a wafer-thin slice of prosciutto from a hunk of ham on the table. Like a voracious crocodile, he dangled it in his mouth, and chewed without a suspicion of elegance.

"Do you want another slice of lasagna? A cold beer?" she asked mechanically.

He shook his head and shot her a penetrating gaze.

"Don't change the subject."

Donatella's eyes darted away then dropped to the floor.

"I know things haven't quite worked out between us."

"What do you mean?"

"You're miserable. I get that. Especially now the kids have grown up and are hardly ever at home."

She raised her eyes to face him with tentative suspicion.

What's changed? It's been like this for most of this pitiful excuse of a marriage.

"I want to make it up to you."

Yeah, right.

Twenty-four arduous years in the shadow of this man, Donatella had experienced every shade of disappointment. A relentless stream of broken promises stabbing her heart deeper each time until she developed a thick emotional membrane to avoid at all costs believing anything this man had to say about redemption.

She had vowed many years ago never to allow him to raise her hopes again, because he always turned around and dashed them. Mauro had never laid a hand on her, but the damage his words and actions had wreaked upon her psyche was far more devastating.

She grinned and tasted bitterness in her mouth.

"Make it up to me?" she repeated casually.

"*Amo'*, what if I could plant joy in your heart again? Make you smile. What if I could give you back something you used to love doing?"

"What do you mean?"

Mauro stood up and wiped his mouth on the sleeve of

his grease-soiled work overalls. He took a few tentative steps towards her and touched her shoulders.

Over the years, Donatella had become immune to his pungent after-work smell of metal, grease and car oil. But there was something particularly repulsive about him today.

"A few years ago I purchased a small shop behind the old Rome exhibition grounds."

"Why?"

"It seemed like a sound investment at the time."

"What for?"

"*Buh*, I had no clue. Maybe a second branch of the auto repair shop for Daniele to run on his own one day? Then the kid lost his marbles and decided to go to school—but don't get me started, what a total waste of time and money that is."

"You always did your own thing without consulting us anyway. Why would your son turn out any different?"

Mauro did not respond to her underlying accusation.

"The shop's on a quiet street in a residential building, collecting spiders and mildew. It's costing me a fortune to maintain."

She threw him a cold glance.

"What exactly does this have to do with me?"

Mauro stared at his feet for a few short seconds as if they were a teleprompter feeding him the script.

"I want to start a business with you. An activity you've always had a passion for. Something you excelled in. Lord knows you waste your day watching trashy television and gossiping with the neighbors."

Donatella ignored his snide comment and latched instead on the other thing Mauro had mentioned: *An activity you have a passion for.* Her long-lost love for still-life sketching and oil painting. Every few years she would take out an empty pad and stare at it hard for a long time as though consulting an oracle. She could visualize the torrent of dark, tortured images trapped in her psyche, but her hands and soul were paralyzed of the confidence to release them.

Mauro's destructive voice had crippled her innate artistic urges. Her natural talent was never nurtured. There was always someone to let her down. First her father, then Mauro and now herself.

But what if Mauro's conscience is finally waking up?

She had no idea how big or small this shop was, or where it was located, but the faint hope of having a studio where she could paint and maybe sell or frame her art rekindled an electric current through her soul she had long discounted as dead. This could be a lifeline to reverse her unilateral march towards a tragic end. She studied Mauro's eyes closely, trying as she had always done to read his intentions.

"What activity do you have in mind?"

He smirked then brushed his grease-stained hands on her cheeks, revealing hard, calloused fingers and filthy nails. A lifetime ago she used to care for his grooming and would tell him what to wear and how to look. She cared how the world saw him. But that was a long time ago.

"Do you remember when the kids were younger and I'd come back home for lunch?"

She nodded, still not sure where he was going with this.

"Daniele and Sofia would be napping on the couch or playing at your feet, with the afternoon sun flooding the living room. A fresh pasta or a succulent roast would always be ready for me on the kitchen counter. And you…standing there looking…angelic. Glowing, and doing something. Do you remember what?"

Donatella shook her head. Most of their marriage was one searing disappointment after the other. She had mastered the art of purging the past from her consciousness like flushing a toilet. Any instance of the image Mauro had described where she would be drawing or painting was nowhere to be retrieved from her memory banks.

"I don't remember," she finally said.

Mauro sighed deeply, like she had hurt him by failing to reconnect with a slice of their family heritage that he apparently had held close to his heart, but still he pressed on.

"You'd be standing ironing the wash as you watched a talk show or a daytime soap. Our clothes would be neatly folded in color-coordinated piles near you. Everything smelling like spring. I loved going to work on Mondays wearing a crisp overall, knowing this was your way to show you cared. Remember what I used to tell you back then?"

She nodded.

Better than the laundromat, he used to say.

Donatella didn't utter a single word.

"You always loved to wash, iron and fold, *amore mio*. Your special talent. And you did it better than anyone else, even saying it was therapeutic for you."

Donatella turned her head to glance away from him. She didn't want Mauro to see the tears about to erupt from her eyes.

"You were a wonderful *casalinga*. You took such good care of me and the kids."

Cutting me open wasn't enough for you, was it? Now you

want to pluck out my beating heart and toss it in the incinerator. When she had wiped her tears with the tip of her sleeve, she turned to face him again. She wanted to look in his eyes now and see for herself if he had any idea how cruel he was.

What a despicable human being.

"I did some research and there isn't a single laundromat in the area. I've set aside about fifteen thousand euros. We'll buy a couple of used industrial washers and driers cheap from a government auction, fix the place up, print some flyers and start a damn business. What do you say, *amo*? You can run the place. Make it your pet project."

"Why would you need me? Aren't these things coin-operated these days?"

"No, there's no money in a self-service laundromat. People don't have the time to waste doing menial jobs."

But the cow you herded from Napoli has all the time in the world, right?

"With your expertise, the laundromat will make a name for itself. You'll be doing something you're passionate about and at the same time earning cash to help out with the expenses. The cost of living is not getting any cheaper in this economic climate. It's time for you to carry your weight around here," he said with a chuckle as he spanked her bottom playfully.

Mauro leaned over and planted a meaningless, empty kiss on her forehead.

"It's long overdue, but this is my gift to you, Donatella."

The sharp knife Mauro had used to slice through the prosciutto sat on the table staring at her, even goading her. A sudden flash of graphic images involving Mauro, his throat and that knife traveled unhindered through her mind.

Donatella wiggled her pelvis to achieve a better aim. She released her bladder and a stream of urine hit the target as planned.

Carefully, she pulled out the plastic stick from between her legs and set it aside on the sink to wait for the result. This was the third pregnancy test she'd done in as many hours. When the first one was positive, she hung up the 'back in ten minutes' sign on the door of the laundromat and rushed to the pharmacy to buy two different brands. The first one could have been faulty.

Back at the laundromat, the second one gave the same result. Pregnant without a shadow of a doubt. So she had no idea why she was doing the test a third time, when the outcome was almost certain.

It had been twenty years since life had grown inside of her, but in retrospect, the signs and symptoms were unmistakable. Not just her missed period, but everything else. The queasiness, the tender breasts, and the white, milky discharge announcing the thickening of her vagina's walls, right after conception.

How can a woman my age conceive after having sex one time, and one time only?

She recalled exactly when it had happened. The warm gush of semen rushing inside her was still as vivid in her loins as it was in her heart. And her spontaneous orgasm preceding his fiery ejaculation.

This wasn't an immaculate or unexpected conception by any stretch of the imagination, but one borne out of pure lust. She scrutinized the two red lines confirming her condition and drifted back to the events that had led to this.

During the darkest moments of her marriage to Mauro,

murdering him and making it look like an accident often seemed like a sound exit plan. She was dependent on him financially, and his death would release her from that bondage.

Despite his shortcomings as a father and a husband, Mauro was a wizard of an auto mechanic and a shrewd businessman. He had transformed his auto repair shop from a microscopic operation to a thriving venture. German brands were his expertise, and before long he had struck a deal with the big two, Mercedes and BMW, to be one of their authorized repair centers in suburban Rome. During the height of the boom years a decade ago, he moved to larger premises in the Garbatella neighborhood, hired a dozen full-time staff, and ventured in the lucrative spare parts business.

Donatella had no clue how much money the auto repair shop was bringing in each year or their net worth as a family. She could only guess, and by her estimates, Mauro could be sleeping on at least a cool half-a-million euros.

Like most Italians, Mauro was probably evading taxes with the same diligence of going to mass on Sunday to light a candle for the Virgin Mary. Which meant the real amount could be even more. These estimates, however, were unscientific, based on crude mathematics rather than any extravagance in their lifestyle. Mauro was a stingy bastard and had curbed their existence as a family at the fringes of the lower middle class.

If Mauro were to drop dead—especially if she were to hasten that outcome—she and the children would inherit everything. Their lives would be instantly transformed, and whatever Mauro was stashing away would ultimately surface as part of an inheritance settlement. Of course, it wouldn't just be cash lying idle in banks, but real estate as well.

When Mauro had first presented the laundromat as a long-overdue gift to Donatella, her desire to slit his throat from ear to ear was overpowering. Probably the strongest she'd ever felt it.

Twenty-four years of dependable hurt at the hands of this swine, and Donatella had wrongly assumed she had seen the worst of him. But this she hadn't seen coming. Her own husband rewarding her quarter-of-a-century of service to their family by further perpetuating her role as a domestic slave. And the nerve of him to package it as a surprise and suggest that washing, ironing and folding clothes for complete strangers would be a 'source of joy' for her.

But she didn't kill him.

Not because the desire had waned or because there was an iota of remorse or pity in her heart for him. She only balked because she feared him. Physically, it would have been impossible to grab the knife and lunge at Mauro without him reacting swiftly and taking her out first.

Even if she could kill him in a fit of rage for the immediate rush of gratification, it wouldn't serve her long-term interests. Mauro wasn't worth going to prison for. Not even a day. She thought of her children, Daniele and Sophia, who would be irreparably damaged if their mother axed their dad and served time for it.

Like all decisions he had taken on her behalf, Mauro didn't wait for Donatella to weigh in on the laundromat proposal. A week after making the announcement, the establishment was all but ready to launch.

Except for the odd plumbing and painting jobs, the machines, the business licenses and the marketing efforts to promote the laundromat were all in place. Within a month of first proposing it, the *Lavanderia di Mauro* was open for business.

For the first few weeks running the place, Donatella was seething on the inside. Business was slow to start, which gave her ample time to probe her predicament from every possible perspective. The very basis of the laundromat was rotten and spoke volumes of the low regard in which Mauro held her.

In time, when she had burned through all the self-pity she could muster, and when business started to move a little, a few possible advantages to her situation presented themselves. Seeing less of Mauro every day, for instance, was a huge incentive.

Running the laundromat would bring her into direct contact with cold hard cash, for the first time since she had fled Napoli. A bulb lit up in her mind when she held the net sum of fifteen euros in her hand from her very first sale. If she played her cards right, she could skim a little money on the side for an escape fund, a little voice whispered in her head.

Before long, the voice in her head was no longer little.

Three months after launching the venture, Donatella's perspective had shifted. The laundromat had picked up and was generating decent revenue. Still, Mauro maintained draconian bookkeeping and always looked over her shoulders.

It took her some time and thinking, but Donatella eventually found a loophole.

Mauro only looked at the register, which meant any off-the-book sales she made could potentially be hers to keep.

And so Donatella began to refine a system to distract clients from requesting receipts. Light flirting, little chocolate hearts and candy, idle gossiping and indulging talkative souls until her ears would wither away and fall. But it was worth it if it meant she could pocket these underground sales. All she had to do was keep the laundromat profitable on paper to fend off Mauro's suspicions.

A day arrived when she had amassed two thousand euros for her escape fund. Donatella opened a savings account at the nearby Banca Popolare del Lazio and deposited the amount. Hardly anything, but it meant the world to her. A beacon heralding a brighter future. At this rate she could save forty, maybe fifty thousand within five years and make a run for it.

Getting out of the house and meeting new faces was also transformational.

The laundromat was on a quiet street with hardly any commercial activities. As the new kid on the block, Donatella soon became the focal point of the area, both for the residents and her fellow patrons running nearby establishments. A fetching woman with a smart idea satisfying a neighborhood need was bound to be a cause for much interest.

An entire cast of diverse and colorful characters began to trickle in, sometimes for business, often for friendly banter, but always out of curiosity.

Appearances seemed to matter, so Donatella began dressing the part. She discarded all her baggy and faded outfits and rediscovered makeup. She dropped a few extra pounds and once again was able to squeeze into her tightest dresses. Even her hair came back from the dead.

At first, it was the elderly. Everything starts with little old ladies in this town. They'd stop on the way back from the market and seem bewildered to find a laundromat had materialized on their street—even though it had been there for months.

A few days later they would come back, but this time to test-drive the laundromat on some expendable items, usually belonging to their husbands. Decades-old shirts with horrific stains, nasty-smelling wifebeaters and boxer shorts requiring neurosurgery rather than detergent to resuscitate them.

When Donatella worked her magic on these dispensable units, the matriarchal gnomes would come back with items of higher value like curtains, blankets and towels. And when she succeeded with those as well, they would return for the grand finale and most exacting challenge. Their Sunday best.

Passing all three stages gave Donatella's laundromat the much-coveted *nonna* seal of approval. The good word of a grandmother went a long way in the community. Little old ladies speak, and their endorsements or wrath can either make or break a small business.

The burgeoning satisfaction of running the laundromat was only dampened by how fast things between her and Mauro were deteriorating. His real motive to want her shackled to the laundromat for most of the day was to get the house all to himself for his morning trysts.

Not that he really cared if Donatella ever caught him red-handed—the bastard didn't even try that hard to clean up or cover his tracks. Used condoms languished in their bedroom trash can. Other women's underwear insensitively left in their laundry basket. And foreign hair follicles everywhere. Even in her own brush.

Her presence at home in the mornings was a logistical and financial inconvenience that would require him to get a hotel room whenever he was in the mood.

A year after launching, business was booming and Donatella

was skimming up to forty percent of the revenue, without raising Mauro's interest. Despite a mediocre economy and Donatella's cut, she was turning over a handsome profit for Mauro, who never once suspected the scheme she was running behind his back. Probably because he didn't give her credit for having the innate intelligence or cunning to hatch such a scheme.

Having clean clothes and linen was still a necessity rather than a luxury for many Romans, even during hard times. As the population aged, and with more women joining the workforce, there was a growing need to outsource much of the housework.

At one point, Donatella's prospects had improved so unexpectedly, she had to revise her target escape fund to an ambitious sixty thousand euros to be raised within not five, but three years.

Growing in tandem with the business was Donatella's confidence. Like a plant that had been tucked away in a dark corner for centuries, Donatella embraced the warm rays of freedom. She bloomed like a flower, emerging a self-assured, sociable woman loved by her clients and respected by neighboring businesses.

Franco, the owner of a bar on a parallel street, dropped off a free *macchiato* every day after lunch. Alessandro, the hair dresser, washed and dried his towels at the laundromat, and every now and then gave her a free hair cut. Then there was Luciano, the dental technician from across the street, who was always up for a friendly chat with incisive political analysis about the dismal state of their country. He seemed to be clued in about the scandalous affairs of Italy's overpaid, over-sexed and underperforming caste of corrupt politicians. The sort of smut you can't read in the papers.

Luciano most likely fancied her, but probably felt too exposed in the area to act upon any such urges, which suited her fine. Donatella wasn't the least bit interested.

Donatella's paying customers, however, provided her with the most intriguing windows on the world, and made her realize just how sheltered she had been under Mauro's insular universe.

At the laundromat, everyone was equally vulnerable. Dirty laundry in every sense of the word was exposed to Donatella.

The men who were having sex at the office and came to clean what they had soiled in the line of fire. Or the group of Brazilian transvestite prostitutes who shared a rented apartment not too far from the laundromat. After weeks scratching her head, she finally figured out that the handsome bronze-skinned guys who dropped the clothes off in the morning were the same hot chicks who picked them up in the afternoon. Their lingerie was more erotic and feminine than anything she'd ever owned, let alone worn.

When she wasn't deducing salacious tidbits about her clients from their laundry, the clients themselves were pouring their hearts out to her. At times she wondered if someone had surreptitiously added 'counseling' or 'shoulder to cry on' to the list of services printed on the sign outside.

Perhaps the relative anonymity of the laundromat, or Donatella's mothering disposition, encouraged random strangers to open up to her with little to no discretion. In return, she doled out level-headed advice, which made them come back for more.

In the year since she started running the place, she had seen and heard it all. Cheating wives, tortured men leading double lives, and even women like her who felt their happiness was tied to the untimely deaths of their abusive husbands. And sad, lonely seniors who found more compassion at the laundromat than with their middle-aged children, who still lived with them, waiting for the day they departed to cash in their inheritance.

But of all the people who had walked through her doors, there was one particular customer who intrigued her the most, and who would end up turning her life upside down. His name was Akbar and she had first met him four weeks before discovering she was pregnant.

Donatella listened as Akbar introduced himself and explained in accented but decent Italian the urgency of getting his shirt cleaned. It seemed as if his whole life depended on it.

The young man couldn't have been older than twenty-eight she guessed. Probably Bangladeshi just by his skin tone and features. Not that she would have been able to tell the difference if he was Indian, Pakistani or Sri Lankan. But the only South Asians she'd ever seen in Rome were Bangladeshis.

Rome was brimful with all colors of immigrants, some legal and most not. A massive population of young Bangladeshi men was seemingly rampant, as if the entire demographic of unemployed males in their twenties and thirties from that country had been transplanted here—at the car wash, selling fruits and vegetables at the market, or working for wealthy Romans as drivers and human drones running errands and doing the heavy lifting.

Unlike North Africans or Nigerians, these young South Asian men were docile and generally trouble-free. They were never in the news for violence or rape, and always seemed to keep to themselves, preoccupied only with finding gainful employment. Many times she'd spot them on the street walking in packs of four or five, chatting in their bizarre, melodic language on their mobile phones, talking to their kin back home no doubt. Their parents, wives, children and siblings. An entire ecosystem depending on them to work like ants and repatriate money for subsistence.

Akbar wanted his shirt cleaned within a few hours. An employment agency had called him unexpectedly to attend an interview for a job as a driver for a diplomat at a foreign embassy. Or something along those lines.

A clean, ironed shirt would impress his potential employer. Most likely he lacked the time or money to buy a new one for the occasion. She cocked her head toward the massive piles of clothes deposited just this morning, and was about to break the bad news to the young man that it couldn't be done, when something happened inside her.

He was silent after pleading his case, with a warm smile flowering on his face. An entirely organic expression, riveting in its innocence, and not artificial like the sort most Italians can perform on cue. It triggered a primeval instinct within her. Perhaps pity for the young man's predicament. But she and pity were best friends and this didn't seem quite like it. Even if it was pity initially, it had now transformed into something unexpected and profound.

As she peered in his eyes, she saw straight into his soul and sensed his every emotion in real time. His hopes and aspirations to get this job. His fears he may not get it and end up on the prowl again, not knowing from where his next euro will come.

Despite his vulnerability, this young man didn't possess the faintest trace of protective emotional layers, the sort people grow around their hearts to shield themselves from the brutality of life. There he stood like an open book for her to read at will. Not blinking or twitching or nervous. Not even fidgeting or glancing at his watch or cellphone, despite the urgency of his situation. Like an obedient child waiting to discover his fate, but prepared to accept it with humility.

The transparency of his soul left her feeling uneasy and inclined to turn him away. Yet the more she honed in on the insides of this man, a different kind of powerful emotion began to simmer inside her. For the first time since he'd set foot in her laundromat, she saw through his brown skin and perceived him only for what he really was. A man. And a damn attractive one.

Akbar's jet-black hair was abundant, straight-as-a-razor and brushed to one side. His was a dimpled, symmetrical face with exquisite formation. Starkly different from the Italian templates she was used to. His nose tiny and minimalist, designed only for the purpose of breathing, rather than attracting undue attention to the face to which it was attached. Akbar's teeth were as white as his soul and his chin chiseled and powerful. His Adam's apple left no doubt about his masculinity, even virility.

Dressed in a faded tan T-shirt, black jeans and sneakers, his humble attire was offset by a bulging physical form, nurtured by years of grueling labor no doubt, rather than expensive sessions with a pretentious personal trainer. These were the muscles of a real man gifted by God and perfected by nature. Donatella imagined him squatting in a rice paddy or laboring over a vegetable plot farm from a young age. Repetitive tasks required to build this sort of physique.

Roughly about her height, maybe a few centimeters taller, Akbar had unblemished skin. Soft as an apricot, begging to be touched and caressed to reveal just how silky it was. Not a single hair on his bare arms. Never before had she seen a man this smooth.

Donatella nodded with a nervous smile and extended her hand to take the shirt from Akbar. She would do her best for this young man to get to his job interview looking sharp.

After handing the shirt over to her, Akbar reached out and squeezed her hands in gratitude.

On any other day, she would have balked at this unexpected physical contact from a stranger. But there was nothing dirty or opportunistic about Akbar's warm touch.

Logged into his psyche as she was, Donatella could feel the young man sprouting inside her and filling her cob-webbed heart at an alarming rate. Perhaps his unexpected gesture was one of respect and courtesy in his culture. But what she didn't expect to feel was a sudden desire for Akbar's touch to mean something more than just good manners or grace.

An insane thought released in her mind was now running havoc on her heart and knees. A long time ago, Donatella's sexual desires had been at the forefront of her perception. Well before Mauro had trampled on her womanhood and left it for dead.

Standing across from Akbar, her emotions had traveled across a turbulent roller coaster within a few short minutes. From initial suspicion of the immigrant who'd walked into her shop, to curiosity, to transient feelings of pity, and now ending with this unexpected rush of wanting something more. Donatella had regressed to an insecure girl with wayward hormones, standing in the orbit of the boy she was attracted to. A man, a woman, and a universe of possibilities that could transpire between them if she chose to play the game differently.

What the hell am I thinking?

Donatella wasn't oblivious to the appropriate course of action. *Take the damn shirt from the guy, ask him to come back in an hour, and let him go.* But obstinacy, even madness had infected her mind, whispering a more ludicrous proposition. Her violent pent-up sexual hunger and repressed womanhood were exploding to the surface unashamedly. Her yearning for independence was equally at the frontline, prodding her to throw the first punch. Because whatever was going through her mind was just as related to her burning need to rebel against Mauro and make the biggest cuckold of him. The very possibility of doing it with a dark-skinned *straniero* was intoxicating and delicious, dripping with poetic justice when she considered Mauro's malevolent views on race and tolerance.

Donatella felt giddy inside. *Does this boy have any idea what's going through my dirty mind?*

She absorbed, even inhaled his tropical smile. Those earnest eyes and his tough, strong body. Everything about him was pulling her closer to a forbidden realm. There was no illusion in her mind about what happens once she allows herself to cross over to the other side. There is no coming back from that.

She glanced at the storage room in the rear and then at Akbar, and made a snap decision.

This was the opportunity she'd been waiting for.

I am going to fuck him.

Donatella spoke in slow, purposeful words, if anything to calm the fire raging through her body.

"Your shirt will be done in an hour. I'll make an exception for you. But in return, I need a tiny favor." She batted her eyelashes, pouted her mouth then traced her tongue around her lips, trying to strike a fine balance between seduction and subtlety.

Akbar nodded with blanket acceptance and a selfless smile. Whatever body language she had tried to exude seemed to fly over his head.

"I have a large box of detergent in the storage room I want to move here. It's heavy and my husband never helps. With anything." *Is this my voice speaking in double entendres? What am I, possessed?*

"Of course, Signora."

Back in the storage room, Donatella pointed to the box in question, which was a lot smaller than what she had made it out to be. Barely a few pounds heavy, really. Akbar glanced back and forth at the box then Donatella, perhaps questioning the logic of why his assistance was required. She must have come across as a spoiled *Romana* compared to his tough, load-bearing women back home.

He smiled and shrugged like he had given up trying to understand this odd puzzle and would humor her anyway. Akbar squatted to pick up the box as ordered, but before his hands reached it, Donatella moved with remarkable stealth.

She tapped him on the shoulder to get his attention.

He stood up again. Confusion clouded his eyes when he turned to face her. As if the puzzle had just become a little more complex.

With her finger on her mouth, Donatella released a low, "hush." Her other hand was still resting on the young man's shoulder when she floated a few steps forward until her lips were almost touching his. His exhalation on her skin and his accelerated breathing were the exact signs she needed.

With a crafty move that astonished even her, Donatella grabbed his pelvis and pulled him closer to her. There was an instant and unmistakable bulge in his pants pushing against her. She had forgotten the wondrous sexual vigor of youth. The swift diversion of blood from the rest of the body to the sexual organs upon the slightest suggestion.

The thrill of an illicit erotic incursion left her knees wobbly, like a freshly cooled *panna cotta*. A warm wave of giddiness rippled unrestricted through her cells, liberating reams of repressed instincts. She drowned in the innocence of his honey-colored eyes and dilated pupils.

Donatella was ready for this, to surrender to his exotic gravitational force. Whether she was the bait or the catch didn't really matter. This man was within her grasp now, caged and helpless, and she wasn't about to release him until she had her way with him.

Akbar's tongue was virginal and tasted like spring marinated in an exotic eastern flavor. A tangy deliciousness she'd never savored, but one she wished she had discovered a lifetime ago. How odd to feel this inexplicable yearning and nostalgia for something she'd never consumed before?

His tongue responded with tentative clumsiness at first as he probed the inside of her mouth. But even his obvious lack of experience was titillating. Akbar may not have kissed a woman before, but the boy was a fast learner and developed his own slow, confident moves.

The sexual instinct. Every man has it, no matter the color of their skin.

Donatella's sense of space and time was gradually, but willingly, diminished. Yet even as her control over her senses was being compromised, her confidence as a woman was erupting at the seams. Mauro's long offensive to erode her intimate needs seemed but a mere footnote now, compared to the potential volumes of lovemaking at her fingertips.

Why have I waited all these years to do this?

Akbar's stubborn erection was knocking hard on her with irrepressible determination. She pulled back from his lips and peeled his T-shirt off to reveal a chest as smooth as his arms. A cheap but not unpleasant deodorant mixed with light, musky sweat. Donatella pushed her nose into his armpits and inhaled him to her core, releasing a long moan, textured with ancient yearning.

She cracked her eyes open to catch a glimpse of Akbar's face, curious to know how all this was affecting him. Entranced, she found him. Drugged on desire, with his eyes fluttering like a newly liberated butterfly.

Donatella took her time to taste every part of him.

She licked his small brown nipples, which firmed up into rock-hard pebbles. Like a cat, she suckled on them with slow rhythmic precision, moving back and forth to savor the entire surface area of his bullet-proof chest.

He groaned from a deep place and his body shuddered uncontrollably under her bewitching spell. She had struck gold with his nipples. They seemed to be a hot erogenous zone for him. But the way his eyes widened as her tongue worked his areolas suggested one thing—that this humble part of his body could bring him so much pleasure when licked, sucked and bitten was probably breaking news to him. He rolled his eyes back then closed them, and continued to growl and moan from the depth of his being, getting even harder and pushing even stiffer into her now.

Akbar kept repeating a word in Bengali under his breath, which sounded like *Isbara*. Donatella had no idea what that word meant, but hearing an unfamiliar language repeated hypnotically was arousing and implored her to take bolder risks. She traced her tongue down Akbar's titanium abdomen, taking her time to salute his navel, before squatting on her feet and undoing the zipper and the button of his jeans. With Akbar's pants down to his ankles, she glanced up to absorb his divine presence.

Mauro had been Donatella's first and only lover. She had never seen another man in the flesh, let alone a circumcised one. The exhilarating vision of Akbar's gravity-defying, rock-hard performance suspended in mid-air left her pulsating and moist.

His naked, bronze-tinted body was a glorious vision she could hardly stop staring at. Never once in the past had Donatella coveted a man of color. Akbar was like an emissary of a new species of men she had been oblivious to and deprived of all her life. This powerful revelation rushed through her veins like an expensive narcotic.

With one hand grasping her trophy and the other cupping her victim's scrotum, Donatella continued to do with her tongue what she had started on Akbar's lips and nipples. Once again, the taste, texture, smell and how this made her feel were like nothing she'd ever experienced before. Like she'd been abducted into a parallel dimension where her sexual hunger was amplified by many factors.

Working her lips and her tongue gently, rotating between fast and slow repetitions, she could feel Akbar's thighs trembling against her face and his moaning growing louder now. Her saliva mixed with his early liquid releases created a moist sheen that was at first distracting, but ultimately delightful to marvel at.

She moved her hands to grasp his iron-tough buttocks to achieve a better anchor with her lips. This seemed to boost the current vibrating through Akbar's body. So she withdrew. Slowly. She wasn't about to relieve this customer before he completed the cardinal task he'd been preordained to perform.

Fumbling in the supplies closet for improvised bedding, Donatella found an old moving blanket the workers had left behind when Mauro was renovating the shop. With feverish clumsiness, she sprawled it out on the cold concrete floor and stripped down naked.

Akbar's mouth was wide open in disbelief as she guided him down to the floor so he was lying flat on his back, his erection pointing straight to heaven. She straddled her willing victim. His muscular thighs against hers thawed more than her body, unshackling her heart as well.

Donatella lowered her face to kiss his lips again and whisper dirty words of desire in his ears. Even if he didn't grasp her Italian, the thrill for her was to hear her voice being slutty with a man other than her husband. And whether he understood or not, Akbar's heart was wild and frenetic when she laid her head against his chest.

Curling up against his body, she dunked her breasts straight unto his face and into his mouth. Like a baby, Akbar was programmed to latch, but like a man he knew exactly what to do with them.

He raised his hands from his sides and took control of her swells, licking and brushing his face against them like a wild boar. At times he bit through her nipples harder than she was used to, but the pain of his pearly teeth cutting into the one part of her flesh with the most nerve sendings was oddly satiating and she felt no need to temper or stop him snacking on them.

When the moment was right, she put her finger on her lips and once again hushed with irreverence so her lover would pay attention now. The grand finale was just around the corner. Sliding her crotch down his body, Donatella wiggled into the perfect position. With her heels dug into the floor, she raised her pelvis above Akbar's firm penis, which she held at the base with a single hand. One confident squat was all it took for her to achieve the perfect entry.

Akbar must have been much larger than average, although her only benchmark was Mauro. It didn't take much for the Bangladeshi to surpass the furthest point Mauro had been able to touch inside her.

When Donatella felt that sliding down any further would be unbearably painful, she remained locked in position, against every instinct programmed in her pelvis to pump up and down. She hovered at the nexus of pain and pleasure and savored every bit of it.

All she desired at that instant was to feel Akbar safe inside her.

Hard.

Warm.

Protective.

All encompassing.

Divine.

And complete.

Donatella was alive for the first time in a long time. Air flowed through her lungs of its own volition, without her having to struggle to breath. Light enveloped her body, even though her eyes were shut. She pinned his arms to the floor as if to keep him from escaping. To keep him there for eternity. Until their bodies withered away.

Donatella erupted in a massive, galactic orgasm. It left her convulsing, cursing and screaming at the top of her lungs. She crash-landed hard with her head lying on Akbar's earth-toned chest before she almost passed out.

It could have been five or fifty minutes during which Donatella was banished into a trance-like slumber.

When she began to descend, Akbar was still hard inside her. She moved up against his body to observe his eyes. They were wide open now and twinkling. He'd been laying vigil by her side to protect her while her soul had momentarily escaped her body. But there was something different in his eyes now, a new fire of a man intent on completing a mission.

Carefully, she withdrew from Akbar, motioned for him to get up and then shifted positions so she was now lying on her back, under him. No more words or hand gestures were required for her young lover to understand what his natural calling was, and what he needed to do next.

The instinct was animalistic and stamped on his genes. The gentle, docile man she had seduced with little resistance was transforming into a ravenous sexual being, fulfilling the prophecy for which he was created by God or nature.

His strong hands pressing down on her pelvis kept her in position as he penetrated through her with no advance warning or mercy. Like a car revving up or a guitarist tuning his strings before a performance, Akbar's thrusts were at first exploratory. Then, when he had found his perfect groove, he started pounding her harder and faster than she had ever thought a human body could move. With every overwhelming thrust, Akbar grunted louder and more forcefully, releasing decades of uncultivated raw sexual energy trapped in his body.

A tapestry of unimaginable pleasure, sweet pain and terror spurted through her as Akbar kept up his relentless offensive. His delivery was so powerful, so focused, all she could do was surrender to him and scream her lungs out.

She relished and feared the thought she could be trapped under his body forever. That he would never stop. But before she could have any other thoughts, another far more violent orgasm burst through her body like fireworks. And yet another.

Donatella hardly possessed the energy or the vocal chords to scream any louder. Only muted air now was coming out of her throat like the Lord had temporarily disabled her voice. Right before she crash-landed for the third time this morning, Akbar's hand pulled hard on her hair as he too began to empty his heart, soul and entire being inside her with ferocious power. Gushes upon gushes of warm stickiness filling and fulfilling her, as the man riding her trembled like a dangerous volcanic eruption.

The annoying buzz of the doorbell awoke her, but she ignored whoever it was until they gave up and left.

What time is it? How long have we been here?

It smelled like sex everywhere. How she missed that.

Next to her, Akbar hadn't been a figment of her imagination after all, curled on one side, facing away. She ran her hands through his hair but he did not respond.

"*Amore?*" she whispered.

Nothing.

She turned around and snuggled next to him, her face

touching his. His eyes were open, and a stream of tears was gliding in slow motion down his face.

She caressed him.

Still no signs of life.

Donatella kissed his lips and licked his tongue.

He didn't react.

"What's wrong?"

"*Isbara*," he finally murmured, as if the mere sound of the word was universal and sufficient for Donatella to understand his intent.

She kissed him again, this time tasting the saltiness of his tears.

"*Isbara*?"

He nodded.

"What does it mean?"

He stared at her with befuddlement, then said, "God."

"What about him?"

"He hates me now."

"I sincerely doubt it. Why do you say that?"

"I've sinned. And I've missed the job interview." More earnest tears flowed out of his eyes with audible sniffles.

She moved her face closer to Akbar and hugged him tight. Harboring debilitating feelings of guilt and shame was her particular area of expertise. Her finger traced down his spine and it made him tremble.

Donatella planted small kisses on his lips then held him tight like a mother would a diseased child. Everything will be okay, she reassured him. He didn't have to worry about God because she promised to have a chat with him on Akbar's behalf.

When his tears subsided, Akbar smiled and for the first

time since his conscience had flared up, he kissed her back. Whatever she had promised, he had chosen to believe. Having already given her his body, he didn't put up much of a fight and surrendered his fate to her will.

She drew imaginary circles with the tips of her fingers on the small of Akbar's back until he slipped into a deep sleep.

Donatella admired her own naked body with a different outlook. She too would close her eyes now and slip into a blissful place, warmed not just by the explosions that had rippled through her body a short while ago, but also by her lover's long breaths against her still-tingling skin.

The life growing inside Donatella was Akbar's. In other words, for the first time ever, her name was up on the marital scoreboard against Mauro. Sure, her husband still held a massive advantage against her, but the long journey to vanquishing the son-of-a-bitch had started on the day she gave herself to another man. One way or the other, she pledged to run Mauro to the ground.

Over the last twenty years, everything in Donatella's neighborhood had changed except one constant, a billboard across from her apartment advertising the services of one private eye.

Prime ministers rose and fell, the lira was replaced by the euro doubling the cost of everything overnight, even *mortadella*, and Fiat gobbled every other national auto manufacturer. But Inspector Guido Marinelli's billboard was eternal.

The billboard itself had been replaced a million times to account for the elements and vandalism. Guido's image, on the other hand, was immortal. His was a perfect mop of seventies hair. Green wire-frame glasses sat effortlessly on his crooked Roman nose, no doubt to inspire scholarly confidence. A quarter of a smirk was stamped on his face, implying he knew things you wouldn't even begin to dream of.

The picture must have been taken when Guido was in his forties. His facial expression was entirely casual, almost absurdly so. Everything about the billboard suggested Guido wanted you to believe in the innocence of his offerings, or that busting cheating spouses, or exposing thieving business partners, were as innocuous as getting your teeth whitened.

Donatella had often wondered why she never ran into him in the neighborhood. Getting a haircut, having a coffee at the bar, or even snooping around as his job must have required him to do.

Guido, she concluded, was a mythical creature who only lived on that billboard. But ridicule him in her mind as she had in the past, his timeless billboard had proved to be a most effective marketing tool. When Donatella had finally developed a need for a private eye, the only face she could think of was that of the man on the billboard.

In the private eye's waiting room, across from his visibly botoxed secretary, feelings of sordidness by association crawled inside Donatella's chest the minute she sat down on the threadbare couch.

There was something decidedly sleazy in the air. Perhaps the incremental energy imparted by Guido's clients and their miseries had given the space its own tortured soul.

James Bond posters, fugitive from the eighties, were plastered across the walls and didn't exactly inspire confidence.

But the crowing set piece of making the whole scene somewhat off was Guido's fifty-something personal assistant, dressed like a horny teenager and chewing florescent bubble gum as she leafed through low-brow magazines. Every so often she would eye Donatella with a modicum of suspicion or disdain, not that it mattered. With every passing minute, Donatella regretted her decision to come here.

More than an hour had elapsed when a tearful woman stormed out dramatically of Guido's office. A few minutes after that he finally buzzed Donatella in.

A suffocating smell of older man's cologne punched her between the eyes when she walked into his office. Hardly an improvement on the toxic cocktail of other smells: tobacco smoke permeating the walls, the chemical funk of toner ink and moldy carpeting.

Guido was crouched at his desk behind a mountain of documents that looked more like props and less like real work.

At first glance, his resemblance to his billboard avatar was uncanny. But the longer she studied him, the more the real Guido appeared to be a bad attempt to replicate his younger self. His hair dyed too bright, his face lifted too tight, and his implanted teeth unnaturally white.

Maybe he and his geriatric Barbie get botoxed together, two for the price of one?

The real Guido sitting across from her was at least thirty years older than his billboard edition. Despite being a caricature of his old self, the private eye emitted an aura of vintage cunning that was mildly reassuring. She couldn't quite figure out what, but something about him implored her not to discount him just yet and to ignore the loud voice in her head begging her to bolt out of there in a flash. Against her better judgment, she trusted her more subtle instinct and decided to give him a little bit longer.

"Take a seat." He didn't blink or take his eyes off her once, and that made her feel instantly uncomfortable. Donatella tried to manufacture a smile as she sank in the armchair.

Guido lit up a cigar, not bothering with the frivolities of asking her if she minded. Any uncertainty about his age was laid to rest as she honed in on his translucent hands with bulging, spider-webbing blue veins.

"Cheating husband?"

Donatella nodded.

"What else. He beats you up? Rapes you? Anal sex against your will? Does he molest the kids?" he said, not sounding convinced of any of those sensational accusations, but probably throwing them about for shock value.

"No. Nothing like that."

Guido blew a few smoke circles in her direction as if they would help him probe her more judiciously. He bit his lips and rubbed his chin a little.

"Emotionally abusive. Manipulative. Highly secretive. A well-rounded son-of-a-bitch. You need material evidence of his cheating and a laundry list of all his assets. Everything he's stashing away so you can clean him spotless on the way out. How close am I?"

Guido's assessment of her needs was terrifying in its accuracy, but he wasn't going to get any compliments from her. Nothing about him suggested his ego was lacking any stoking. Donatella just smiled and pursed her lips.

"Get the silver package for a thousand. It includes a full report and a detailed log of his affairs and his lovers for a week."

Donatella's eyebrows shot up at the word 'lovers.'

"Trust me, Signora, even though you're thinking it's one woman, there's usually more, often many."

"I don't care. He could be sleeping with half of Garbatella. I just need whatever evidence you dredge up to be rock solid in court. Will it be enough?"

"Depends on how magnanimous the judge is. And, of course, for your husband to really be cheating on you. Many times it's just in a woman's mind, these matters. Are you prepared for that possibility?"

"Oh, don't worry, he's cheating on me. I am one hundred percent—"

"Your divorce lawyer—is he any good?" Guido cut her off.

"I...I don't—at least—"

Guido's eyes widened and he slapped his open palm hard on the glass surface of his desk, like he was squatting a fly.

"You need one! Don't go cheap if you want to avoid getting screwed over," he erupted.

"Of course. I—I plan to," she lied. Donatella hadn't thought as far ahead as the legal proceedings of a divorce.

"Without knowing the caliber of your lawyer, I recommend the gold package instead. For seventeen-hundred you also get photos of the lovebirds in public areas. Nothing explicit, but highly suggestive. Holding her hands. Caressing her ass. That kind of stuff is gold in court. It shows he's cavalier and doesn't give a shit about being caught in public."

"I want an open and shut case, leaving no margin for doubt or interpretation," Donatella said firmly.

Guido sighed then put out his cigar and appeared deep in thought for a while.

"Here's what I think," he finally said. "You need the platinum package. For twenty-five hundred you get the bedroom goods. High-quality photographs—and just because I think you are a decent lady—I'll throw in the sex tapes for free. His attorney will claim our photos are doctored until he sees the videos. That will certainly shut his filthy mouth and force him to knock some sense into your husband to settle fast, and settle generously."

Doubt started creeping in Donatella's chest about how easy Mauro would make this for her. "What if you can't find anything? My husband's not an idiot, and I am certain he'll notice if someone's shadowing him, let alone pointing a camera at his penis."

"I get twenty percent up front and the balance when I deliver the damning evidence. If you're not happy with what I dig up, don't pay me and I'll just keep the initial down payment. In all my years in private practice, I never once stuffed a job."

Donatella didn't want to overthink this. She sighed and ignored her many doubts and decided to jump in the deep end of Guido's pool. "I'll pay in cash then."

She reached in her handbag to fish out for her wads of euros.

"Wait." Guido held up his palm to stop her.

"You don't take cash?"

"I take nothing *but* cash, lady."

"So?"

"There's something else you need to know."

Donatella bit her lips and looked hard at Guido. She saw something unexpected in his eyes.

He likes me? Or does he feel sorry for me? Maybe both.

"You're probably thinking I am a huge risk."

Donatella shook her head, but he was, of course, right on the money.

"Maybe you look down at my entire profession. Charlatans and crooks the lot of us. I blame the movies for that."

"No, no. Not at all—"

Guido didn't humor her interjection and carried on. "Maybe the only reason you came to see me is because I'm the only private investigator you know. In other words, you're here because you're desperate. You have no one else to go to."

"That's not true—"

"I don't care either way, to be honest with you. But I must warn you I'm the best in this business, a trained professional with many years of experience. I keep up with the times and invest in the latest technology. I have amazing contacts throughout the police force and my reputation precedes me. I deliver results."

"Of course. I…wouldn't be here if I had any doubts about your experience, Signor Marinelli," Donatella said with half-hearted indignation. "Your billboard had always caught my attention."

"You don't understand, Signora Forleo—" he peered at his notepad to make sure he had her name right. "I am not trying to sell my services. I want to dissuade you from hiring me."

Donatella shrugged, not quite understanding.

"Women like you, desperate to unveil the truth about their husbands, come through my doors every day. You'd be naive to think you'll get closure or move on, when you have evidence he's fucking around."

"What do you mean?"

"There's no turning back after you sign on with me, is what I am trying to tell you. There's no unknowing the terrible truths I am going to reveal about the father of your children and the man you were once madly in love with. The truth is always more despicable than your wildest suspicions, is what this job has taught me."

Guido's thin lips contorted to form the same quarter smirk

she recalled from his billboard face. An expression suggesting he knew and saw things that would cause one's hair to stand on end.

"I am ready for this and prepared for whatever you find. There's no doubt in my mind he's cheating, I just need it documented so I can get rid of him once and for all."

Guido shook his head.

"That's what you all say."

Three weeks later, Guido summoned Donatella to an over-priced café in EUR, the heartland of Mussolini's ambitious, but still-born urban expansion project. Donatella knew it more as the joint where dirty old men with material means showed off their fancy cars and seemingly underage designer girlfriends.

Maybe the onlookers were thinking the same thing about her sitting across from Guido, although she hardly looked the part.

He wore a white blazer over a purple shirt, and his face was masked by a pair of camp green shades. The light in his office, the first time she saw him, must have been deceptive. Now under the unblemished Roman sky there was an explosion of gray follicles on his head, or perhaps he had forgotten to dye it. In natural light, he also appeared a lot paler with near-translucent skin.

A smug-faced waiter buzzed by and Donatella barely managed to catch his attention to order a *marocchino* coffee with heavy cream. Ever since she found out she was pregnant, she had tried to diminish or eliminate her favorite beverage, but today her nerves demanded a serious caffeine fix.

Guido had two manila envelopes at the table, perched near

a half-empty glass of café latte. A sudden rush of trepidation and fear quivered through her body as she sat across from him.

What if Mauro was cheating on me with one of my friends? Or a neighbor in the building?

He handed her one of the two envelopes.

"This is everything you need to know about his affairs and his assets. Nothing too exotic as far as the women are concerned. It's no one you know, if that's what's turned your face white as *panna*. They're expensive, high-end call girls. And you were right, it happens at your house when you're at work. About two to three times a week."

"Expensive?" All these years she had formed a mental image of Mauro's sluts as being of the cheap and nasty variety.

"Oh, yeah. Prime cuts, too. Had I known you're married to such a prosperous man I would have charged you double," Guido said with a dreadful cackle.

A few of the other patrons abandoned their conversations and shot a glance towards their table, as if to check the sound had not come from a dangerous, escaped animal.

"How rich?"

"It's all in the file, but I'll give you a summary." He pulled out a little notepad from the inside pocket of his blazer and pushed his glasses as far down his crooked nose without them slipping off.

"Mauro's known personal assets in the European Union amount to an astonishing six million euros."

Donatella's heart almost came to a screeching halt.

Bastardo! Where the hell did he get all this money from?

"About two million is pure cash held in time deposits and savings accounts. He's got another three million invested in property—a town house in London, an apartment in Berlin and a small vineyard outside Florence. He also has four commercial properties across Rome, one of which is your laundromat."

"And the other million?"

"Stocks, options, luxury cars and a boat. A really nice one."

Donatella took a sip of her sweet coffee with a fatty layer of cream floating on top, and with the revelation of Mauro's unexpected worth, her heart palpitated in her throat and the room spun ever so slowly. The information Guido was feeding her was surreal. The magnitude of the amounts was giddying.

"You said 'known' assets. Could he be hiding more?"

"I guarantee it. But not in the EU. It'll be anywhere impossible to trace. Switzerland, the Caribbean, even the Middle East or Asia. He's sitting on a cash cow with the spare parts business. Which brings me to his commercial assets. The most conservative estimate suggests they're worth three to four million even at the height of this depressed economy. And—"

"What?" Donatella snapped.

"That's just his legitimate activities."

She shot him a bewildered look.

Guido looked around with orchestrated suspicion to make sure everyone else was minding their own business. His voice dropped a few decibels.

"I don't have material proof, but your husband is under the radars of the *guardia di finanza*."

"Tax evasion?"

Guido chuckled and shook his head. "Tax evasion? Seriously, Signora? Every Italian is under investigation for tax evasion by the *guardia di finanza*. Newborn babies are under investigation for tax evasion. Where exactly do you live?"

Donatella shrugged.

"This information is from an old friend at the *guardia*."

"Keep talking."

"Let me ask you a question. If a law-abiding citizen wants to upgrade their car, what do they do?"

Donatella was taken aback by the sudden rerouting of the conversation. "Ah...Sell it, I guess, then buy a new one and pay the difference?"

"Exactly. But not everyone is straight like that."

"Please explain."

"Some people prefer that their car goes 'missing,' and their insurance company pays them out. It beats the royal hassle of having to deal with selling it and the risk of not getting the best price."

Donatella's head started to spin again.

"That's where people like your husband come in. They're hired by dishonest owners to steal their cars so they can then turn around and cash in the insurance policies. It's a scam, and your husband is the fulcrum that brings it all together."

"So what happens to the stolen cars?" Donatella whispered.

Guido smiled as if the best part was yet to come. "They break it down to the smallest constituent parts, then ship them overseas where the vehicles are reassembled and sold in the black market. Sometimes even introduced as legal imports by way of corrupt government officials in these countries. There is a huge market for this kind of racket in the Middle East. Especially places like Iran, which is languishing under long years of economic sanctions by the West."

"And Mauro does this?"

"He doesn't just do this, apparently he's the best."

Donatella thought hard about what Guido had just told her. "If the *guardia di finanza* are on to him, why haven't they arrested him? It would certainly make my life easier."

Guido sighed as he sipped the last remaining foam from his glass, and then smacked his lips in satisfaction.

"Because he's protected, of course. He's paying top-notch bribes."

"To whom?"

"Everyone whose palm needs to be greased for Mauro to operate effectively and with peace of mind. It's an entire substructure that goes as far up as how deep your pockets are and what level of brazen crime you want to normalize. No wonder this country is going straight to hell on a high-speed train."

Donatella's head hung low.

Guido's initial warning, which she had slighted, came back to haunt her. The truth was far bleaker than what she expected. She had prepared herself to learn of Mauro's bedroom indiscretions, or that he was hiding a few hundred thousand euros here or there. But the man Guido was describing was someone she had never met, and it stung hard. The audacity of Mauro's betrayal wasn't just limited to fucking high-class *puttanas* three times a week. He had completely hoodwinked her and their children and was leading a parallel, dangerous life.

"If this information is speculative, how important is it for me? I can't even use it in court."

"It's more important than you can imagine," Guido said.

Donatella did not understand, and it must have shown on her face.

"Allow me to explain." Guido leaned forward. "I am telling you this information so you proceed with extreme caution against this man. Your husband is not a just a philandering bastard. He's a hardened criminal working and associating with some terrible people. If you're going to go after him, a simple divorce case is not going to cut it. He'll have you knifed and filleted before your divorce lawyer's paralegal starts typing a single letter in your case. With men like him, you have to go for the jugular and take them out before they get wind of what's about to happen."

Guido was suddenly quiet, with his hand resting on the second envelope on the table. He puzzled over Donatella's face, scrutinizing her intently, as if struggling to understand something about her. After deliberating, he bit his lips and handed her the second envelope.

"What's this?"

"When I take on a case, I don't just touch the surface like some of the other rookies I am ashamed to call my peers in this profession. I do my job, and I do it well."

Donatella wasn't any wiser about the contents of this second envelope, but Guido's introduction was foreboding, to say the least.

"If you want to get rid of him, you have to ambush him and you need to be brutal about it. In this envelope is information about the man you know as Mauro, your husband. These are his origins. Did he ever tell you why he had to leave Napoli so urgently?"

"We were eloping, so we needed to do it fast and before my family could suspect."

Guido nodded in approval. "That's a good line. I would have believed it too."

"Please, I can't bear this anymore. What do you mean 'the man I know as Mauro?'"

"Mauro's been harboring a dark secret for as long as you've been married to him. It's the real reason he had to escape Napoli and change his name legally soon after you moved to Rome. If you want to take him out, the contents of this envelope are possibly the only way to do it."

Donatella's hands trembled as she reached out to take the package, of which Guido was not yet prepared to let go. They were both holding it at the same time.

Her throat was parched and she could hardly speak, let alone breathe. Everything she had heard so far suggested Mauro—or whatever his real name was—had been leading a shocking second life of crime and untold wealth.

What Guido was alluding to with this second envelope was an even deeper layer to the man she had married. She wanted to slap herself for being so stupid, but then remembered how young and insecure she was when he had spun his web around her. Mauro was twelve years older than her, and her innocence—no, stupidity—must have been one of her most attractive qualities.

"I must caution you, Donatella. This path here has only one possible outcome for Mauro, and it's not pretty. He is, after all, the father of your children. You have to ask yourself if you are willing to live with the decisions you make."

"What other option do I have?" Donatella hissed under her breath.

Guido reached out and caressed her face. His hand felt cold, like a dead eel. "You're a very nice lady. I like you. So I'll tell it to you straight. You only have two options, both equally detestable."

"I don't understand."

"You can choose to carry on living the life you've had with him so far, as if nothing ever happened. Just suck it up and hope he dies of a stroke or gets entangled in something horrific related to the sewer in which he operates. Or, you may follow the path laid out in this envelope and terminate him."

"What?"

"You heard right. I'm giving you your best shot to take him out, without having to do it yourself. But—"

"But what?"

"After you do it, will you be able to look your children in the eye knowing you were responsible for their father's most horrible, most painful death? It's a hard choice, but only you can decide. A life of shame or a life of guilt? There's no third option."

When Guido loosened his grip on the envelope, Donatella had made her decision.

Every Thursday morning, Donatella and Akbar made love at the back of her shop. They had become experts now on evading detection. When they were done, Donatella would slither out first and reopen the laundromat. When the coast was clear, Akbar would then emerge holding a bag of laundry, pretending to be a client. He would linger for a while, then leave.

The Bangladeshi had sprouted inside of Donatella just like his child. Could this be love, even though all they ever shared was sex? Whatever it was, it felt addictive. Donatella was unable to fantasize of a future without Mauro and not fill this vacuum with her brown-skinned lover. Sure, it was an insane proposition. Even if she could get rid of Mauro, she still had to think of her kids and how they would react to such a revelation.

Donatella was three months pregnant when she confessed to Akbar about the child they had made together.

Fear and confusion clouded his eyes. No doubt, as a man, he was programmed to perceive such an announcement as possible entrapment. She held his face in her hands and hugged him tight. Speaking in Italian clear as water and earnest as her feelings for him, Donatella wanted to leave no doubt in his mind.

"Don't be scared, *amore mio*. I expect nothing of you. I can raise this child on my own. No one needs to know you are the father, if you decide to leave us."

"You are married. What about your husband?" he inquired with doe-eyed purity, as if the concepts of divorce or separation were plug-ins missing from his operating system.

"Not for long. I am going to escape Mauro's hell very soon. I have a plan..."

Akbar wrapped his hands around his head, like the weight of the world was about to come crashing down on him.

"I am not like you."

"What do you mean?"

"I have a big family in Bogra to take care of. I'm not rich—"

"Let me ask you a question," Donatella said as she placed her palm on his warm chest. "But answer me from the depths of your heart."

"Yes?"

"If we could escape somewhere far where no one would judge us, and if your family in Bangladesh was taken care of and never had to worry about money again. If it was just the two of us and our child, Akbar, would you want to be with me?"

Akbar thought about this stream of possibilities, and then inhaled a vast amount of air. He did not answer in words, but raised his head and devoured every inch of Donatella's neck, with his hands grasping her buttocks firmly, pulling each side wide open and driving her crazy.

"I will make you the happiest man alive, *amore*," she purred in his ears, eyes closed.

When they had both put their clothes back on, Donatella took out an envelope from her handbag. Over the past three months, she had painted a grim, although somewhat exaggerated account of her relationship with Mauro, to ensure Akbar was primed to revile and fear him with equal vigor.

"Listen carefully," she whispered for added dramatic effect. "If we want to be together, there are certain things we need to do. We need to follow a specific plan."

"I don't understand?"

"Mauro is not just a terrible husband. He's also an extremely dangerous man, Akbar. I cannot just leave him to be with you. I have to…disappear first. And if you want to be with me, we have to devise an air-tight escape plan to avoid his venom."

Akbar nodded, but with no less bewilderment sketched on his face.

"I want you to go back home and pack your bags and get ready to travel tomorrow. You are flying back to Bangladesh."

"What?" His face turned pale as if he had just seen an apparition.

"Don't worry, it's only temporary. I need you out of Italy and far from Mauro's grasp just in case things go wrong."

She opened the envelope and took out its contents.

"In here are three thousand euros in cash, and a plane ticket in your name to Dhaka, via Dubai, flying tomorrow. You will remain there for three months. This money should cover your expenses to support your family while you're there and out of work. After ninety days, fly back to Rome, but don't come here to see me. Instead, go to the Banca Popolare del Lazio two streets behind and ask to access the safety deposit box in your name. They'll want to see your ID, of course."

Akbar was absorbing everything, and seemed to be taking frantic mental notes.

Donatella handed him the key to the safety deposit box in question, and explained it was held jointly in both their names. Once she'd figured out her escape destination, she would access the box and leave him exact instructions on how to find her, along with an airline ticket and money for his onward journey.

"Outside Italy?"

She wrapped his arms around her waist and nodded as her mind drifted to any number of remote spots she could start fresh with her lover.

"My residency permit only allows me to travel within Schengen countries in Europe," he reminded her.

"I know. It'll be somewhere on the continent where you can safely get to me. We'll stay there for a few years until the day I can pass on to you the Italian citizenship. After that, we can go wherever our dreams take us."

Akbar was speechless. Donatella planted a soft kiss on his lips as she pinned him to the wall, to seal the deal. He never said a word, but his tongue dancing around her mouth left little doubt he had signed on to her insane plan.

Twenty-four years ago when Donatella and Mauro were escaping Napoli, the only thing she could think of was how she would never miss this toxic wasteland. With every mile Mauro drove north towards Rome, Donatella could breathe lighter.

Whatever life would throw at them, they would work it out together, and it would pale in comparison to the purgatory of a Neapolitan existence. At least these were her thoughts back then.

Over the years as Mauro robbed her of the essence of happiness, her estranged family and the Napoli of her childhood came back to eat away at her insides.

Still, no matter how bitter the nostalgia stung, Donatella never once suspected she would make the journey back, let alone on her own.

This wasn't a grand homecoming or a quest to make amends with her parents and siblings. Donatella had no such compulsions. No plans to walk by her family's *gelateria* in the historic center, to check if her youngest brother, Francesco, was behind the counter, to find out what he looked like now as a man, when the only memory she had of him was as a boy. Or to determine if he and her other brothers had forgiven her, or if they had inherited their parents eternal wrath for how she shamed the family by eloping with Mauro. She had no intention to saunter on the *lungomare* to inhale the filtered air blown by Mount Vesuvius across the Gulf of Napoli. Not because she didn't crave these things, but Donatella didn't possess the luxury to indulge her nostalgia. Her drive south was a critical, dangerous mission requiring absolute focus and anonymity.

Following the instructions Guido had given her, Donatella parked her rented Fiat 500 across the street from a fishmonger in the heart of Scampia—a violent and economically depressed neighborhood, exemplifying the very worst of the city's organized crime epidemic. Before fleeing Napoli, she had never once set foot in this urban cesspool.

This was not a part of the city any woman would want to wander about alone. Hard-core drugs were not just traded in broad daylight, but casually used in the public eye. There were more prostitutes and hit men per capita than teachers or police officers. At various times in its relatively modern history, bullets flying across buildings was not considered abnormal.

For the last four decades, two feuding organized crime families have been raging a bloody turf war that terrorized the residents of Scampia, producing hair-raising episodes of violent murders.

When Donatella stepped out of her car to walk across to the fishmonger, raw human misery filled the air. This wasn't even the most desolate part of Scampia. The streets were paved and there were no mountains of overflowing rubbish. But the unmistakable stench of something sinister hovered above her head. An amorphous presence prodding her to do what she had to do and then get the hell out of there quick.

She had clamped her steering wheel, but instinctively turned back to double-check she had locked the car before making her way to the fishmonger.

Inside the shop, an old man sat on a battered wooden chair staring into nothingness.

Oppressive neon lights on the ceiling made Donatella irritable. There was something about the glare of neon that invoked a sense of oblivion and mediocrity.

Behind the counter, a few limp fish were on display on a thin layer of ice. Around them, bouquets of parsley were intended for decorative purposes, but failed on every count to live up to that promise.

On the other end, a mishmash of tangled squid and

a handful of microscopic shrimp didn't appear any more inviting.

The old man didn't even flinch when Donatella had walked in. Wednesday mornings were slow in the fish business. Fresh produce was delivered on Tuesdays and Fridays.

This gruff *nonno* must have been stationed here on slow days when few or no customers were expected. Donatella started doubting the efficacy of Guido's instructions, but had no option but to forge ahead with the plan he had laid out for her.

"Good morning," she said with a wry smile.

The old man nodded his head and reciprocated with a single grunt but still no eye contact.

"I'm looking for wild clams."

"Come back after lunch," he responded with casual indifference.

She feigned interest in the paltry products on display then turned to face him again.

"How about shark fin? I was told I could find the finest *Pinna di Squalo* in town, right here."

Jumping to his feet with surprising agility given his age, the fishmonger quickly lost his geriatric ambivalence. Instead, he honed in on Donatella with terrifying focus, like he feared in one swift move she could empty the contents of a firearm in his skull.

"What did you say?" he hissed as he moved up close.

She scanned the shop to make sure it was just the two of them and whispered, "I said *Pinna di Squalo*."

"Keep talking," he said, fire shooting out of his eyes.

"I come with vital information for him. Information he'd been hunting after for the last twenty-four years." Donatella tried to sound confident, but inside, her heart was sprinting back and forth around her chest cavity. Her eyes blinked like a dying lightbulb, her hands frozen and clammy.

"Wait here." The old man disappeared in a room at the back of the shop and never returned.

A few minutes later, two young muscle heads stormed into the shop. One of them shuttered it closed as the other approached her.

"The blue 500 parked outside. Is it yours?" he barked.

"Yes," she managed to utter.

"You'll leave it here and come with us. I need to frisk you and check your bag for weapons and bugs before we go for a drive."

When they had determined Donatella wasn't carrying anything nefarious, the three of them exited the shop where a black jeep was parked outside. One of them jumped in the driver's seat and the other, who had frisked her, sat next to her in the back.

With no prior warning or asking her permission, he wrapped a tight blindfold around her face. This made Donatella claustrophobic and instantly aware of just how perilous this situation had suddenly become. Her heart wasn't just sprinting, but spinning out of control. Her mouth was dry, and fainting didn't seem too far off.

Any number of hours could have elapsed when they finally removed her blindfold. The ride had been smooth and lulling, enough for her to calm her nerves, even weave in and out of sleep. Judging by the length of the journey, she figured they had taken her out of town.

When they finally emerged from the car, the afternoon seagulls and the smell of iodine in the air gave it away. Perhaps they were somewhere on the Amalfi coast.

They walked for a while on sand before the two men asked her to sit down on a chair, cuffed her, removed the blindfold and walked away.

Another empty chair had been placed in front of her, closer to the shore. For a few minutes, she gazed at the horizon of a calm Mediterranean and considered how her day had started. The fact her throat hadn't been slit or she wasn't lying dead at the bottom of the sea, yet, was somewhat reassuring.

She turned her head as far around as it would go with her hands tied to the chair, glimpsing an unexpected but imposing white mansion about five-hundred feet inland. There was nothing else nearby on either side. Whoever lived here must have also owned massive stretches of land around it. She turned her head to once again stare at the abundant swathes of turquoise water. This was like no other seaside she had ever seen in Napoli.

Donatella closed her eyes momentarily and focused on the sound of lapping waves.

"What do you want from me?" a voice whispered.

Donatella cracked her eyes open to find the old fishmonger she had seen earlier at the shop sitting across from her.

"It's you?"

"One minute. Speak. My patience is notoriously thin."

"Are you Don Di LoRusso? Also known as *Pinna di Squalo*?"

"Fifty-five seconds left," he said as he glanced at an expensive wristwatch that sparkled under the sun. If she was the sort who paid attention to these things, she would have noticed earlier the incongruity of a spare-tire fishmonger wearing a watch probably worth double the value of her car. This was her man.

"Twenty-four years ago, the Montanari family ruled Napoli. You and your brothers, the three sons of Giuseppe Di LoRusso, had pledged allegiance to them and worked under their protection. That is, until an internal crack in their leadership structure weakened them. Your family saw this as a once-in-a-lifetime opportunity to secede and start your own splinter crime dynasty."

The old man listened quietly, with no visible reaction to her accusation that he and his brother were criminals. The impatience on his face had all but subsided now. He was listening.

"But the Montanaris didn't take too well to that. They closed rank and overlooked their differences, deciding instead to come after you and your brothers, to set an example to those with faltering loyalties within their organization. They pledged to kill not you or your brothers, but one son each from your lineage. Two of your nephews were murdered, but you managed to smuggle your only child, Giacomo, to America.

"To smoke him out, the Montanaris abducted your son's girlfriend, Fiorella Verde. But he never surfaced, because you never told him. Eventually, they raped her, shot her in the head, stuffed her in a car and set it on fire in the middle of the Scampia park."

The old man's head hung low and for the first time since she'd met him, his poker face had betrayed him. His eyes seemed moist, and his face stoic, struggling to avoid the inevitable emotion of a father who had to bury his own flesh and blood.

"You wanted to keep this away from Giacomo but he found

out anyway. He couldn't live with the guilt and jumped off the George Washington bridge in New Jersey, taking his own life."

The last remaining patriarch of the Di LoRusso clan held his hands against his head as the avalanche of painful memories Donatella was releasing seemed to cut deep through his heart.

"The Montanaris saw this as sufficient retribution and agreed to end the feud between your families, if you vowed to stay out of the business.

"Peace reigned for a decade, until the Montanaris once again imploded due to renewed infighting. This time, the authorities jumped in and finished the job you and your brothers had started. They wiped them out, leaving a power vacuum. Within a few years, your family rose to fill that gap, under your leadership. Methodically, you proceeded to kill every remaining male of the Montanari clan and their associates, both in and outside of prison. Except one man."

Donatella paused to ensure Di LoRusso was paying full attention.

"I am listening."

"The man who raped, shot and set fire to Fiorella. He wasn't a Montanari, but one of their hired guns. A young criminal called Toto Galazzo. Legend has it that the Montanaris gave him safe exit out of Napoli and set him up with a new life and a new name, as a reward for his loyalty. You hold this man responsible for your only son's suicide. You've spent your entire life since searching for Toto."

Di LoRusso closed his eyes and breathed with focus. Although nothing he said or did suggested it, Donatella could sense a burning cauldron of rage bubbling within him.

"Don Di LoRusso. The man you've left no rock unturned to

find, Toto Galazzo, has been my husband for the last twenty-five years."

Di LoRusso's eyebrow's shot up like the whiskers of a predatory cat.

"I know him by a different name, because up until a few months ago, I had no idea who he really was."

"You wouldn't be the first person to come forward with a false lead," he goaded her. "I've lost count of how many people I've slaughtered who tried to take advantage of me."

"Uncuff me, please. I have something to show you."

"I'll do no such thing."

"Then reach into my purse and take a look at the photograph inside. It's a recent one of Mauro."

Di LoRusso followed her instructions cautiously.

"You've worked with Toto in the past and must remember what he looked like. Wouldn't you say the man in this photo resembles an older version of him?"

He held the photo against the sky.

"*Oh Dio santo!*" he roared under his breath. "Where is this piece of garbage hiding, and why are you telling me this?"

Donatella inhaled a deep, satisfying lung-full of air.

"I am willing to give him up to you. In return I ask for one thing and one thing only."

"This land is mine," he said, waving his hand at the expanse of powdery sand and blue waters. "You don't get to make conditions here." He strode towards her, while pulling out his cellphone to summon his men.

"Then you will never find him. I came here willing to die. Like Fiorella, I will perish with my secrets. There is nothing you can do to me that I am not already prepared for. My car is a rental under a fictitious name, and I have no identification on me. Ask your men, they searched me. If you have me followed, I'll know. If I don't return home safely today, a friend will alert Toto that he must disappear. You've spent twenty-five years fishing for him. Of all people, you should know best how well he can disappear and hide."

"What do you want from me?"

"Your word of honor that if I give you Toto, you'll not come after me or my children. I know how things work here. A vendetta is never against one man, it always includes the family and progeny.

"I beg you, Don Di LoRusso, in honor of your son's spirit ,to accept my offer. It's Toto you're after, not my innocent children. And not me. I married him under false pretenses and would have never stayed with him if I had known what he had done to that poor girl or what he had done to your family."

"Why would you want to give up your own husband? What's in it for you?"

Donatella cracked a tiny smile. The moment she'd been waiting for, the one she had risked her life for, had finally arrived. What she was about to say would either make or break the deal, her only chance to speak her heart with searing conviction and hope this fox would buy it.

"Because he ruined my life. He promised me love, companionship and respect, but all I ever got was heartbreak, abuse and infidelity."

"Sounds like the turd I remember."

"I wake up every day feeling death may be a better condition than living under his tyranny. If Toto dies, I live again. He is a terrible father to his children, and they are better off without him. My life will be worth living again without him."

Di LoRusso turned to consult the sea. He paced around like a caged tiger for what seemed like an eternity, as he contemplated what she had just off-loaded on him.

"You have my word," he finally said as he turned to face her.

"Thank you, Don Di LoRusso. In exactly two weeks from today, Toto will be checked in at the Montebello Splendid hotel in Florence. Promise me there will be no collateral damage when you pick him up. I don't want any innocent blood spilled as a result of our transaction. He won't be expecting you. Clueless, like a chicken about to be slaughtered."

Di LoRusso nodded, the fire in his body language betraying how much he loathed being told what to do.

Donatella couldn't extend her hand to seal the partnership she had just struck with one of the most violent men in the history of Napoli, so she did it with her eyes.

No sooner had La Tintorería Grazia on Carrer dels Alts Forns in Barcelona opened for business, than the locals had quickly grown fond of its bubbly Italian proprietor. Eight months pregnant and running the business on her own, Donatella was quick to adapt to a new life, a new language and a new name.

Her Polish assistant had taken the morning off to vaccinate her daughter, so Donatella was bustling around doing the light tasks. Now in her final trimester, she got tired quicker and was a few beats slower than usual. All too aware of her forty-two years, Donatella wanted to give Mother Nature a helping hand to make sure this pregnancy remained incident-free until the end.

Five months had passed since she last saw Akbar. Their agreement was that he would come back to find her ninety days after she had sent him away to hide in his native country.

Initially she had contemplated getting in touch with Guido to ask him to dig around for the father of her would-be child, or at least find out if he ever made it back to Italy. Although she yearned for him to be by her side, a part of her had also accounted for the possibility Akbar was too young and inexperienced to want to buy in to what she had tried to sell him.

He gave her the most important gift of all, a miracle baby girl now four weeks shy from popping out. But rational as she could try to be about the prospect of losing Akbar, it didn't stop her from never forgetting he was the only man she ever loved. The only man who knew how to pleasure her in bed.

When she had liberated herself from Mauro, Donatella had promised Guido to never look back at her old life in Rome. Not just for a surgical cut with every crushing memory this would have invoked, but for her own safety and that of her children, Daniele and Sofia.

The kids were now living in England, also under new identities. She had saved them the truth about their father, and instead spun an elaborate fairy tale to explain why they needed to go in hiding.

Although Donatella resisted getting in touch with Guido in her pursuit of Akbar, there was one last thing she owed the private investigator. A letter she had written to him on the flight from Rome to Barcelona but which she had never sent.

Donatella was too busy poring over her Spanish-language instruction book to notice a last-minute customer walk in.

"Are you able to do a rush job? I have an interview in less than an hour and I need my shirt washed and ironed."

Her heart jumped to her throat, ready to exit her body as Akbar's soft Italian words registered their meaning.

Standing at the entrance of the shop, with a rucksack on his back, a small suitcase in his hand, Akbar was a most glorious halo lit by the afternoon sun behind him. She rushed straight in his arms and kissed his hands, his forehead, his lips, his neck, and held him against her bulging belly.

"I thought I would never see you again..." she managed to say through a rain of tears.

"I always knew I would," he replied with a smile. There was something different about him. He looked manlier, more battle-worn. "My mother died. I had to stay longer than three months. I couldn't call or write to you, as we agreed."

Donatella hugged him tighter to console his loss and convey with her actions she would try to fill whatever void his mother had left behind. From now on, she would be his family. His woman, his companion, the mother of his child, his everything.

"She's a girl!" Donatella squealed, pointing to her belly.

Akbar kneeled to the floor and kissed the bulge in which his daughter was encased. He held Donatella's hand and peered up with a twinkle in his eyes.

"She'll be beautiful like her mother. Can we name her Amina?"

"Of course. It's a beautiful name. What does it mean?"

"'Honest.' It was my mother's name."

Later that evening, Donatella left Akbar sleeping at the apartment and slipped out. The trip from Rome to Barcelona was short, but his journey to get to her had been a lot longer.

He was home now, safe, and ready to be loved and nurtured by her.

When she had first met him and seduced him, she had never thought Akbar would amount to anything more than a garnish to her rebellion against Mauro's tyranny. But the more they made love and she got to know him better, the more he entrenched himself deep in her heart. Getting her pregnant was but a sign from above of their entwined fates. As Amina grew inside of her, so too did Donatella's love for her new man.

A gentle breeze caressed her skin as she strolled through a quaint street with small art galleries and a handful of brasseries.

She had decided it was time to mail Guido his letter. With Akbar back in her life, this was the last thing connecting her to a world she had entirely abandoned.

Guido's appearance and demeanor had left her unsure of his motives and competence the first time they met. But he had proven effective, and had a soft spot for her. Not in a romantic or sexual way, but Guido was her mentor and guardian angel. He had arranged their identity changes but asked not to be told where she and the children would ultimately settle down, just in case someone ever held a gun to his head trying to siphon that information.

Her sense of smell was acute. Whiffs of coffee and something delicious from the bakery wafting from a corner street bar stopped Donatella in her tracks. She ordered a herbal tea and a mini pastry, then sat down to read her letter to Guido one last time before she mailed it.

Dear Friend,

How can I begin to thank you? I came to meet you as a client, and we became family. Your advice, expertise and care have guided me to the life I've always wanted to live, free from the oppression of my ex-husband.

I know you'll be red in the face, fuming and swearing in your best *Romanaccio* about how you had warned me against getting in touch! So I will try to keep this letter as vague as possible. Frankly, I very much doubt anyone else but you will read it. But who knows, right?

When we met at the bar, you gave me that second envelope, which ultimately freed me. Do you remember what you told me back then?

You prodded me to think twice about whether I had the stomach to use this information to attain my goal. Would I be able to look my children in the eye, knowing what I had done to their father?

There were only two options available to me, you had warned. Either accept the status quo, or sacrifice my husband for my freedom. To live with shame, or live with guilt. Those words never escaped my mind after you spoke them.

Back then, I was so desperate to get rid of his cancerous hold on my soul, I felt certain I could sentence him to death and never look back.

And I did what I had to do. I traveled south and met with the devil himself to strike an unholy deal to serve my interests. I told him exactly where to find my husband, knowing by doing so I had signed his death certificate.

It was thanks to you that I finally discovered that for the last twenty-five years, the curse of my life was tied to a saga of endless bloodshed. My marriage only ever came to be as a direct result of the senseless murder of an innocent girl, which led to our escape from our Godforsaken city.

My friend, although I respect you, I write to say that you were wrong. I had a third option, and I chose to exercise it. One that would allow me to live with my head raised high, accepting neither shame nor guilt as my fate.

I confronted my husband with my discovery of his dark past, and revealed how I had met the man who wanted his head.

I warned him against doing anything rash to harm me, and bluffed about a fictitious confidante who I had supposedly instructed to go to the police, the news media and the devil in the south to give him up if I somehow ended up dead or missing.

Nothing less than a divorce and a handsome share of his assets is what I demanded.

I told him he could never again see the kids, for their own safety. With the brightest smile radiating through my heart, I looked the bastard in the eye and told him I was carrying the child of my brown-skinned lover, with whom I would spend the rest of my life.

The defeat in his eyes on that day instantly disinfected every festering wound he had branded on my soul. He did not say a word and never once spoke to me again, even throughout the divorce and transfer of wealth procedures. Like we had exchanged roles. I had become the oppressor and he had become the abused prey.

You were right. I could not destroy my husband in my children's eyes. I made him out to be a hero, for their sake. I lied and told them he had been a witness to a terrible mob crime twenty-five years ago, and had escaped our hometown under a government protection program. The criminals he had helped send away had served their time and were now out to get him.

The kids were traumatized at first, but they believed me, and ultimately accepted we had to adopt new identities to escape the country. They came to terms that it would be a very long time before they saw their father again, if ever.

Knowing you, I am certain you may be thinking I allowed my ex-husband to get off easily, right?

Perhaps.

After all, he never answered to his horrific crime. But in a manner of speaking, he will never be free again. The life he had has been disrupted forever.

He's probably in some foreign country where he can't speak the language, where he finds the food inedible, and the weather is God awful, looking over his shoulders waiting for that bullet to come.

But that's not all.

Before I departed, I bequeathed anonymously a substantial amount of his money to the family of that young girl he had raped and murdered.

Why?

Because at some point in any long cycle of senseless violence, someone has to stand up and sever this diabolical cord.

I chose to be that person. Not because I had any compassion for my ex-husband, but because enough is enough.

With respect and love,

Your client.

THE JEWISH NEIGHBOR

The one dollar bill in Umayma Yaghshi's hand was the one thing left in her possession reminding her she was once a free woman. Every morning she would hold it against the light to read the Arabic inscription handwritten on the bill.

George Washington stared at her, a frilly scarf tied around his neck and his soft tufts of sugar-white hair hardly matching his youthful face. His intense eyes betrayed a melancholy she had once-upon-a-time confused for indifference, even arrogance. For many years she had studied his face as part of a daily ritual until he too had grown inside of Umayma, just like the man who had given her the dollar and dedicated the inscription to her.

Umayma was pulled out of this bitter-sweet river of memories by her three-year-old stepdaughter, Layal, tugging at her coat, reminding her they were running late for school.

She stuffed Layal's water cup and snacks in her lunch box, buttoned her tiny coat and wrapped a scarf snug around her neck. They dashed out of the door with Layal strapped to the stroller.

The walk to the Highgate Montessori Preschool was usually pleasant, but this was an arctic November day in London and a few men in fluorescent outfits fixing a big chunk of the road slowed them down even more. *Maybe I should have covered Layal's head with a thicker hat*, she panicked.

A few months after she had arrived in London to be his bride, her husband Kamal had shown Umayma his temperament when Layal fell ill with swine flu. In an irrational fit of rage, he accused Umayma of being the classic negligent stepmother. Her face still tingles when she recalls the back of his hand striking her jawbone, pushing her to the ground. The madness in his eyes has haunted Umayma since, like a guillotine hovering over her head if she ever crossed him again.

She had married him exactly a year ago even before meeting him. Kamal had escaped Syria in the eighties for his political activism against the ruling regime and built a successful life in Britain. Umayma never quite understood what he did for a living. He worked with money, he told her, but the exact dynamics of his job were 'too complicated for her to grasp,' he had said condescendingly. Whatever his vocation, Kamal must have been quite good at it given his wealth and affluent lifestyle.

His first wife had died relatively young, although Umayma was never told how. When he was done mourning, Kamal reached out to his sisters in Damascus to arrange for a new bride. A devout Muslim, he was seeking permissible companionship with a young and energetic new wife who could also help raise Layal, his youngest child who had come unplanned when Kamal had turned fifty. His two older sons, twins, had left home to attend college in St. Andrews and Oxford.

Kamal's sisters had interviewed a handful of women on his behalf before finally settling on Umayma as the perfect candidate. There were no men left alive in her family who would bargain for a high dowry. She must have also come across as desperate to get out of the country. Umayma lived in Baramkeh, one of the poorest neighborhoods of Damascus and a favorite spot for shelling by the army and rebels alike. The golden opportunity to escape the bloody civil war ravaging Syria had prevented her from inspecting the finer details of the marriage proposal back then, an error of judgment for which she was now paying a hefty price.

In Damascus, Umayma had been an English teacher in a private school in the upscale neighborhood of Mazeh when Kamal's sisters first proposed to her. Although she wasn't exactly one of those airbrushed Levantine goddesses who had ruled the city before the war, Umayma wasn't unattractive either. Hers was a more organic beauty with soft features, almond shaped and colored eyes, a soothing voice, and a slightly plump figure with feminine curves. At thirty-four, she was twenty years younger than him, wise enough to raise Layal and young enough to still be desirable in bed.

At the first interview with Kamal's matchmaking sisters, Umayma struggled to accentuate her best physical attributes without coming across as slutty or overeager. Granted, her bulging breasts were impossible to hide, but everything else appeared shapeless under the black tunic she wore for modesty, because modesty was a trait deemed of cardinal importance to this particular buyer, as she had been forewarned by interlocutors who had introduced her to Kamal's sisters.

Umayma met all of Kamal's physical requirements: a fair virgin with ample bosoms and naturally straight hair. Her buttermilk skin and swelling breasts were two of her best features, and it would be left to a doctor to verify her chastity. Only her covered hair remained a question mark. In the least delicate terms, Kamal's sisters asked Umayma to remove her scarf to ensure she hadn't chemically treated her hair or straightened it with a hot iron for the occasion.

The procedure to get married and approved for residency in the UK was long and convoluted, but not nearly as humiliating as the battery of medical checkups and the virginity test mandated by Kamal. The latter left her in tears and sore in the groin for weeks but was a small price to pay to flee a country swiftly descending into hell, she rationalized. Many of the people she loved most in life had been murdered in cold blood or obliterated in random explosions, including the man who had given her the one dollar bill. Umayma didn't want to be next.

Any illusion of a better life in London was dispersed within the first few days of her arrival. Kamal's elderly parents were living with him in the house and although his sisters had never mentioned it, she was expected to care for them as well.

No sooner had she arrived than Kamal promptly terminated the services of the Bosnian maid who she was now expected to replace. Umayma had to hit the road running, including learning how to shop in a foreign country, manage a huge household, and tend to the disparate needs of her young stepdaughter and her elderly in-laws.

Not being born with a silver anything in her mouth, Umayma had taking care of domestic chores for as long as she held memories. *I am the woman of this house now and it's my duty to care for my husband and his family,* she consoled herself.

What she wasn't expecting to hurt so much was the extent her role as Kamal's wife would be devoid of affection or empathy, stripped of the normal things that one expects to transpire between a man and his wife.

Perhaps out of respect for Layal's feelings, Kamal had mandated Umayma would sleep in a separate room. He never said for how long so Umayma assumed until the young girl accepted her as a second mother.

Yet even after Layal had warmed up to her, Kamal never changed the sleeping arrangements. For months after she arrived he hardly acknowledged Umayma's presence in the house, let alone visited her room to consummate their marriage.

When he finally came in the dead of the night, he raped her, violently.

She woke up to find him mounted on top of her like a bull. Not even granting her the chance to willingly give herself to him like the obedient wife she wanted to be, he tore her lilac nightgown off, forced his hand on her mouth to drown her screams, reined her long auburn hair and penetrated past her knickers through her hymen like a surface-to-surface missile. Never touching or caressing her, never looking in her eyes, never uttering a single word. He used her like a worthless hooker, never tending to the piercing pain of losing her virginity or her blood gushing on the sheet.

When he was about to erupt, he withdrew quickly and sullied her chest and face, then dismounted her and walked casually out of the room. Just before he shut the door he turned to her and said, "I can't always do this," without the faintest trace of humanity or chivalry in his voice.

"Do what?" she whimpered through her muffled tears.

"Pull out in time. You need to get yourself fixed so you don't get pregnant. I'll arrange for it next week. I don't want any children from you."

Umayma nodded obediently, her own hand now covering

her mouth. A week later she was sent to a doctor who implanted something in her to put her fertility on pause, giving her no more say in the matter than a domestic pet being neutered.

Kamal only ever came to her room to rape her after that, like she really was a maid and sleeping with her was a shameless sin he could only commit in secret. Maybe it was more exciting for him this way, Umayma could never tell.

He ordered her to go to bed naked every night just in case he decided to take her on a whim. Short of tearing her clothes off like he did the first time, the act of undressing her must have had a certain tinge of tenderness he seemed intent on denying her.

Rarely, he would fondle her breasts or lick them until they would firm up and fill her with a streak of forbidden excitement. The prickliness of his salt and pepper beard on her areolas was a cruel mirage of intimacy. When he did these things, she tried to engage with him in foreplay to make the act feel less like rape and more like lovemaking. She would try to endear herself to him or invoke some sense of sympathy, but Kamal always knew how to shun her with decisive brutality, as if anything other than taking her violently with little concern for her needs was a buzzkill.

The worst was when he took her from behind. That was real hell.

How could a man so devout commit a sin so forbidden in Islam?

On the day of resurrection, Allah will not look at a man who had intercourse with his wife in her anus. She remembered the religious saying every time he pounded her insides. Faith aside, this was one of the most painful things she had ever experienced. With no lubrication or prior warning, it always left her feeling pillaged and even more ashamed of her lowly existence.

Realizing she was worth no more to Kamal than a slave or a concubine was gradual, but when it finally dawned on her, a fast-burning fear spread through her heart like a wounded, caged animal. What if her only way out was for her life to end prematurely?

Kamal had taken possession of her passport and only disbursed her enough money to attend to the house for one week at a time. She had no credit cards or a bank account to her name and her daily existence was micro-choreographed by her husband, who kept her on a short leash.

She had no friends or peers to confide in. Even his parents did nothing to suggest they believed her status to be any higher than what their son had relegated her to.

Once a month she was allowed a few minutes to call her mother and sisters in Damascus, with Kamal hovering nearby. There was no chance she could vent her true feelings without him finding out, not that it would have mattered. Because Kamal had made it clear from the start, if she ever wanted to escape his tyranny, her only option was to go back to Syria. Without him, she had no legal permission to stay in the country.

No matter how abusive life was under Kamal's compassionless roof, there was no going back for her. The only flicker of hope was to fulfill the three-year residency requirement for British naturalization, then leave Kamal and find a way to bring the rest of her family, assuming the war didn't take them first.

Once they were past the road works, Layal's stroller glided down Bishopwood Road before they turned left on Denewood.

Her stepdaughter's hair was tied in two pigtails bobbing up and down in the air. Layal turned to Umayma and smiled with big blue eyes gleaming with innocence and forgiveness. The youngest person in the house was the only one who treated Umayma with any respect. In turn, she had grown fond of the girl despite her father and grandparents. Maybe because she was three and had no idea of Umayma's humble place in the family, but whenever Layal was alone with her, Umayma could almost forget the complete rut she had gotten herself in.

An unspoken awkwardness always greeted Umayma when she dropped Layal to school in the morning. Today was no different. Other parents must have assumed she was Layal's new nanny and avoided any meaningful interaction with her.

She walked past a few dolled-up mothers of some Arab persuasion who were prone to go particularly out of their way to ignore her, rather than embrace her as one of her own. When she had first heard their Arabic chatter, she tried to engage with them but they simply looked the other way.

Even Layal's young teachers, who should have been trained not to judge, always seemed to regard Umayma with pity. *Poor little peasant girl from the Middle East.*

Umayma's command of the language was excellent but the teachers and staff still spoke to her in slow, clearly enunciated words as if she was slow on the uptake. They never entrusted her with critical information regarding Layal's progress, health and behavior, but instead sent it to Kamal in written form. It almost felt like they too were in the know about Umayma's microbial position in the household.

Walking back from Layal's school, she decided to divert to the nearby Fizroy Park, which she knew would be empty this early in the morning. Sometimes a few young mothers and their children would be loitering in the playground, but for the most part, they kept to themselves and didn't gawk at her black head scarf as if she was an extraterrestrial. When the playground was empty, she would sit on the big swing and rock her misery away as she reflected on happier times. These stolen moments allowed her to momentarily escape the oppressive universe she was trapped in.

Today was one of those rare occasions when Umayma had most of the day to herself. Kamal was taking his parents to get their annual physicals and she had done all the necessary shopping a few days ago.

From the entrance of the park, Umayma saw an older woman walking towards her with a dog. She bit her lips and attempted to smile at Umayma when their paths crossed, but it came across more like a frown.

Even with her limited interaction with other people, she was able to infer some perceptions of the British psyche. Most of them seemed caged in impermeable capsules that greatly reduced their attempts to be warm or personable—a blessing as far as she was concerned. People here kept to themselves and no one pried with malicious intent.

Back home, human warmth was abundant like the sun but it also came with a total invasion of personal space and privacy. The ability to walk in public places around London harboring dark secrets without a nosy neighbor trying to force her open was something she grew to appreciate.

When the woman with the dog had disappeared, Umayma

scanned the park and the playground until she was certain both were empty. She sat on the swing and shot her legs in the air to gain momentum. Almost instantly her body became one with the swing as together they drew imaginary arcs in the air.

The sky above was muddled with dark clouds and the threat of rain. Frosty wind caressed her face and caused her eyes to tear, and before she could control it, Umayma exploded in a fit of bitter crying. She hated her life, she despised herself, but most of all she loathed the injustice of her predicament.

If I had been born rich, everything would be different.

Before she descended any further, Umayma employed her well-honed ability to detour her emotions on cue. She directed her thoughts to anything else that could bring a smile to her face. She didn't want to waste these precious solitary moments doing something she did every day in bed.

Thunder erupted and it stunned her. She remembered stories of people being struck by lightning and dying. If only she was that lucky.

Voices coming from behind and across the park snapped Umayma out of her reverie. Rotating her head discreetly like a periscope, she caught the figures of two men moving slowly and conversing louder than what the English are usually prone to. Their voices reminded her of the drunken youths who crawl by her house late on weekend nights as they emerged from nearby pubs.

Gradually, she decelerated her swinging and sat quietly waiting for the men to pass her by, all along praying she'd remain invisible. She hated confrontations. Not that she was doing anything wrong, but the sight of a foreign woman in a head scarf on the children's swings could be provocative for some.

Her gaze fixed at her low-priced sneakers, Umayma began counting away the seconds, hoping the passing men would walk away in the opposite direction. But as they grazed forward on the grass, their rambling only grew louder, until they stopped abruptly.

She had her back turned to them but sensed they couldn't have been more than a few feet away.

"Hey, look at this—" one of them whispered to the other.

Umayma's shoulders tightened, her heart drummed faster and her eyes blinked rapidly and uncontrollably. Without thinking, she started to recite small protective verses from the Quran under her breath.

Their feet shuffled closer as they circled around and stopped in front of her, forcing Umayma to look up and face them.

Two men in their mid-twenties, one tall and bulked with muscles, the other shorter but equally well-built. Both bleached as white as white can be, padded in faded army fatigues, feet clad in black boots with serious mileage, heads shaved to the follicles, belligerent tattoos, body piercings like weapons and ice-gray eyes with no discernible symptoms of humanity.

"Excuse me. May I ask you a question?" the big one said in a mock educated accent, steam rushing out of his mouth like a smoke monster. A few of his front teeth were capped in gold.

Umayma nodded.

"Do you understand and read the English language, dear?" he said, reverting now to what she assumed was his normal cockney drawl.

Umayma paused to think before she responded. "I was an English teacher in my country," she mumbled, projecting a nervous smile.

She had worked hard to eliminate her Arabic accent, but now under stress, whatever pronunciation tricks she had learned were impossible to summon.

"Jolly well then. I suppose you must have seen all the graffiti near the Archway tube station. Do you happen to remember what they say?"

Umayma shook her head.

They took a few steps towards her until they were mere inches from her face, enough to hear the rage buzzing on their skin and alcohol fuming on their breaths.

"They say 'Go the fuck back to where ya came from ya fucking cunts.'"

The other guy erupted like a mad hyena then joined in a slurred, drunken stupor.

"Why the fuck do you pajama mamas and your sand nigger men like it here so much, anyway?" He had a sniffing tick when he spoke.

"Yeah," the taller guy continued. "What is the attraction here for brownies? Pig meat everywhere. Booze, bitches and Jews. Everything you hate, really."

Umayma turned her face away.

"Flocking here like dirty camels, bleeding us dry and living on welfare. White man has to work double shifts to sponsor maggots like you," the sidekick said.

"I know, I know," the big guy said.

"What?"

"Maybe their ladies come 'ere for a taste of real men?" he said then turned to Umayma. "Innit true, duckie?"

Their voices were still audible but quickly fading in the background against her booming heart and labored breathing.

"Say, what do you think of me and this bloke here, on a scale of one to ten?"

"Fine," she said, immediately regretting her naivety.

"Jolly good then. Fancy a taste of white cock for a change? You know, a real man who doesn't have to wear a suicide bomb to prove he's got balls?"

At the corner of her eyes she spotted the shorter one unzip his trousers and yank out his uncircumcised penis in the air. He dangled it with his hands left and right, in sync with his extended tongue like a tribal war ritual.

"Hey Gavin?" the tall man asked his friend.

"What?" He seemed annoyed to have his rhythmic play interrupted.

"Reckon your girlfriend here's good enough to be one of Osama's seventy-two virgins waiting for him in hell?"

Umayma's body shivered. She gripped the frozen chain of the swing tighter and it turned her knuckles a deathly shade of white.

"Can't see why not—she's got bangin' big tits, a nice round ass and a pouty mouth big enough for both of us."

"Feck off, I'm not double dipping with you!"

In a swift move, the tall one snatched Umayma's head scarf off, clasping her arm so tight she could no longer feel it.

"Listen up, sunshine," he breathed near her lips. "How abouts you save us all the drama of screaming and all that palaver?"

"Please, don't do this…"

"Oh don't be like that. Take one for the team." He pointed to thick bushes in the back where Umayma had seen small boys being taken by their moms to pee when the public toilets were locked.

"You'll take your garms off, and gorgeous Gav here and I

will take our sweet time on your merry go round. If you so much as whimper—" He hissed at her then took out a hunting knife from his back pocket and brandished it in her face.

Umayma put her head down and began shuffling to where he had motioned her to go.

I am done for it.

As they approached the bushes, she broke out of his grip and bolted as fast as she could in the opposite direction, but didn't get very far. Gavin, who was a few steps behind and prepared for her flight, had extended his foot to trip her. She tumbled flat on her face.

Umayma tried to get up but the tall guy gripped her ankles and immobilized her, then flipped her on her back and struck her face with crushing force.

Blood started dripping down the corner of her lips.

"Now you've done it!" he hissed, then slid his body up against hers until he was lying on top with his knees pressing hard on her arms.

Umayma's soul crept closer to the surface of her body.

He undid her coat, lifted her dress to her chin and plunged his hand to grab her breasts, tugging hard at her nipples.

His morning breath laced with strong liquor made her stomach heave.

He wiggled down and tightened his grip on her pelvis to liberate his hands. Then, with a precision that could only mean he had done this at least a few times before, he unbuckled his belt and dropped his pants down. For a fraction of a second he released his tortuous grip on her hips ever so slightly to allow him to pull her knickers off, which he placed on his face and inhaled with his eyes closed.

"Delicious…" he breathed out, his eyes shut but his face pointing to the heavens. "You may be a fucking Arab, but you sure smell fine down there, sister."

Anger at Kamal rather than fear of these men radiated throughout Umayma's chest. What they were about to do was no different to the way he engaged her. These men were rabid street dogs born and bred for this sort of thing, but Kamal was meant to be her husband, her protector.

Umayma had no willpower or energy to resist. Nothing she could do would prevent the inevitable. If she screamed or resisted they would kill her, not that there was any guarantee they wouldn't cut her up anyway after they had taken her.

Her body writhing, she laid her head to one side and shut her eyes, resigned to her fate. Rape, death, or both. It's not like she hadn't been violated before. Bitter but familiar tears ran down her face and a torrent of helplessness gushed through her weak body.

The man on top spread her legs wider, positioned the head of his penis at her entrance, and then wiggled to improve his aim. For a fraction of time, Umayma saw the devil dancing in his eyes, and there was not a force on earth that could retract him from what he was hell-bent on doing.

As he pulled back like a slingshot preparing to thrust in, a shouting voice carried loud from across the park.

"Hey!"

It must be a third accomplice coming late to claim his share of the kill. If there was any justice left in the universe her heart would stop right now to end her miserable life.

"Mind your own fucking business!" the man mounting her shouted back. He pulled out his knife again and raised it in the air to declare his belligerent mettle.

"Let go of her now and walk away—I am dialing 999!" Fortified with resolve and authority, the voice was approaching closer.

Umayma's would-be rapist jumped swiftly to his feet and pulled up his pants, releasing what felt like a container truck pushing down on her.

She gasped for air and saw light bursting at the corner of her eyes. With her head too heavy to lift off the ground, she observed the world upside down and in it a man running towards them at an impressive pace.

Gavin puffed like an exasperated child being dragged out by the ear from a theme park. Like his accomplice, he too was quick to button up.

"Let's get the hell out of here."

"Chicken out? We can take him!" Gavin argued back.

"Don't be a bloody muppet, we need to scram, now!"

Before he scurried away, Gavin kneeled down and whispered in Umayma's ears, "You're never going to be safe in this country."

With the might of a vengeful battalion, he kicked her ribs, the force of the strike carrying with it the wrath of not just the man delivering it, but his entire people. A paralyzing pain overpowered Umayma's body and shut it down.

She came round to find a black cat with striking green eyes resting at her feet. Umayma's ribs were still hurting like hell, but slightly less than what she felt right before the lights went out, probably thanks to some ice packs she noticed attached to her body.

Where am I?

When she was more lucid, only one thought looped in her mind and clutched at her heart—that she probably missed picking up Layal from school. Which meant the school would call Kamal and if he wasn't able to get there in time child services would be notified and life as she knew it would cease to exist.

"Hello?" she called out, her voice weak and unrecognizable.

Subdued classical music was floating in the air along with the smell of something earthy cooking. A soft, lime-colored sheet covered her body. She was lying on a couch in a living room of a house she did not recognize. Her scarf had been tied back on her head and her coat neatly folded near her feet.

Struggling to stand, Umayma only managed to remove the sheet and ice packs, then sat on the couch. The black cut sprung gracefully in the air then disappeared, leaving Umayma to come to terms with her spinning head.

When she was finally able to regain her bearings, she noticed she was in an impressive, spacious room. Charcoal-gray wooden floors lined the walls, and a few pieces of expensive furniture were scattered with understated sophistication, making a bold statement.

Whoever lived here didn't believe in clutter. Bookshelves stood in perfect symmetry along two opposing walls like a public library, with thick hard-covered books. A deep russet grand piano stood in front of expansive French windows, and on one wall, a fireplace with a white quartz mantelpiece was lit, broadcasting warmth and coziness.

On top of the mantelpiece, an oil painting of a coconut tree in a tropical setting seemed oddly familiar. She remembered Layal again and her pulse spiked.

"How are you feeling, Ms. Yasin?"

The baritone voice came from a man who appeared out of nowhere at the entrance of the living room. The same man who had thwarted her attackers, she suspected. He wore an apron, suede slippers and waved around a silicon spatula when he spoke, like a conductor's baton.

Yasin is Kamal's family name. How did he know I am his wife?

Something about him made her want to observe closer. He was probably mid-forties, and was smiling on the inside even though his lips weren't. His soft curls were brown for the most part with only a subtle suggestion of gray. Behind his near invisible glasses, his olive eyes were politely focused on her.

He reminded Umayma of a supporting character in a Turkish soap opera she used to watch in Damascus. An actor she found intensely attractive, not because he was outright handsome in a conventional sense, but because he possessed a slow burning aura emanating from his core. A smiling, knowing, protective spirit, with a low confident voice that never shrieked or surpassed its natural pitch.

I need to get out of here and rush to Layal...

"What time is it?"

Instinctively, he glanced at his wrist but there was no watch. He pulled out his phone from the apron pocket instead. "Three p.m. You have a good hour to pick your daughter up from school. You're usually back by four, right?"

She looked at him inquisitively.

"My study faces the street and I often see you from the window coming back," he was quick to explain.

Umayma's muscles relaxed slightly. He was right about

Layal's schedule. Kamal and his parents weren't expected back home until later in the evening. With any luck, she had ample time to rein in the situation and pretend nothing had happened.

"Who are you?"

"My name is Felix Susmann, I live two houses down from you on the same street." He tiptoed into the living room but remained a few feet away from her, his silicon spatula now tucked in the apron pocket.

"What happened to me?"

"You were attacked by skinheads."

"Skinheads?" She gathered the term was descriptive of her attackers' physical appearance, but the way he said it implied a darker connotation that went over her head.

Felix didn't explain further.

"Nothing serious," he continued, possibly trying to veer the discussion away from the subject of sinister men with shaved heads who raped innocent women in broad daylight.

"Fortunately, I got to you in time."

Umayma felt a stabbing pain in her right shoulder blade and she grimaced.

"One of your ribs may be fractured. He kicked you hard. I've given you strong painkiller shots, but you should get it checked out soon."

"Are you a doctor?"

A smile finally erupted at the corner of his lips. "Not exactly, but I look after my aging father who is quite unwell."

"Thank you, but I must go now."

"May I offer you something to eat or some herbal tea before you leave?"

Umayma shook her head and pursed her lips.

"By the way, I have not reported the matter to the police out of respect for your husband. I know he likes his privacy. If and when you do report it, I would be more than happy to testify if you need me to. Their faces are forever etched on my mind."

Felix pulled out the silicon spatula by force of habit, then tucked it back in before approaching closer. He squatted on his knees and picked up her budget sneakers from under the couch and placed them under her feet.

"May I?"

Umayma barely managed a nod, trying hard to ignore the man who wasn't her husband touching the skin of her sole, or that his hands against her flesh felt oddly satisfying.

Head light, stomach invaded by wayward butterflies, Umayma turned her face away from Felix. He caught her staring at the oil painting.

"Do you recognize it?"

His warm hand lay firmly on her foot as he spoke in a slow, intoxicating voice. When it felt like he was about to remove his hand, Umayma's other foot betrayed her better judgment and did something unthinkable. It moved up and clamped down on Felix's hand to keep it in place on the other foot.

"Yes, I think I know it." Her heart was dancing at a tempo she had not heard in many years. Where was this appetite for stolen intimacy and skirting with danger coming from? Perhaps the kindness flowing unconditionally from this man had temporarily short-circuited the part of her brain that had been trained to equate affection with violent rape. Or that being in this gentle man's orbit was slowly rinsing out how Kamal had conditioned her to feel in the presence of members of the opposite sex. She felt numb at the harrowing possibilities of what could have happened to her at Fizroy Park, like the incident had left her drunk on fear hormones and prone to taking bold, out-of-character risks.

Whatever was happening to her, Umayma saw no immediate need to probe why she was aroused at such an inappropriate moment. Chemicals of desire were infused in her bloodstream, igniting a blaze in her flesh.

"What is it?" she whispered.

When it was clear Felix had understood she wanted his hand exactly where it was, she raised the stakes even higher and removed her placeholder foot and landed it on Felix's other idle hand. Two for two.

"It's what you think it is," he replied with the sheepish grin of a seasoned university professor challenging a precocious student to dig deeper.

Umayma closed her eyes briefly to live every second of what was happening. Her ears were hot and her body soft and moist. The electric current of his skin transmitting through her body was also numbing the pain radiating from her ribs. An involuntarily moan escaped her lips, followed by a clear vision of what the painting signified.

She saw an older man coming back to Damascus from an overseas trip in Saudi Arabia where he worked as an Arabic teacher. She hugged him tight and never wanted to let go of him. Sitting on his lap, he gave her a sweet treat to eat. One she had never seen, let alone tasted before.

"It's the logo of a famous coconut-flavored chocolate bar," Umayma said, then opened her eyes.

Felix grinned.

"My grandfather designed it for the confectionery company that makes it. He used to work for an advertising agency in Germany. During the war he and my grandmother escaped to England. This was his first commission here. They liked it from the first mock-up he made. He painted this many years later at my nanna's request, a few months before she died."

"What were your grandparents escaping from?"

Felix bit his lips and looked the other way. For a short while there was a lump of silence in the air.

"Hitler's gas chambers," he finally said.

It took Umayma a few seconds to realize what this meant. Then it sunk in.

A storm of primal instincts exploded through her.

Fear, suspicion, contempt and pre-molded hatred all at once. Hard-wired reactions she could neither control nor suppress. She shifted her feet away from Felix's hands abruptly.

Umayma's formative school years were under the rule of Hafez al-Assad. A massive state propaganda organism had controlled and manufactured what people were allowed to think, feel and say.

In her mind, Jews and Israelis were one and the same, both the enemy. There were no shades of tolerable gray when it came to the enemy. No space to accommodate exceptions to the rule. The entire narrative upon which the modern nation of Syria defined itself was based on an unshakable belief that Jews had no other purpose but to undermine and destroy Syria and the greater Arab nation.

This man had saved her life, maybe even risked his own. He had carried her on his back to safety to tend to her bruises then given her painkiller shots. Still none of that seemed to have any bearing on her sudden distrust of him simply because he had revealed himself to be a *yahoodi*.

A wall of contempt had sprung between them the moment his lips had revealed his grandparents' history. The fleeting kissing of the flesh between her feet and his hands that had turned her insides into mush invoked shame and disgust now rather than pleasure.

A horrific scenario ripped loose in her mind as her hands clammed up and her vision blurred. What if Felix was a Mossad agent trying to recruit her?

What if this whole rape episode was orchestrated for a chance encounter? A way for him to manipulate her into becoming a spy for the Zionists. She had seen countless Egyptian soap operas and films where Mossad snakes ensnared innocent and unsuspecting Arabs.

I have to get out of this house fast.

Umayma put her shoes on, leapt to her feet, grabbed her coat and found the front door on her own. She rushed out, not looking behind once, not apologizing or explaining her sudden departure.

That night, sleep was impossible to pin down. Umayma had rummaged through the medicine cabinet for the most powerful painkillers and took the maximum dosage. As she lay in bed covered from head to toe in a light sheet, she prayed desperately it wouldn't be one of those nights Kamal was in the mood for her. *Any night but tonight.*

The kitchen floor downstairs started creaking. She held her breath and waited for the tell-tale sliver of light at the door announcing Kamal's dreaded arrival.

A minute passed.

Then ten.

Then thirty.

An hour went by with no sign of Kamal but still she couldn't sleep, not even for a fleeting lapse. The effect of the drugs eventually wore off and Umayma had to cope with the pain stabbing both her body and her soul.

The next day Umayma announced she had tripped at night and fell on her ribs while going to the toilet. Kamal was too busy to attend to her, so he ordered a minicab to take her to a hospital where x-rays revealed three of her ribs had indeed been fractured.

Many weeks after Umayma had healed, Kamal took the family to their holiday house in Cornwall. The twins were home for reading week, a chunk of time off given to university students to prepare for upcoming exams.

The Cornwall villa was smack on the beach on the west end of St. Ives. She had her own room but because the house was smaller and the walls flimsier, Kamal had never in the past come for her in the Cornwall house.

Layal shadowed her older brothers all day, diminishing Umayma's household during the holiday. She had ample time to reflect, sitting by the water's edge, reliving every scene of her tragic life from birth until what had almost happened to her.

The war in Syria had introduced her to the terrible stench of death, but never had it come so close to almost claim her own life. The incident in the park had changed something fundamental in her.

Killing herself was no longer one of her salvation options because life, after all, was worth living. Being under the crushing power of the men who wanted to rape her had also shed light on the absurdity of her marriage to Kamal. He had convinced her she would be desolate without him, and she had chosen to believe it, to accept that her only options in life were two variations of hell—the life of a slave under his oppression or a shameful retreat back to Syria. Instead, a tiny hope began to flicker in her soul that maybe, just maybe, there was another way out.

Throughout her introspection during the Cornwall holiday, there was another man other than Kamal who Umayma couldn't stop thinking of. After the hysterical thoughts that had spurred her to shun Felix's kindness had subsided, Umayma's rational mind started to kick in.

She put his creed aside and judged him purely on the merit of his character and how he had made her feel. Felix was the most valiant, most gallant man she had ever come across. Few men in this world had ever gone out of their way to look out for her well-being and protect her. For as long as she could remember, Umayma's sole purpose in life had been to please and take care of others.

Marrying a man like Kamal was a culmination of a universe that had conspired to make her feel worthless. Then Felix comes along, offering a new script she had obstinately blocked, simply because of the God he worships. Her knee-jerk reaction to Felix's revelation made even less sense now, in hindsight.

Her encounter with Felix was the first time she had come across a Jewish person in the flesh. All she possessed to judge them was the weight of many years of brainwashing by the sophisticated government misinformation machinery.

From the deepest bends of her mind a faint memory

surfaced of a grandparent or an older uncle speaking of a time long gone when Jews were an integral part of the national fabric. A moment in Syria's history when being Jewish didn't matter any more or any less than being anything else. Islam regarded Jews as descendants of the same patriarch, Abraham, and referred to them as people of the book, to be protected and respected. Muslims believed God had sent his revelation first to the Jews through Moses, and hence there was an important link between Judaism and their faith.

She wondered why she had managed to extricate herself from every other piece of misinformation the regime had hard-coded in her, except this reflexive antagonism to Jews. With total impunity and disregard for the sanctity of human life, Syria's rulers had allowed the country to descend into chaos. The only thing they cared about was to protect their own skin.

Was it possible this grand narrative about Jews and Israelis being the fundamental threat facing her country was nothing more but a convenient excuse? A blanket shield for Syria's heavy-handed autocracy to justify its own existence and failures, and to keep plundering its people.

As she spoke to herself every day, she saw her reflection in the mirror and had an epiphany as clear as the sun rising over the Yarmouk River on a glorious summer day. Her reaction to Felix was every bit as despicable as the two men who had tried to rape her. She had judged and condemned him based on false preconceived notions, and had treated Felix with irrational contempt.

Something else continued to puzzle her about their encounter. Right before Felix had rescued Umayma, her scarf had been pulled away. Yet she had woken up on Felix's couch to find it neatly tied on her head. Felix had thought about what the veil meant to her and how she wouldn't have wanted a man other than her husband to see her hair exposed. Even as she lay unconscious at his mercy, he had the decency, even humanity, to respect her beliefs and traditions. Precisely what sort of 'enemy' behaves like that? What sort of 'heathen' goes to so much trouble? Her own husband, a devout and practicing Muslim, had shown no such consideration for her well-being.

Perhaps the most perplexing part of her thoughts of Felix was that Umayma couldn't get her mind off his understated masculinity or his magnetic presence when he had squatted on the floor to put her shoes on. The touch of his fingers on the soles of her feet had made her quiver. Tiny electric waves of pleasure had traveled through her feeble body and reignited her needs as a woman.

Even when she had stepped out of her element and did something sexually forthcoming with her feet, there was nothing dirty about how he reacted. He hadn't behaved like any other man who would have wasted no time to take advantage of her show of weakness. With little words and fewer actions, Felix was the consummate gentleman whose initial instinct was to protect and care for a woman, rather than use and abuse her.

The more she probed within her conscience, the less Felix's religion seemed to matter. She saw him only as a man, and one she was attracted to.

At the end of the Cornwall holiday, Umayma could hardly wait to get back to London. She was desperate for a second chance with Felix. Hungry for his presence, and eager to apologize.

Every day after dropping Layal to school, Umayma would

loiter in front of his house, pretending to check her mobile phone or to adjust her scarf. But the chance encounter with Felix she was hoping for never came.

The cold winter months eventually abdicated to the early signs of spring, but the passing of time had done little to dent Umayma's burning desire to see Felix. To have something to long for after all those years of being lonely and helpless was transformational. Even when Kamal took her, imagining it was Felix riding her instead made the ordeal hurt much less.

Spring bloomed in full but still she had yet to meet her benevolent neighbor for a second time.

Eventually Umayma's mind was forced to drift away from Felix for a while as her chores at home began to expand.

Kamal was involved with a group of men organizing to support the rebels in Syria. Twice a week, a dubious gathering of her compatriots, along with Egyptians, Tunisians, Iraqis and Pakistanis, convened at home for long nights during which Umayma was expected to cook up a feast for them to eat before they worked. Their secretive business with Kamal left a hollow feeling in Umayma's gut. None of them came across as neutral supporters of the Syrian people. Their beards and mannerisms smacked instead of a more sinister predisposition, most likely highly radicalized Islamists.

The rebellion in Syria had first started as a grassroots movement of idealistic young men and women daring to dream of a future free of their tyrant, only to be hijacked and polluted by fanatic groups, just as intent as the government to take the country to the brink. Al Qaeda and its franchises from Iraq had seen an opportunity to meddle in the mud and were running a ruinous and dirty campaign in her country.

Why was Kamal associating with these types?

Umayma kept her eyes open and her ears alert to what was taking place at these meetings. She may have been a simple woman but an idiot she was not. Although Kamal forbade her from interacting with his male guests, it wasn't impossible for her to pick up on what was being discussed at these gatherings behind closed doors.

Deep in the night and in the heat of their discussions, Kamal and his friends would often let down their guard, just enough for Umayma to eavesdrop from the kitchen. Over time she was able to build a clear narrative of what they were up to. This was a war council.

Kamal and his friends were funneling money into Syria to fund rebel operations against the government. Terrorist acts to be precise. Ruthless explosions aimed at maximizing collateral damage, to terrorize the public and further discredit the regime. Not that the government was playing any cleaner. Two sides of one murderous coin.

As time passed, Umayma's interest in Kamal's affairs with these men of questionable standing departed from her initial concern for her country and became more inspired by the outright hatred festering in her heart for Kamal.

Back in Cornwall when she had decided she deserved a better life than what he was giving her, a seed was planted in her soul that was now starting to bear fruit. The only way to escape a man like Kamal was to identify his biggest vulnerability and stab him straight in the heart. All she had to do was stay alert and remain on the lookout for the right opportunity.

Summer came by and Umayma was back again lusting after Felix. Her attempts to convince fate to reunite her with him hadn't progressed one iota, although her need to see Felix had grown beyond wanting to apologize for how she had reacted. What she really desired was to be near him so her heart could race freely and her stomach flutter with the juices of bodily desire, just like how he made her feel the first time they met.

This was not merely a juvenile fantasy she had built around the first man to extend her some civility and kindness. Her female intuition recognized her feelings as a deeper yearning that came surprisingly devoid of any guilt over openly coveting a man other than her husband.

One Monday morning when Umayma was cleaning the windows with old newspapers, she saw Felix, or at least three quarters of his face printed on a torn sheet of The Independent. Was he some sort of celebrity or public figure? The part of the paper that had the story was torn so she couldn't tell.

Waiting by the sidelines for something to happen wasn't taking Umayma any closer to her object of desire. If she really wanted to see him again she would have to take more decisive action. She wasn't the type to show up at a man's doorstep and launch into a confessional. There had to be some other way.

Umayma made a delicious semolina desert called hareese every weekend. Layal was practically addicted to it. One Sunday, she saved some in a Tupperware container and the next morning after dropping Layal to school she left the sweet treats with a note on Felix's doorstep. She expressed her gratitude and remorse for what had happened between them and requested a meeting to explain herself.

I'll be at the cereals section at eleven a.m. tomorrow at the Sainsbury's supermarket on Archway Road, she told him.

Like an adolescent throbbing with the newfound impulses of love and sexual want, Umayma's heart was about to leap out of her chest as she stood waiting for Felix between shelves of sweetened grains in colorful boxes. Her face flustered, she contemplated running back home a million times a second. Whenever someone walked by, her lungs stopped breathing, leaving her light in the head and close to fainting.

Then she saw him giving her his back, one aisle across in the rice and pasta section, comparing brands. She took a breath as full as the galaxy and forced her dough-like legs to take her to Felix one nervous step at a time.

When she was standing but a few inches behind him, she tried to get herself to say something but her voice had long abandoned her. Overdrafting her last reserves of pluck, she raised a timid hand and tapped him on the shoulder.

"Can I help you?"

The man who looked like Felix but wasn't him must have thought Umayma was out of her mind when she dashed out of the supermarket. Running back home, a cocktail of disappointment and self-immolation haunted her.

What an idiot! How could I think for a second he would accept to see me again? I humiliated him and he's giving me a taste of my own bitter medicine.

On the way back she stopped by Felix's house and found the gift and the note she had left him were no longer there. He had received her message but had chosen to ignore it—yet another stab to her already defeated heart.

Later that night, when Kamal came for her, she did not fantasize about Felix. As she lay there being hammered by him, a cold emptiness had crept inside her. The man she needed was ignoring her and the man she loathed was screwing her. How much more irony could life hand her down?

For many weeks after being crushed at the supermarket, Umayma tried to exorcise Felix out of her soul but to little avail. Ever since he had rescued her from rape and possibly death, Felix was still the first and last person Umayma thought of every day. The raw feelings this man invoked in her were like nothing she had ever experienced, and what a ridiculous notion that was, to fall in love with a man you barely knew.

Umayma woke up one night gasping and screaming in her sleep. In her nightmare Kamal had discovered her in bed making love to Felix and was suffocating her with his hands. She begged for mercy but there wasn't an ounce of empathy in Felix's glassy eyes, as he stood motionless, failing to come to her rescue.

When her breathing had slowed down, she got out of bed frantically and wrote a long and impassioned letter to her neighbor. Having nothing else to lose, Umayma unlatched her heart, allowing unbridled passion for him to gush out like a waterfall.

The next morning she delivered the letter to Felix's house and as usual she hovered around the property for a little longer than necessary, hoping to run into him.

She had come to memorize every detail of the house's

external façade. Unlike any other day, there was a forlorn, abandoned energy about the property and it left a sinking feeling in her heart. Like whatever fond memories she had of what had happened between her and Felix inside were now so remote, they may have very well never occurred. Just a figment of her imagination.

Ten days elapsed and Felix had not taken any action to suggest he had read her letter or that it meant anything to him. She noticed an unfamiliar car under Felix's carport, an expensive German machine like the ones driven by the oligarchs in Damascus.

At the corner of her eye, she caught movement inside the house. She ducked for cover behind the mailbox. From this vantage point she made out a figure of a person at the far end of the room, moving in confident, purposeful strides. When the figure approached closer to the window, Umayma could tell it was not Felix, in fact, not even a man. A stunning brunette dressed like a socialite who had stepped out of a lifestyle magazine, and behaving like the queen of this castle.

For a few weeks later, Umayma resorted to every last trick she knew to try to get Felix out of her system. Nothing seemed to work. Even after seeing another woman in his house who clearly belonged to Felix's world far more than she did, the temperature of Umayma's passion for her neighbor had not dropped by even the slightest degree.

There were times when she was able to temporarily suspend her obsession with Felix, like when she escaped with Layal into a fanciful world of childhood innocence and dreams, or when

other pressing thoughts were at hand. Her determination to
rid herself of Kamal's scorpion clutch was shaping up to be her
number one priority. The faint possibility of a life free of him
was an unexpected alternate future in which it was Kamal
who dropped off the cast list, not her.

Umayma couldn't slaughter a chicken let alone murder
a human being, even a rapist and terrorist financier like her
husband. Not to mention she lacked the resources to do it
in a clandestine way to avoid getting caught. Kamal was
undoubtedly a man in possession of a closet overflowing with
skeletons like his affiliation with dangerous men engaging in
dubious activities. Still, try as hard as she could, she didn't
know exactly where to start her campaign to end him.

That is, until she came across a poster one day near the
bus station that lit her path forward by a million lumens.

*It's probably nothing, but if you see or hear something
that could be terrorist-related, trust your instincts and call
the confidential anti-terrorist hotline. Our specially trained
officers will take it from there. 0800 789 321. Your call could
save lives.*

The problem was always going to be Kamal's prudence.
Men like him don't get to where they are in life by leaving
loose ends lying around for others to exploit.

To her credit, though, paying attention had always been
one of Umayma's strongest suits, and her memory was
photographic. Whereas most people ignore the mundane
details, from a young age, Umayma had come to understand
how sometimes the difference between getting what you seek
in life and falling short comes down to recalling inanities.
Like the village idiot who sweeps it all at a quiz show just

by remembering mindless facts rather than possessing any real intellect.

One afternoon before one of his infamous dinners with the war council, Kamal was busy working in his study when she served him sugary mint tea and a small plate of buttery ghraybe cookies she had baked.

He seemed entirely absorbed poring over a printed map and what appeared to be an internal schematic of some sort of building. Kamal was making notes and charting marks. On the top right of the schematic, the address of the building in question was printed in bold letters: Eight, Belgrave Square.

When she had first arrived to London, Umayma had to visit the Syrian embassy for some additional paperwork required for her residency. Kamal had written the address for her on a piece of paper: Eight, Belgrave Square.

Little speculation was required on her part to conclude what her husband was up to. Kamal wasn't busy building or creating anything, but quite the opposite. For a while now she'd been certain her husband and his friends were bankrolling terror attacks inside Syria. They had the means and the depravity of spirit to engage in such activities.

This, however, was different. A potential weakness in his operation she'd been waiting for. Although she possessed not a smidgen of proof, yet, she was certain beyond any doubt Kamal was plotting to bomb the Syrian embassy in London. *Trust your instincts*, the police poster had said. Now she had to come by some confirmation before making the next move.

That night, she perked her ears and listened for dear life. Her heart fluttered and her soul soared when she finally heard confirmation of what she had initially suspected, just by recognizing the address of the Syrian embassy in London. Kamal was the initiator of the plot, and he proposed his idea to the council. It took some back and forth discussions, but in the end, and after initially disputing the viability of the attack, rather than its depravity or how many lives it would terminate, even the hardest skeptics came round.

The band of murderers agreed to meet the next day to plot the finer details of their crime. Without having to wait too long, Umayma's chance to catch Kamal red-handed had fallen from the heavens straight into her hands.

This is how you fight for your life. First, you create a diversion. The next day, before the evening meeting, Umayma walked into her husband's study to interrupt him.

"We ran out of mango juice," she stated.

Kamal ignored her at first and continued working on his map and schematic with autistic focus, exactly as he had done the day before.

"What?"

"We're out of mango juice."

"Sheikh Hamza likes to have it with dinner, you know that," he snapped back, still focused on his work. Hamza was the oldest man in the group and Kamal feared and respected him more than his own father.

"You could have bought some yesterday when you went shopping," he said, peering up with livid eyes.

"You only told me they were coming for dinner again this morning. They never come two nights in a row. Plus, no one else in the house drinks it when I buy it and we end up throwing it. It's *haram*."

There was a short silence as Kamal better processed this information. "Have you taken care of dinner?"

"Yes. Everything is set. I just need to fry the kebbeh and dress the tabouleh when the guests arrive so they're served fresh."

"Then go. Go to the supermarket and buy the mango juice quickly," he ordered.

Umayma grabbed her purse and mobile phone, replaced her house slippers with gym shoes and covered her hair with a powder-blue scarf. Making sure no one was looking, she took out the cartons of mango juice she had hidden, put them in a shopping bag and rushed out of the house.

Second, you arm yourself with the best weapons you can find, by any means necessary. Forty-five minutes was all she had to get this job done.

The mobile phone shop was right across from the supermarket. A tiny operation served by Asian men with gel-slicked hair and funny accents. Umayma came here every fortnight to top-up her locked-down, limited services phone Kamal had allowed her. The sort of phone plan parents gave their untrustworthy tweens. She flashed a sweet face to the young man behind the counter.

"My daughter's school is holding a concert in a few days. I wanted to know if my phone can record the sound."

"Sure, let me check," he said as he took the phone from her. He fiddled with the menus for a while then nodded. "This is a fairly new smartphone, so yes, you certainly can."

Umayma batted her eyelashes and smiled.

"May I ask why you would just want to record the audio instead of using the camera? You have a pretty good one."

Umayma shrugged to make him feel important and in control. "I am not very good with technology," she said with a giggle. *Men are so predictable.*

"I can show you how, it's fairly easy."

The young man proceeded to give Umayma precise and simple instructions on how to use her smartphone to record audio as she had first requested, and video as he was suggesting.

"The microphone and the rear camera are at the back of the phone, so make sure to point it towards the stage, and not to cover either with your fingers. You have an additional memory card slot, which means you can record for many hours while the battery lasts. Given this is a new phone, your battery life should also be quite decent."

Umayma rehearsed the steps in front of him until she was certain she had gotten the hang of it.

Third, you infiltrate behind enemy lines and plant your explosives surreptitiously. Back home, Kamal was taking a nap and his parents were out for a stroll. Umayma slipped into the study where the band of warmongers would convene later that night after stuffing their faces with her delicacies.

She froze in position and couldn't think of a suitable place to plant the phone. Kamal had banned her from coming in the study alone. When she had to clean it, he was always hovering nearby and he locked it when he wasn't home.

Come on, Umayma, you can do this.

Umayma looked away from her insecurities, grabbed a chair and stood on it in front of the bookshelf. Checking the phone was working, she pressed record and tucked it between the bounded books on the top-most shelf.

The home phone erupted suddenly like a siren, startling

her. Kamal sometimes took his calls in his bedroom or in the privacy of the study, which meant he could storm in any second now. With every menacing ring, Umayma felt Kamal breathing down her neck and her plan falling out of the sky like a crashing plane.

This was not the time to falter. She waited a few seconds then checked the test recording. The frame was cut, so she repositioned it with a slight tilt. The ringing was now loud thuds in her head, but she had no option but to pretend she couldn't hear it to get the job done. As quietly as she had entered, she walked out of the study then finally allowed herself to breathe.

Later that night she played the damning evidence recorded by her phone over and over again. Every single conspiring bastard in that room had been filmed in high definition making plans to bomb a foreign embassy on British soil, biting the hand that had fed them so generously. Now emboldened beyond return, Umayma knew she needed further material evidence if the case against Kamal was to really stick.

The next morning when he had left the house for the day, she searched every inch of his bedroom for the key to the study and found it stashed in his underwear drawer with a collection of porno magazines.

When his parents snoozed in the afternoon, she broke into the study and retrieved the map and schematic of the embassy that carried Kamal's incriminating notes. Using her new best friend, her phone, she snapped an endless number of pictures of the two documents and anything else she could find that looked remotely of relevance. Anything that could help screw Kamal.

Finally, you shoot to kill without a speck of mercy. They came in the middle of the night as they usually do and were civil and compassionate. Female officers attended to Umayma and Layal. Kamal's parents were handled with care like glass objects. Even Kamal himself was spoken to cordially like a suspect who could potentially be innocent, rather than the terrorist bankroller he most certainly was.

With Umayma's recorded and photographed evidence in their possession, and her signed testimony, neither Kamal nor any of his rotten partners were going to get away with what they were plotting to do.

Kamal shuffled out of the house in handcuffs, his head stooping. He turned to Umayma with broken eyes and whispered, "Forgive me. I beg you, please look after Layal and my parents."

She saw humility in Kamal's eyes for the first time. Feigning distress, she rushed to him like a loving wife and pleaded with her eyes to a female officer standing nearby.

The officer hesitated briefly, then nodded and granted Umayma permission to embrace her husband.

With a tight hug, she pulled him closer and planted a tiny kiss on his temple. The smell of his skin nauseated her. Kamal seemed bewildered when she squeezed his hands. Before she let go of him, she moved her lips close to his ears and whispered, "Beware the wrath of the meek."

The Highgate Nine, as they came to be known in the media, were convicted of conspiracy to commit terrorist attacks on British soil.

A family court deemed Layal's brothers too young and her grandparents too old to care for her. Umayma became her sole custodian and the guardian of Kamal's legitimate business interests and massive financial assets.

The informed opinion of social workers, psychologists

and numerous interviews with the young girl deemed it in the best interest of Layal to be under the care of her stepmother. Without their son's protection, Kamal's parents opted to return to Syria, where they preferred to spend their last days.

To acknowledge her valor and service to her adopted homeland, Umayma was naturalized as a British citizen by the Home Office a few months after Kamal's conviction.

Was it stupid to reveal to Kamal she was the one who turned him over? Perhaps. But the pleasure of looking in his eyes as it dawned on him what had happened was something she could not deny herself. And with Layal in her sole custody, Umayma had gambled Kamal would never risk conspiring to harm her from behind bars and losing his daughter to foster care.

When the 'for sale' sign went up on the front lawn of Felix's house, Umayma began to think of him again every day. Throughout Kamal's trial and the ensuing process of taking over his life, Umayma hardly had any time to dwell upon her complex web of feelings for her neighbor. She figured he must have moved or left the country, both being much better reasons for why he hadn't responded to the two letters she had sent him—even if he was married or seeing someone.

On a few occasions, an attractive real estate agent in short skirts and high heels would come by Felix's house to show it to potential buyers. One day Umayma felt bold enough to go up to her to ask what became of Felix.

"Is Mr. Susmann selling his house?"

"I am sorry, who are you?" the agent asked with moderated suspicion.

"I am his neighbor," Umayma said, pointing to her house.

"So I take it you don't know?" the woman sighed and tilted her head to one side.

"Don't know what?"

"Mr. Susmann passed away eight months ago."

The colors of autumn were spreading like fire for a second time since she had first met Felix. Umayma was sitting in the garden sipping mint tea when she heard the doorbell. Instinctively, she touched her hair to tighten her scarf but remembered it had been a while since she had removed the veil altogether. She had figured if God had wanted it concealed, he may as well not have given her any hair to start.

"Registered mail for Umayma Yaghshi," the postman said, peering up from behind his glasses, confused how a woman living in this house had not only opened the door, but with her hair exposed.

It was her finalized divorce papers from Kamal.

One November morning after dropping Layal to school, Umayma decided she could no longer run away from her demons. In her heart of hearts she knew that unless she made her way back to Fizroy Park and sat on the swing, her new-found freedom would forever taste incomplete.

The park was her ground zero, and she'd never been back since the day Felix had rescued her a year ago. Two men had tried to rape her, spurred into an aggressive sexual frenzy by a racial hatred she could hardly understand.

Umayma had already been killed many times over by Kamal. Threatened by these men, she had lacked the courage to shout or scream or even fight for her life. Surrendering and taking it as it came had felt like the only honorable thing to do back then. Except, as she now realized, there is no honor in giving up and playing dead. There never was, there never will be.

Umayma took slow steps to the swings, breathing deeply. Once again the playground was empty. Frozen air penetrated through her clothes, aching her bones. Despite the frost, the skies were open and the sun beamed down generously.

Eyes closed, Umayma listened to every sound she could perceive. The distant hum of the motorway, the singing birds, the chirping crickets and her own lungs heaving rhythmically.

Umayma must have dozed off on the swing. When she opened her eyes the sun had been swallowed by thickening, ash-gray clouds and the sky was spitting out rain.

A creeping sense of doom burrowed in her chest. Something other than the rain had woken her up, and it felt morbidly familiar.

Someone was standing behind her.

Who was it?

Her heart ricocheted back and forth in her chest.

A hand landed on her shoulder.

It's them again!

What had started out as gentle rain exploded into a torrential downpour with thunder crackling ominously above her head.

The hand on her shoulder remained there.

This was the moment everything in Umayma's life had been leading up to. A final opportunity to fight for her dignity even if she was killed in the process. A chance to stand up to the next man in line coming to plunder more of her self-esteem.

She will scream her lungs out in one loud, resounding 'No!'

on behalf of every woman in her predicament. Never again would a man take from this woman what was never his in the first place.

Umayma shot up to her feet and turned to face her greatest fear, with a raging fire growling in her belly.

A ghost stood before her.

Not as pale as white can be, but a smiling spirit.

Soft brown curls with hints of gray and olive eyes stared at her through white-framed glasses, speckled with the rain splashing against them.

Umayma ran her hands through Felix's hair before she allowed her hungry lips to be drawn to his.

He hugged her tight with strong arms and she prayed their bodies would merge into one.

At no point did it seem necessary to stop and question how she was kissing a dead man. If Felix was a ghost, she too wanted to die.

Supernatural or hallucinogenic, whatever the explanation of his presence, it couldn't possibly be any more important than what Umayma was feeling right now.

Love flooding her heart. And the very real taste of Felix's lips, the smell of his hair and his skin, the warmth of his stubbled face, the firmness of his body against her soft curves. Finally she was home.

Right here under the rain, secure and protected by Felix, alive or dead, nothing else seemed to matter.

When his tongue inside her mouth tasted like it truly belonged there, Umayma finally understood.

"You're not a doctor," she whispered in his ears, as she held his face, while interspersing kisses on his salty lips.

His eyes beamed. "I am not a doctor. I write books. But I am able to give painkiller shots."

"You looked after your father, didn't you? It was your dad, the other Mr. Susmann, who died."

She hugged him tighter to console his loss.

Umayma's heart contracted and a dark memory cast a long shadow on the sweetness of the moment.

"You ignored every letter I sent you. Why?"

Images of her in the supermarket waiting for him in vain flashed shamefully in her mind.

"I only got them today."

She pulled away, not entirely understanding this explanation.

"What do you mean?"

"This is not my house. When my father died a year ago, right after we met, I returned to New York."

"And the woman I saw inside, is she your wife?"

Felix held her hands tight. "That would be Ms. Susmann, yes," he said with a devilish glint in his eyes. "My sister…"

"She did not read them and tell you?"

"We're English. We mind our own business and never pry."

"I wish she had."

Umayma grabbed his head and kissed his lips passionately, grinding her body against his.

"Do you not think of me as a crazy woman, to have felt these things for you after just a brief encounter?"

"I did. You terrified me. I thought you were completely batty."

Once again that stabbing pain tearing through her heart.

"But—"

"But what?" she begged, hoping for the right answer.

"I am just as crazy. Ever since you arrived in this country, I'd see you through my window coming and going. All I could ever think of was an inexplicable need to come out and say hello. Just to stand before you and greet you. Nothing more, nothing less. Then when I carried you back to my house and laid you on the couch, something powerful possessed my heart. An inexplicable feeling that you belonged to me, not him."

Umayma's knees were wobbling and her lungs starved for air.

Felix continued. "That day when I saw you heading into the park, I decided it was finally time to introduce myself. I was prepared for you to slap me or tell me off but I wasn't ready to see you being harmed."

"You risked your life to save me, only to have me insult you with my ignorance and intolerance. Why would you still want to know me after what I did?"

Felix didn't speak any more, but allowed his hands, his lips and his whole body to tell Umayma what she yearned to know. That what was didn't mean anything, and what is and what will be is all that really mattered. Forgiveness can come in many shapes and form, but none sweeter than a slow, eternal kiss.

That night, near a slow-dancing fireplace and burning amber incense, Umayma lay naked on her side on Kamal's bed, with Felix's body fused around hers. Their silhouette was breathtaking. Like two perfectly matched spoons.

Her hair sprawled wild against her body, Umayma was glowing on the inside. The immediate thirst for Felix had been quenched repeatedly. She now had a lifetime to satisfy her long-term hunger for this man, her man.

Careful not to wake him up, she reached out to the night table and grabbed her purse.

She pulled out the one dollar bill her father had given her when she had turned eight. He had just returned from Saudi Arabia where he was working as an Arabic teacher. She held it against the light of the fireplace to read the inscription on it.

Umayma, you were born free. Never let a man convince you otherwise.

She had never asked her father what those words meant, but lived her life trying to understand them.

With a deep sigh, she folded the dollar bill and placed it in the fireplace, watching it being consumed by the flames and disappear into ashes, just like her father's body.

The man sharing her bed was now the only thing in Umayma's possession reminding her she was finally a free woman.

CRUSHED

Of all the girls who turned me down in high school, only Ashley Sakowski broke my heart. I never blamed her for snubbing me, but I loathed her for leading me on and making me think I stood a fighting chance.

Back then I was your archetypal geek. Smart and into computers in a creepy, OCD way. Tousled hair, waxy complexion and pudgy. Horn-rimmed glasses a given. Nothing I wore had the slightest suspicion of cutting-edge or cool. I dressed to cover my nakedness, not to make a statement or appeal to anyone. Simply stated, my chances with the opposite sex were at best comatose on arrival.

I fell for Ashley and came crashing down like a big sack of shit in the worst possible way. The self-immolating, warty, messy, sleepless-nights-crying-in-bed, I-can-hardly-breathe, kill-me-now sort of way. The type of love that forces you to surrender your dignity and self-esteem at the door.

As a teenager, hitting on girls was a combination of self-indulgence and masochism on my part. Just a horny dork being fresh, knowing I stood no chance, and that the harder I tried, the more I would get burned.

With Ashley, and for the first time in my life, it was my heart doing the talking, aching and yearning rather than just my loins. I fantasized about spending the rest of my life as her appendage.

A.M. KHALIFA

I knew hell would freeze over first before that would happen, so I settled instead for the lesser pleasure of worshipping her from afar. Every night I would retreat to the safety of my fertile mind to spawn elaborate fantasies and conversations with her. Pathetic things like picking out names for our unborn children and the fabric colors of our curtains in our future home.

Then one day when I was minding my own business and being the insignificant high school microbe that I was confined to be, she began talking to me in the hallway.

"We should hang out," she declared, as if I was a piece of bread cleared of the suspicion of being moldy.

And hang out we did.

She was sweet and funny and attentive and pressed my most sensitive buttons.

How was a kid like me supposed to avoid not falling for her? She casually said things like, "I prefer the understated good looks of a man with brains, over a good-looking guy who lacks IQ firepower."

I melted like butter under her innuendos and physical contact. She liked to brush up against my skin as if by accident, then stare at me with sultry, deep eyes filled with endless possibilities.

For the first time ever, a woman was conversing with me as if my opinions really mattered, or as if my life was interesting and worth dwelling upon.

Then, as abruptly as it all started, it all stopped.

Ashley led me to the water's edge, but right before I could quench my thirst, she waved a wand and replaced the freshwater stream with a parched desert.

She ejected me without the mercy of a parachute.

Overnight, I went from being her soul mate back to invisible dweeb.

During our short-lived three-week interaction—I could hardly call it a relationship, really—she had hinted she may even take me to the school prom. In my needy, inexperienced, love-starved mind, I prayed she would use the event to declare her undying affection and kiss me in front of the whole school, turning this frog into a prince. To rescue me once and forever from Loserville.

Not that you didn't see this coming, but it was, of course, a ruse. Ashley was failing her computer science class and needed someone to help her with the assignments. Unwittingly and because I was smitten blind, I saved her from a big fat F.

It must have been a no-brainer for her: Flirt with a nerd to get him to serve your academic interests, then, when you're home free, dump him back to the swamp from whence you found him.

I wish this story had some original twist I could delight you with, but what happened next was text-book high school angst. Not only did Ashley terminate any contact with me like I ceased to exist, but she went to the prom with one Jake Balantine, a perfect human specimen. He was everything I wasn't—a beautiful, physically superior jock with formidable social power. They dated through high school. When they were college juniors, he got her knocked up and they got married, I later heard.

They say our tragedies and heartbreaks define us and transform us into stronger, future versions of ourselves. That's probably true in my case, as you will soon find out, but none of that changes the fact that heartbreak stinks, and if you could live without being rejected and humiliated, you wouldn't be worse off for it.

Like a man, I stomached Ashley-gate and moved forward. I heeded the lessons from the scam and vowed I would never be taken advantage of again.

After high school, life started to incrementally improve for me. I got accepted at MIT to study artificial intelligence. There I finally found myself in a setting where being brilliant mattered more than being beautiful. In time I began to blossom to my full potential.

I don't know about you, but I always had this image of places like MIT being a colony of brainy rejects, and that a guy like me would fit right in. Nothing could be further from the truth. Instead, I found smart, socially adjusted kids who wanted to hang out. The world outside high school was not a black and white division of geek versus jock empires. There was every shade of normal and a galaxy of amazing people who began rubbing off on me. The better I adjusted in life, the more I looked back at high school with indifference.

I started taking better care of my body and paying more attention to how I presented myself to the world. It's truly remarkable what contact lenses, the rays of the sun on your skin, a year at the gym, an expensive haircut and some attention to your wardrobe can do to transform an awkward boy into a confident, even desirable man.

Underneath my nerd disguise lived a pretty good-looking young fellow who I had kept imprisoned all my life. Perhaps because I hailed from a family of scientists who cared more about ideas than appearances, I had never learned the fundamentals of looking the part. It was at college that my perspective shifted.

By my junior year, I had shaved off my maladjusted exoskeleton and morphed into a social super hero. I had taught myself about everything you need to thrive in high society. I read voraciously and learned from history. I allowed music and art to refine my sensibilities and soften my heart. I paid attention to emotions rather than just quantifiable ideas. And I surrounded myself with a network of high-stake players and supportive friends who always challenged me to reach my best.

In high school the operating standard was to trample on the weak and worship the strong. At MIT and beyond, I found people who inspired me because they believed in me. My confidence began to skyrocket and my checkered past mattered less and less in my mind as I set out to conquer the future and change the world.

I dated like a junkie, dipping my cup in every well I came across until the void of deprivation I had grown up with was filled and patched forever.

In my senior year at MIT, I fell in love with the woman who would become my wife and my partner. Melinda Brand.

It all started when I went back home to Oakland to spend Thanksgiving with my family. Both Melinda's parents and mine were friends from their high school days, all four of them brilliant minds in one capacity or the other. And all four of them were intrigued why Melinda and I had never hung out in high school, even though we were in the same grade and apparently mirror images of each other, whatever that meant. The answer to that seemed obvious in my mind. I barely took notice of Melinda, or any other girl-nerd, precisely because they were the female iterations of me. Two invisible souls can hardly perceive one another.

During college I had become shrewd about wiggling out of my parents' never-ending campaigns to set me up with good girls they thought were perfect for me. My standards had understandably evolved and I could no longer trust their definition of good girls to line up with mine. Not to mention I was doing pretty fine pulling any number of stunning ladies all on my very own.

Still, the name Melinda Brand never seemed to go away.

Hoping I could get my parents to stop badgering me about her, I finally caved in during that last Thanksgiving break before I graduated. It seemed like a fair trade-off: I'd give them a lousy hour of my life with the Brands over for coffee at our place, hoping this would be the end of their Melinda Brand campaign.

I came home on the day, thirty minutes late, almost certain my nonchalance and rudeness would send a clear message to that Melinda character not to get her hopes up. I simply wasn't going to be interested.

As I emerged from my car, I caught sight of a young woman in rust-colored leather getting off a Harley. Yet another distraction from the hell waiting inside my parents' house.

She parked in front of our neighbor's front lawn, her long hair cascading down to her waist as she took off her helmet. Her body cut through the air with grace as she made her way to the front door, which made no sense. This was the house of the Berthold's, who had two boys my age. And if they did have a daughter who looked like this, how the hell could I have missed her growing up?

"Nice ride. Bobcat?"

"I'm sorry, do I know you?" she said, probing right through me with laser green eyes.

I am usually subtle when sizing up a woman with the intent to make a move, but as I approached her, it was obvious this one was an outlier. Taller than most, ample where it mattered, curves carved in heaven and pouty lips. And those eyes…

I took off my shades and caught a suspicion of a smirk on her face, like she too was secretly admiring what she saw.

"Larry," I said, extending my hand in peace.

She bit her lips and chuckled.

"Larry. What kind of name is that?"

"A regular name, only a gazillion times more awesome."

"If you were an accountant or a country clerk, sure."

"Happy to change it, if you like."

"Really?" She smiled.

"Really. I just have one condition."

She tilted her head to the side, her eyes focused on me.

"And that would be?"

"I take you out for dinner tonight."

"You don't say."

"I just did."

"Let me get this straight, Larry. You'd change your name for one lousy date? Exactly how desperate are you?"

"Desperate is a loaded word. I prefer…motivated."

"Sure you do."

"I'm a gentleman like that."

"What would you change it to?"

"Let me guess, you'd prefer Igor, Winston or Maxwell."

"Actually, would you consider Stanley or Herbert?"

"High school crushes?"

"Way better. Idols. Stanely Cohen and Herbert Boyer invented DNA cloning—"

"Which allowed genes to be transplanted between biological species. Their work gave birth to genetic engineering," I finished her sentence for her.

"I am impressed, Herb."

She winked at me with the confidence of a middle-aged hairy biker and the measured seduction of a high-society hooker.

"While we are on the subject of herbs, shall we say eight?"

"Eight what?"

"Pick you up for dinner, tonight."

"You're not planning on letting it go, are you now?"

"Our entire species would have been extinct if the male variant took no for an answer."

"Now you're turning me on, Herb," she said, running her hands through her hair and biting her lips in mock arousal. "Keep talking evolution and we could skip dinner altogether..."

"Except we need to eat."

"So just dinner?"

"Well, dinner and drinks, dinner and life-changing conversation, dinner and the best time of your life," I said, returning her wink.

She eyed me from top to bottom.

"If it's okay with your parole officer, and we'll stay within the range of your ankle bracelet, I'll say yes."

"Smart girl."

"Wait. Only if it's dinner and those things you mentioned, but nothing else. Are we clear?" All the while she did not move her eyes away from me.

"Oh, come on! You think all men are wired that way?"

"I don't think it, I know it," she giggled.

"Well, I could be gay. New research suggests homosexuality may be a form of improved human evolution."

"Could very well be. Which is why I don't think you are gay. Don't take this the wrong way, but you don't strike me as the poster child of advanced Darwinism."

"Ouch. Harsh."

"I study biomedical engineering at Harvard. I've seen the male source code and it's not pretty. Fortunately, nothing I can't fix in a Petri dish."

"Show off."

"Me? Look at your smug smile and that convertible you drive. You've left nothing for your mid-life crisis."

"Oh, you're too quaint," I sniggered.

"Say, what do *you* do, Herb?"

"I am a senior at MIT—"

"We're practically neighbors. Doing what?"

"Artificial intelligence. My dream is to build an improved human brain, free of all our existing flaws."

"You mean you want to improve female logic, just admit it."

"You did, I didn't," I said, my eyes beaming, unable to hide how much I was enjoying this exchange.

"Typical man. Instead of fixing what we already have, you want to scrap everything and build from scratch."

"You know… I'm already looking forward to dinner," I said as I scribbled my phone number on a gas station receipt I had fished out of my back pocket.

"Shit, you really are called Larry!" She screeched as she looked at the piece of paper.

I didn't quite get her excitement, but when I saw her

pulling out her own pen and scribbling her details, I fell for her a tiny little bit more. She walks around with a pen. Now how hot is that?

"I'm Melinda, by the way. Melinda Brand."

I froze. She stood there grinning like the joke was on me.

Instinctively, I turned back to look at my parents' house, where I had thought Melinda Brand was desperately waiting for me.

"Wait. Melinda, Melinda?"

"Melinda, Melinda."

"The Melinda?"

"The one and only."

"The Melinda I thought I was ignoring as she sat in my parents' house waiting while I insensitively chatted up the most beautiful woman I've ever laid eyes on? That Melinda?"

"Stop. Now you're making me blush and I fucking hate it when that happens. Evolutionary defect."

"And you swear like a sailor. I'm thinking we skip dinner and elope."

"Don't flatter yourself, Herb. There's a long line ahead of you."

"Wait—what were you doing walking up to the wrong house, Melinda, Melinda?"

"Shit, this be da wrong abode?" she said with a sheepish smile, and a terrible Jamaican accent.

"Harvard, my ass."

"I said genetics, not geography."

That night over dinner, I broke my promise to Melinda.

It wasn't just food, drinks and conversation. That night we planned the rest of our lives together. We chose names for our unborn children and picked the wall colors of their rooms. Pathetic, right?

Ten years later, the seeds of love Melinda and I had planted were embodied in the three monkeys we added to our cast of characters. Our love flourished, our careers were soaring high, and nothing could dent our happiness bubble.

Melinda was heading a research team funded by Google to wrestle Alzheimer's to the ground. Keeping it in the family, the artificial intelligence startup I had founded with my college buddy Earl, from our dorm room at MIT, was acquired by Google. Earl and I never had to work another day again, but we really wanted to. Good thing Google hired us for even more obscene amounts of money to build the brains of future robots.

Before we knew it, the years rolled by and Melinda and I were getting invites to our fifteenth high school class reunion. The historic geek in me panicked at first. I had to look in the mirror to remember I had morphed from an unsightly caterpillar into a beautiful butterfly.

Because I only ever knew Melinda as the hot, brainy Harvard head-turner, I found it impossible to believe she too had belonged to my people and was feeling the same heat. It turns out that no matter how successful or beautiful your metamorphosis, memories of high school have that ability to randomly terrorize you.

In the end, and after we had dissected it six ways to Sunday, we agreed we owed it to our fellow geeks to show the rest of our class just how remarkable we had turned out. But who was I kidding, one of the main reasons I wanted to go to that stupid reunion was because a part of me secretly wished Ashley would be there, and that she had turned into a crazy cat lady living on welfare.

I had never spoken of my teenage romantic misadventures to Melinda, and never wanted to probe hers. I figured there wasn't much to report on either side. Just like me, Melinda sowed her oats in college after she too had blossomed, making up for lost time. Except, of course, I had Ashley's skeleton lingering in my closet.

There are times when you couldn't script a happenstance better than real life. At some point in the evening during the class reunion, Melinda and I found ourselves chatting to no other than Mr. and Mrs. Balantine, Ashley and Jake. There we were, the four of us, sipping delicious Brunello red and nibbling on blinis.

I swear to God I would have taken out my checkbook and donated a million dollars to charity just for the gift of looking into Ashley's eyes when it finally dawned on her who I was. We were all adults now, and a few bottles between us later, we were immersed in grown-up topics like kids, schools and nannies.

As much as I would have liked Ashley and Jake to have turned into pathetic middle-aged morons, both of them were still quite attractive in their mid-thirties and had done relatively okay in life.

One thing, however, had changed. That confidence once flickering in their eyes during high school had been greatly diminished if not switched off. I had a theory why.

When you grow up beautiful and popular in high school, leaving that artificial environment to step out in the real world presents a major shock to your system. In the real world, your good looks and social skills are minor weapons in your overall arsenal of life tools. Being smart, being successful, being empathetic, standing up for what you believe in, and being a productive, caring member of your community weigh much more.

For the heartthrob jocks and bombshell babes like Ashley and Jake, real life can be a bit of a drag. I am not suggesting if you were born pretty it automatically makes you hollow in every other respect. All I am saying is that it takes getting used to when you realize you need other things of substance to move you forward in life.

Ashley and Jake seemed happily married on the surface, but painfully average in every sense of the word. Okay, maybe even above average if I want to be fair.

She started her career after college as an on-screen reporter for a local network and worked her way up to evening news anchor. Ashley was even a bit of a celebrity in her community, with her own YouTube channel as she was proud to show us on her phone.

Jake, on the other hand, sold banal industrial automotive components for a boring-sounding Irish company. Not sure I quite understood what, or cared, but apparently he was good at it. By any standard, they had done well and probably earned decent money and lived in a big house with its own basement gym, or some other upper middle-class indulgence. Bland, unrecognizable social fodder—the polar opposites of the gods they once were in high school.

They weren't, for instance, working to cure Alzheimer's or building an improved iteration of the human brain. You see, Melinda and I had started life as underdogs. Our appearance and confidence came after high school. It was hard-earned. We never counted on our looks or charm to get us anywhere in life. Looks and charm came later, as a late-blooming bonus, not principle weaponry.

As the night came to an end, relief and closure radiated through my heart. Finally I was going to let go of my Ashley Sakowski demons. What a drag that life is never so straightforward, always throwing you a curveball when you least expect or want it.

Right at that awkward moment when the four of us were saying goodbye, deciding whether to shake hands, half-hug, or go European and plant cheek kisses, Ashley took the lead and embraced me tighter than I expected. At the corner of my eye, I glimpsed Jake doing the same with Melinda, probably to even things out and make everyone feel less weird about it. But I'll tell you what did feel odd: Ashley surreptitiously planting a little note with her number in my jacket pocket.

There's nothing worse than the tiniest bit of doubt contaminating a strong moral position you've adopted. There I was basking in my victory over Ashley and everything she stood for back in high school, when she introduced this little chink in the armor. What could she possibly want with me that she couldn't say in the open and before our spouses? Did she want to acknowledge or speak about our notorious three-week history? Apologize maybe? About fucking time, of course.

Here's the bigger problem, though. No matter how successful, how accepted, how loved, how beautiful, how secure I had become, the minute Ashley had shown a renewed interest in me, irrational and incongruous ideas sprung in my mind. My little head was eager to play, my crushed heart was desperate for a second chance, and my bruised ego was after blood.

I'll spare you the mundane details of how the brain justifies the unjustifiable and will jump to the point of the story where I am about to walk in the restaurant to meet Ashley for dinner. Weaving between the tables towards her, I felt the wound in my soul carved out by this woman flaring up.

Ashley wore a lavender strapless dress like a model in a lifestyle magazine, selling something obscenely expensive. With every step in her direction, the illusion of control I thought I had evaporated faster than uncorked vinegar. Unresolved sex and love hormones wrought drama on my body. My head spun, my pulse raced and every pleasure sensor in my brain lit up like Christmas.

This is going to be a disaster.

Dinner turned out to be a delicious four-hour concerto of riveting emotions in which Ashley played every note masterfully.

First, she disarmed me by apologizing for being so forward, and explained that what she had to say concerned only the two of us. We had unresolved history, she called it. She saw no need to hurt our spouses. All she wanted was to hold my hands and look me in the eye and say sorry for being such a cruel bitch. Her words, not mine.

Then she gave me the explanation I had once-upon-a-time yearned for. A heartfelt confessional about how she was suffering panic attacks at the time, for which she took funky meds that forced her to behave like crap. Still, she felt accountable and had to take responsibility for her 'shitty actions.' My words, not hers. She was ready to come clean after all these years.

I didn't mince my words about how I had felt then, but, and I really believed it when I said it: I held no grudges. If anything, I thanked her for emotionally vaccinating me early in life against heartbreak and emotional anguish.

If our conversation had ended then, there was every chance I would have never thought of Ashley Sakowski again. But the rest of the evening took on an even more unexpected turn. She didn't just open her heart but she laid it on the table. Jake was an okay guy who provided for her and their two girls, but the fire between them had long been extinguished. Even if he was cheating on her, she didn't have the courage to poke around. For many years she'd been feeling invisible, and conflicted by her desire to stay for the girls or leave to satisfy her unfulfilled need to be loved and desired.

Who would have thought I would find myself giving life advice to the woman I once held responsible for all my miseries?

I am not the sort of guy who can kick someone when they're down on their knees begging, regardless of how much they had hurt me.

"You need to find a job or career you are really passionate about. It seems to me you just ended up in television right out of college because it was easy," I counseled her.

"You hit the nail on the head, Larry. My real passion is behind the screen. I never want to be a pretty face again. My dream is to write and produce shows of substance. I know I can't change the world the way you and Melinda plan to, but I don't want to be stuck in prime-time purgatory for the rest of my existence."

What if girls like Ashley, who were total dickheads in high school, are just regular people underneath it all, dealing with their own insecurities, dreams and fears? She ends up as a television anchor because everyone expected her to monetize her good looks. Yet, there she was bearing her heart and telling me she wanted to be loved for greatness other than that of her cleavage.

The more we spoke, the more I enjoyed it, and the more I enjoyed it the sooner I began to convince myself Ashley was nothing like the monster I had made her out to be in my mind.

Whatever she had done to me in high school, dubious meds or not, we were seventeen back then for the love of God.

Then it struck me.

I didn't have to sleep with Ashely, fall in love with her again, or hurt her to settle the score and expunge her from my system. I could just as well extend her some compassion and let her go.

Still, life is that conniving, curve-throwing bitch that it is. How I wished Ashley would have stopped there when we were both still ahead from doing anything foolish.

For the next three weeks, Ashley did the unimaginable. She pursued me with frightening determination.

Life was too short to waste on a relationship less than explosive, she said of her own marriage, and by allusion of mine.

We owed it to ourselves to be with the people who made us the happiest and who excited us the most. If only she had been smart enough to recognize my worth back in high school, she would have saved herself ten years of blandness with Jake, she confessed. I was the one she really wanted to be with, and given the opportunity, she would show me that I too would want to spend the rest of my life with her.

"How?" I said.

"Sex, of course," she said casually. "The ultimate litmus test."

By tasting her, I would realize beyond any doubt why we

could never be apart, she rationalized. The more I tried to talk her out of it, the harder she came on. Just one night together was all she was pleading for. If I didn't enjoy it, well, at least I would achieve closure knowing I finally conquered her, after all those years. Win-win, she described it.

Any time a story reaches the point of a no-strings-attached sexual proposal from a woman to a man, what happens after that will never please everyone. But I want you to know that when I walked into the Palace Hotel in San Francisco to book a room for Ashley and me, the thought process that had led me there was not entirely based on unfettered animal instincts.

You're probably judging me in a negative light because the honorable thing to have done would have been to squarely turn her offer down and get on with the rest of my life. And I don't blame you for thinking that. But stick with me, the stakes are about to be raised a lot higher.

Ashley strutted across the lobby of the hotel and time shifted to slow motion. Show-stopping is the only way I could describe the vision of her body floating towards me. Her hair was tied in a ponytail that danced around, catching the afternoon rays of the sun. She wore the shortest black tunic dress with no sleeves like it was her skin.

The last time I had seen her legs was during track and field day in high school. They had now become the lower limbs of a real woman, having been spread many a times to allow the seeds of life in, and just twice to allow babies back out again. Long, tanned and sculpted with enough tone to excite any man with the slightest bit of warm blood flowing through his veins.

I was nursing a highball, sitting cross-legged on a leather chair when she stopped in front of me, her knees pushing into me.

She extended one hand to take mine so we could go up, and with the other one she pressed a finger to her lips to indicate the time for words had now officially ended. The rest of the night would be all action.

I am not the sort of guy to kiss and tell, but there are some details of what happened between us that night you need to know if this story is going to make any sense to you.

Let's get one thing straight, the universe operates with a patent hatred for vacuums. Voids have to be filled. Any time a man comes across a woman whose sexual needs aren't being met, regardless of how he feels about her, he will be compelled to equalize that deficiency. Men smell sexual hunger on women like hound dogs smell blood. Ashley's unsatisfied need to be loved, caressed, kissed and taken in every possible way was burning electricity through the air, even before we stepped in the room.

I say these things not to brag about how my one-night tryst with Ashley could very well have been the best sex she'd ever had. The gold standard upon which she will forever hold her husband to—or whichever man she ends up leaving him for.

For three slow hours we rocked the universe. We fucked in every possible position, and with the stamina and erotic madness of much younger kids.

I harp about it because I want you to know when I stripped naked and screwed the breath out of this woman, I had no intention of hurting her, or anyone else. I was simply following her cues and doing what nature was requiring of me, to fill the void.

The fact I did end up hurting Ashley had nothing to do with me, and everything to do with the sort of person she really was. The real Ashley, not the character she was playing to ensnare me.

We lay on our backs floating in the afterglow of magnificent sex.

"You…" she whispered, snuggling her face in mine and twiddling my nipples with her fingers in a manner that was oddly arousing again.

I giggled, eyes still closed.

"You're incredible…"

"Nah, I'm nothing special. The only thing going for me is my great taste in women, even back when I was seventeen."

"You're sweet to say that, you know."

"It's the truth. You're amazing, Ashley. Everything I dreamed you would be. I am glad I listened to you."

She turned around and got on top of me, her thighs straddling my body as she dipped her face to kiss me.

"How about we do this every day, sir?"

My heart spiked, my chest heaved louder, but other than that, not a peep. Not a single word from my lips.

"No? Wouldn't life be special if this is how sex was done every day? Done right."

I turned my head away, then turned her around so we were again lying side by side.

"Of course."

"Be mine. All I want is nights like this every now and then. You can keep your life, and I keep mine."

"Jake doesn't know how to satisfy you?"

I could see blood coloring her complexion.

"Why ruin this perfect mood?"

"Am I?"

"Jake is the last person I want to talk about tonight." She reached out to hold me down there. Her slow kisses tasted like spoonfuls of heaven on my lips, revving me up again. I resisted, and moved my face away.

"Ashley, we need to talk."

"About what?" she whispered.

"This was an amazing night."

"I don't think I have ever screamed this loud…"

"Yes, this is how sex should be, but with the people you love."

"You hated sleeping with me, didn't you?"

"I'm not saying that at all. I loved every bit of it, and it was extra special because it was you. The part of me that once loved you will keep thanking me forever."

"I thought the deal was if you enjoyed it you would consider being with me? No one has to know. Our secret."

"A deal is something agreed upon by all parties. This was your proposition, and I tried to talk you out of it, even though I now don't regret it. We're both adults here. This was truly special, but it ends tonight. There will be no 'us.'"

"Fuck you," she said as she sat up in bed and moved away from me.

"You're sexy, you're sensual, and you can get any man you want. We both know it."

"Bullshit. I was just an easy lay. Either that or you're still bitter about what I did to you."

"You can believe what you want, but it's not true."

"You're like any other scumbag. A cheater and a liar thinking only of where to stick your dick in next. I don't buy any of your stupid lies about your perfect marriage to that idiot, either."

The show was quickly coming to an end. I got out of bed and started getting dressed.

"Let's keep this civil, Ashley. This was always about you and me. No need to say nasty things about the people we love."

"What do you know about love? Go to hell. We are cheating on our spouses! How's that supposed to be civil?"

"Cheating? That's a bit melodramatic."

"You want to know why I really slept with you, Larry?"

I nodded.

"Pity. I don't care how you look now, in my mind you will forever be that loser who slaved to do my assignments and didn't even get a pat on the back."

"You enjoyed sleeping with me, you just said so yourself."

"You're not getting off that easily. I'm telling your wife everything."

I stared at her, eyes widening, unable to believe how low she was intent to drown us.

"You wouldn't."

"I would. I can and I will. Unless—"

"What?"

"You think of a suitable compensation to keep me quiet."

"You're blackmailing me?" An involuntary laugh came out of my mouth.

"Call it whatever you want, but you're not sleeping with me and walking away without paying for it."

"I'll play along. Let's say I pay to shut you up, what's stopping you from outing me anyway?"

"We'll do it like they all do in this town and draw up and NDA. I know lawyers who specialize in sexual favors."

"There is such a discipline?"

She ignored me.

"What if I say I don't think you could sink that low? What if I tell you Melinda will never believe you?"

"Listen, jerk. You've got until Friday to come up with a proposal. Five figures at the very least. And just so you know I'm not an amateur, I've got photos of every time we met, including us walking up to this very hotel room."

"You hired a photographer to trail us?"

"Hell, yeah. But even without photos, Melinda will believe me. We're both women. I'll say exactly what I need to tell her to rip her heart out."

I placed my hands on my head and turned to gawk at the ceiling.

"Ashley, Ashley, Ashley...You never cease to amaze me. I have to say, I didn't see this one coming."

By now she too had crawled out of bed and was picking up her clothes from the floor.

"You think because you've moved up in life and learned a few tricks, you are suddenly a different person? Once a loser, always a loser. I wanted to give you an opportunity to be with someone in a league way higher than yours, but you're just too stupid to see what you're missing. A cash payment works out just as good. It means I never have to sleep with you again."

"Now that's hurtful."

"That's called a bitter lesson in life."

"Somehow, I only ever get those on your hands."

"Whatever."

I pulled out my phone and handed it to her.

"What are you doing?" she said.

"I've made up my mind. Ain't payin'."

"You'll regret this. It's not just your wife who'll find out you are a cheating bastard, but the whole world."

"You'll get burned just as bad."

"I work in television. I'll ruin your name with hearsay. I'll raze you to the ground."

I sighed and bit my lips.

"I don't care, Ashley."

"You have everything to lose. I swear to God I will unleash a shit storm on you, Larry. And it wouldn't be the first time I do it to settle a score."

"Nah, you won't. In fact, why not call Melinda and tell her right now and get it out of your system?"

"You're bluffing."

"Try me."

"I'll do it."

"That's what I want you to do."

"There's no turning back."

"You keep saying that."

"You still have a chance to get out squeaky clean."

"I'm good, thanks. Go ahead and call her. I have the number pulled up. Just press on the call button."

"You're lying. This is somebody else's number. Very clever." Her voice started to quiver.

"Put her on speaker phone, and let's have that conversation, all three of us like grown-ups."

Ashley's face lost any hint of color as she held my phone in her hand. Either she thought I was absolutely bonkers, or that I was carrying the biggest balls ever known to man.

I had her cornered. I could hear her breathing louder, and for a split second I really thought she would back down.

Then rage or arrogance flashed in her eyes and she pressed the dial button, declaring all out war. She just couldn't resist.

"Hey baby. How was dinner?" Melinda answered, her voice bright and perky on the speaker phone.

"Dinner was great," I said. "Then I met Ashley Sakowski. Remember her from our class reunion?"

"Of course."

"We're in a room at the Palace Hotel and she asked to talk to you. You're on speaker phone, by the way."

"Hey Ashley," Melinda said casually.

"Go ahead, Ashley, speak. I believe you had something you wanted to share with Melinda?"

Ashley had turned into a wax statue, and those don't usually tend to say much.

"Seems Ashley is a bit lost for words, baby."

"Of course she is. My hubby's a stud. You must have overwhelmed her."

"Yes. She and I just had earth-shattering sex. That's what she wanted to tell you."

"Okay, great. Do you know what time you'll be back, the babysitter needs to know? No rush, though, take your time."

"I'm on my way home now."

"Righto."

"And you?"

"I need to pass by the lab for a few hours. Can you pick up some yogurt and eggs? I think we're out."

"Will do. Before you hang up, how was your evening?"

"Meh. Huge disappointment. I think I got the short end of the stick, literally and figuratively."

"Sounds like it from what Ashley has been telling me. Tiny?"

"Yeah, but that wasn't even the problem. Serious performance issues. Couldn't get it up most of the time. We cuddled, he cried a little, we cuddled again, he cried some more, then he left. Sweet guy, though. Much more mellow than when I first met him. How was Ashley?"

"What are you both talking about?" Ashley interrupted, her eyes shifting erratically.

I shrugged. "Isn't it obvious?"

She cupped her mouth.

"Jake," Melinda volunteered.

"Melinda was in a room at the Ritz Carlton with him. They were planning to fuck, Ashley. Sounds like they didn't get up to much."

Once again, if I hadn't gotten it for free, I would have paid a seven-figure amount to see the look on Ashley's face, standing there after the cold bucket of ice known as defeat came down on her.

Sometimes, despite every effort you exert to avoid hurting people, they just goad you into doing it. Sometimes, when you try to be the better man, you have no option but to be the rascal.

After all was said and done, the underdogs got the final laugh. Melinda and I never set out to vanquish Ashley and Jake. It all started out as an experiment.

Jake will probably be fine if he remains ignorant of the larger truths. His mediocre life will chug along at its mediocre pace until he and Ashley walk away from their crumbling, mediocre marriage. That is, if they don't kill each other first.

Ashley, however, may never recover from this.

Let me tell you what really happened, because, unlike

Ashley, you deserve to know. I need to take you back to the night of the class reunion. Driving back home after we had spent the evening with Ashley and Jake, I was quiet and contemplative.

"Are you okay?" Melinda asked, rubbing my arm.

"There's something I need to tell you about Ashley, the woman we just met."

"I'm listening."

"She broke my heart."

There was a long silence.

"I knew it."

"She used me to help her out with her computer science assignments then chucked me in the trash."

"Go on."

"There's something else you need to know. Something happened tonight," I said.

"Wait, Larry, I have to come clean as well."

"What do you mean?"

"You're not the only one who was used and abused in high school."

"I don't understand."

"Jake did exactly the same thing to me. He was failing chemistry and I tutored him for four weeks. Got him up from a D average to B."

"They had a pact!" I screeched.

"Maybe. Trading the promise of sex for other life-critical advantages is part of our survival manual. We're wired for it."

"She slipped me a note with her number when she was hugging me. She wants to meet me privately," I said.

"Jake didn't have a pen, so he made me memorize his e-mail address. We're in the same boat."

"When exactly were you planning on telling me this?"

A flood of emotions rushed through my brain, jealousy not being one of them. Ashley and Jake had scammed us once as a pair, and were now trying it again as free agents, each of them potentially willing to cheat on the other. They wanted to use us to spice up their lives. Relive their past glory.

I exited the highway and drove to the closest coffee shop.

"I have the craziest idea," I told Melinda.

Over two steaming coffees, Melinda and I began to scheme.

"Sex and sexual attraction are the hardest aspects of human intelligence to replicate. The wires and the impulses required to get us buzzing are complex beyond comprehension. We're struggling with the infidelity module at work, but the machines are just not grasping it."

"What do you mean?"

"People cheat for a variety of reasons, none of which is quantifiable or easy to replicate. If you're married and getting plenty of sex at home, why would you cheat?"

"The thrill?"

"Try getting a computer to distinguish between the thrill of having sex with your spouse, and that of cheating on them with someone else. For the last two years, we've only ever gotten an artificial brain to cheat once, and I think it was a fluke."

"That's just great. You're trying to get artificial intelligence to inherit cheating."

"We're not building angels. We need to emulate the entire gamut of the human condition. If I can't get my computer to cheat, then how can I make it strive to be loyal?"

"What do you want?"

"We have two willing guinea pigs, male and female, begging to be experimented on."

"Who?"

"Jake and Ashley, of course, who else?"

Melinda broke out in laughter and in the process splashed my face with soy latte. "You're insane! You can't play with people's emotions like that. That's against the ethics of science."

"All's fair in love and war. They fucked with our minds back then, and still want to. Fifteen years later and they're back at it, wanting to break a perfectly good marriage. I'd say they've lost their ethical protection," I reached out and caressed her face.

"Hmmm. Machiavelli always turns me on…"

"All I am asking is that we just respond to their advances in a manner that encourages them, and document how they respond back. I will feed the data to our infidelity module and try to write an algorithm that may help us crack it."

Melinda nodded. "You and I would be the control variables, since we are technically cheating as we indulge them, but also not really cheating since we both know what's happening."

"True, but we're only going to indulge them as far as the intent to cheat, and then extrapolate anything that happens after that from the overall data sets."

As we both sipped our coffees, an elephant walked in the room and sat next to us, but neither of us dared acknowledge it. It was Melinda who caved in first.

"Shall I say it?"

"I'd prefer it, yes. I'm the one slinging a penis in this relationship, so if it comes out of my lips first, you'll always doubt my integrity."

"That's sexist. You could just as well worry that I am manipulating you to get what I want."

"Baby, we are both scientists. Just say the damn thing..."

"Fine. In order for this experiment to be viable, we need to indulge them all the way to the bedroom and really get them to cheat on each other. If possible, we also need to find out how they justified the cheating in their heads. Not what they are saying, but the truth. Safe sex a given, of course."

"Shit. That sounds terrible."

"It does, doesn't it?"

"Forget it."

"No, it's the only way. What if..."

Melinda ran her hand through her hair. "What if we treat the sex part as a fringe benefit, and remove any guilt attached to it?"

"What do you mean?" I said.

"I don't know about you, but that creep really hurt me. My entire transformation after high school was inspired by that experience."

"Ditto."

"When I saw him today at the class reunion, and after he approached me, I felt a little bitter, but a little flattered."

"So did I."

"What if the only way to get these two out of our systems is to do what we were promised back in high school, but never got?"

"That sounds good in theory, but it's still cheating. I don't want to cheat on you. I don't want you sleeping with another guy, least of all that numbskull."

"This is anything but cheating."

"Swinging?"

"Not even. This is redemption."

"You just want to fuck Jake!" I said then planted a kiss on her lips.

"I do, but not any more than what you want to do to Ashley. Let's be honest."

"I always say the universe hates vacuums, and is constantly balancing inequalities."

"Exactly."

"You and I could have very well slept with Ashley and Jake back then, but we didn't. There is an imbalance of justice looming over us, and we have a chance to fix it. Help nature course-correct rather than work against it."

"And if we were always meant to sleep with them, it shouldn't matter if it happened back then, or will happen in the future. Time is an irrelevant variable here."

The science was sound, but the potential pitfalls scared me.

"What if we sleep with them and end up loving it? Wouldn't it end up ruining our relationship?"

"It could, but I'd be happy with that. I'd rather know now that there's someone out there you would prefer to be with than five years down the line."

"You're brutal."

"I'm rational."

"You're a robot."

"I'm your wife. The geneticist in me has a theory, too, you know."

"What theory?"

"I'm betting that stripped of the rush of doing dirty

things in the dark, the sex we may end up having with these two will not be good enough to force us to question our relationship."

"What if she makes it extra dirty for me? What if Jake is hung like a donkey and reads Fifty Shades?"

"None of that will matter. You know what will, though, no matter how much we try to rise above it?"

"What?"

She hugged me tighter.

"Revenge."

"That's another thorny model. One step at a time, Dr. Brand."

"One step at a time indeed, Herb."

Melinda got up and sat on my lap and kissed me. For anyone caring to look, we could have been two high school lovers unable to keep our hands to ourselves.

EXTRACTION

I gave Dina and her husband Sammy less than forty-five minutes to go through their Cairo apartment for the last time before their identities were erased as part of Interpol's witness protection program.

Forty-five minutes, dammit. How can anyone do it? To savor your memories one last time. Bid farewell to the only life you thought you would live until the end of your days, not knowing what will happen next. The future no longer a space for you to dream but a huge, gaping black hole of multiple unknowns.

Where could you possibly begin?

One year ago, Dina and Sammy were a standard issue, upper-middle class Egyptian couple. He was a respected journalist and she a successful pediatrician.

Life was sweet in Cairo. An apartment overlooking the Nile, two healthy children and a full-time nanny, a summer home on the stylish Mediterranean coast, and a European vacation every other year.

Then, one day Sammy wakes up tired of filing banal stories on newly constructed bridges and every other hollow achievement of the Mubarak regime. The paper he works for is government owned, so there's little space for him to exercise any journalism that doesn't have 'ass-licking' as its primary goal. He feels a yearning in his soul for a loftier ideal to live up to. A social conscience is budding within him and it's starting to itch real bad. The kids and Dina are responsible for this. Being a family man had transformed Sammy. He wants to be the sort of father who can make the world a better place for his kids to inherit.

Not long after, Dina comes home from work one day, her face desaturated of any color, like she had shared a cab ride with the devil. She'd seen and heard things that spooked her. She tells him of a twelve-year-old girl who had hemorrhaged to death after coming through the triage of the hospital where Dina volunteered every Wednesday. Organ pirates had cut her open and snatched a kidney, then did a terrible job stitching her back up.

The illegal trade in human organs was a chronic plague preying on poor, marginalized souls living in the most destitute shanty towns of Egypt. What if this was precisely the story Sammy needed to tell, Dina suggests.

He agrees. Soon after, he started poking around, with Dina serving as his scientific and medical reference. He had barely scratched the surface when he was convinced that the story was far grimmer than he and Dina had initially thought. Sammy decides to go undercover posing as a rich industrialist, in the market for a spanking new kidney.

Three months later, a private, left-leaning paper ran Sammy's damming exposé. Sammy had uncovered an intricate and horrific criminal operation, and from that day onwards, nothing would ever be the same again for him and his family.

His story focused on a government-funded summer camp

for underprivileged teens from Cairo's poorest slum areas. For the last decade, Sammy discovered, the government-appointed medical staff members at that camp were operating a clandestine harvesting farm for fresh kidneys, destined for the lucrative European market.

The scam went something like this: Every camp season, about ten of the healthiest teenagers of the hundreds attending were identified as suitable organ donors. One day after a routine health checkup provided by the camp, the parents of the children in question are informed privately, by one of the resident doctors, that a life-threatening growth was discovered in one of their children's kidneys.

An immediate removal of the diseased organ is the only way the child can survive, they reveal. But the catch is, of course, that the procedure is costly and must be performed at a private clinic. In other words, there's no hope. And just when the parents have all but lost faith, the camp doctors come through at the last minute with a phantom offer from an anonymous philanthropist to fund the surgery.

How could they run such a tight operation without ever being busted for ten whole years, Sam posed the question, and answered it. Easy, apparently. The camp doctors insisted on absolute discretion as a condition for the provision of the procedure. They did so under the pretense that if word got out they were playing God with who gets to live or die on the dime of rich benefactors, someone was bound to cry foul and derail the whole thing.

The scheme was diabolical as it was ingenious. It preyed on endemic ignorance and a parent's instinctive love for their flesh and blood. Ten kids providing ten kidneys every six months.

The kids and the parents feeling grateful for what they believe was a divine intervention and the chance of a lifetime. And somewhere in the world an ailing rich bastard get the spare parts he or she urgently needs, brazenly jumping all queues.

The operation would have lasted forever if Sammy hadn't butted his head in.

But that wasn't all he unearthed. The rot ran far deeper than the camp's corrupt doctors. Two senior government health officials who were previously deemed infallible in the public eye were also implicated as co-conspirators. They were at the top of the pyramid, interfacing with the international buyers, who as it happened represented respectable medical facilities in cities like Bucharest, Doha and Lagos.

If it had been limited to international whitecollar crime or government collusion, the repercussions may have ultimately faded, with little impact on Sammy and Dina's lives. But as with any underground criminal racket, the whitecollar culprits are only part of the equation. Invariably, there is always a darker hand sullied in the murkier aspects of the business.

Whether it's the money movers, the delivery service or the rogue doctors who plunder the organs, Sammy's investigative journalism had blown the top off a global network of exceptionally organized criminals that cast a wide net from Cairo to Kabul.

Despite Sammy's airtight reportage, every single allegation he brought to the forefront was ultimately discredited. Not a single case was filed, let alone convictions handed down. Not one career derailed or a reputation tarnished. No government official taking his life in shame.

Sure there was public outrage, which resulted in the camp

being shuttered, no thanks to any prosecution or state action, but because even the poorest and the least informed parents had heard of Sammy's story about the 'camp of horrors.'

I wish the story would have ended there and whatever storm Sammy instigated had eventually subsided. Sadly, that's not how it works when you take it upon yourself to provoke a deathstalker scorpion.

Long after the flames of Sammy's exposé had burned out, the counteroffensive began.

First came the defamatory campaign. Anything from allusions in Cairo's venomous yellow press that Sammy was a a communist, to blatant accusations on television talk shows suggesting Sammy and Dina were part of a nefarious fifth-column conspiracy to undermine public confidence in the state. When that didn't resonate much, they hit them with the religious card, claiming they were apostates. Self-proclaimed theologians began citing out-of-context words Sammy and Dina had spoken publicly or published as incontestable proof of their blasphemy.

Before long, Dina and Sammy found themselves embroiled in a soul-draining campaign to defend their good names, and a legal sewer requiring them to respond to a torrent of frivolous lawsuits, brought against them by a seemingly endless stream of 'concerned' citizens. Concerned citizens my ass, hired guns was more apposite.

When the smear campaign ended, the terror kicked in.

It started with their Siamese kitty. The poor thing was found skinned on the windscreen of Sammy's car.

Four days later, Dina's private practice in a gated community on the outskirts of Cairo was fire-bombed to the ground, in the dead of the night. A week later, when their children's nanny hadn't turned up for a few days, they discovered her lying face down in a pool of blood at her home, with her throat slit. She'd been carved out. Her kidneys, heart, liver and lungs brutally removed for added irony. The message couldn't have been more pointed—they were closing in on them, and it was only a matter of time.

That's what A-list criminals do when they want to take someone out as retribution. They don't kill you immediately. They start chipping away at you slowly before they bring out the guns. As if to tell anyone taking notice that pretty doctors and middle-aged journalists should mind their own fucking business, and not poke around in matters that don't concern them.

Terrified, Sammy and Dina took their children and went into hiding in Alexandria. Hearing of their plight through trusted mutual parties, Interpol reached out to the family and offered to enroll them in their international witness protection program. Desperate and with no other option that would ensure their safety, they signed on.

The children left first, airlifted out of the country to be placed under temporary protective custody. Sammy and Dina would follow after a plausible double suicide was staged at their apartment. The plan was to reunite them with their children and provide new identities for the family. A new life somewhere far, somewhere safe.

Initially, they were given a few weeks to liquidate their Cairo existence and see everyone they cared for one last time.

But twelve hours ago, things took a turn for the worse.

We informed them of credible intelligence we received that

the organ mafia had detected their hiding place in Alexandria and would soon be coming after them. Remaining in country was no longer an option for them. The operation to extract them had to commence immediately.

That's where I fit in. I was assigned as the lead coordinator on this emergency extraction, working with my colleague, Victor Patel. I wouldn't have chosen this job if I had a say in the matter, but when you're dealing with international crime, you don't have the luxury of picking and choosing the cases that suit your sensibilities.

There are good days and there are bad days. This is definitely one of the bad days, but not the worst. As a father myself, I've become quite sensitive over the years to the plight of any family with children having to deal with this sort of crap. I spent twenty years as a narcotics police officer before this job, and it was always the kids who touched me the most.

I trailed them on this final tour of their apartment, as they weaved from one room to the other.

"Remember, computers, external drives, mobile devices and digital cameras stay behind."

They knew this already but still seemed miffed.

"Pretty much anything they can use to track you down after you go off the grid," I said, reminding them of the logic behind the harsh regulations.

There was a fine line I needed to tread. While I wanted to give them some space to absorb this moment, I also needed to do my job.

"What are you going to do with them?" Dina asked.

"My colleagues at Interpol's digital forensics unit will

back up your data then exterminate these devices. You'll get your documents on the other end. Don't worry," I said with a smile, like I was delivering the only good part of what was otherwise solemn news.

"Can we take our photo albums?" Sammy asked, even though I was in the same room with him five days ago when one of my colleagues had answered that precise question. But I couldn't blame him. The mind starts lagging when it's stressed.

"Unfortunately, not. Photographs must be destroyed. We can't back them up. And while we are on that topic, no documents either. Nothing made of paper—remember, the only reason we are here is for both of you to see your home one last time, not to take objects."

"Why can't we take our photo albums?" Dina pressed on.

"You just can't, ma'am. Please don't make this any harder than it needs to be. Delays will only jeopardize the operation and your safety."

I tried hard not to roll my eyes as I recited a stale script I had committed to memory. One I had delivered hundreds of times in the past on similar jobs to decent folks with nothing but terror in their eyes, after they had unwittingly fucked with the wrong customers.

They began to protest my instructions about the photographs, as I knew they would.

I responded preemptively, reminding them it was very likely their home was breached by whoever wanted them rubbed, long before Dina and Sammy began to feel threatened.

"We're dealing with the highest caliber of sophisticated criminals. We must allow for the possibility—remote though it may be—they used microscopic, spray-on nano particles that act as GPS beacons," I explained, now trying to sound as casual as an airline host reading the safety procedures prior to take off.

"What does that even mean?" Dina asked.

"Tiny, robotic particles that attach themselves to paper surfaces, only to reveal their location to whoever planted them in the first place. Invented by the Japanese, adapted by the Chinese, and stolen and commercialized by the Russian mafia."

"Sounds like science fiction," Sammy sniggered.

"You wouldn't even begin to imagine how dangerous the combination of money and a criminal predilection is."

I was right, of course. In this line of work, I've witnessed firsthand the brazen actions of the criminal masterminds of our time. I am not talking about the rookies who kill and terrorize to create noise, but the real deities of global malfeasance. The sort of criminals who never get caught, because no one knows they exist in the first place.

"I know my colleagues from digital forensics have completed their extraction protocol with you, but if there is any part of your online footprints you may have forgotten to extinguish, now would be the best time to do it. I have a laptop set up here for that purpose. Let's go through what you've done so far one last time, shall we?" I fired my words at them with military precision.

"Officer Olson, my wife and I have already been through this with Officer Patel about a hundred times—" Sammy protested.

"A hundred and one won't kill you, sir," I snapped forcefully. "But one loose end will."

With the waning resolve of a defeated man, Sammy began to recite what I wanted to hear.

"We erased and terminated our e-mail accounts. Cancelled

our credits cards, and banking and brokerage profiles. Killed our online subscriptions and memberships. Deleted our social media profiles, including photo and video sharing sites. We've scoured the Internet and removed any contributions either of us may have posted to online forums. What else?"

Dina took the baton from him. "I've pulled the plug on my medical blog for parents, and other than what's already in the public domain, Sammy is pretty much a ghost who never existed, at least online," she said.

Both their heads slouched to the ground as the full implication of what this meant seemed to have smacked them in the gut.

"Well done. How about your suicide notes?"

Dina pointed to the coffee table.

We entered their eldest son's bedroom. Dina appeared visibly moved. It had been more than a week since she last saw her children. She pulled down a small picture frame that housed an image with oval shades of gray against a black background. Dina held it to her bosom.

"This is Timmy at twelve weeks," she whispered as she showed me what I quickly understood was an ultrasound image of her son as a fetus.

"He was seven centimeters and jumping around like crazy," she said, wiping a lone tear with the tip of her sleeve.

"I fell in love with him even before I knew I was pregnant. I saw him in my dreams even before I had met Sammy," Dina said, then reached out to hold her husband's hand.

"Your first child, Officer Olson—nothing compares to that," Sammy added, as if to excuse his wife's display of raw emotions.

But he didn't need to explain anything. I tried hard to stand firm, but I couldn't stave off the goose bumps or the tight knot forming in my stomach. I have three boys myself, and I can't imagine what it would do to them if I too had to uproot their life like this. Displacing them from the safety and comfort of the only shelter they knew. No more grandparents, friends, or any meaningful reference point in their lives. Not for a brief while, but forever.

"You know what he told me before your colleagues took him?" she asked out of nowhere.

I bit my lips and shook my head.

"Timmy said he was proud of me and his dad. We were fighting for children like him and his sister. Children who didn't have a voice. Then he hugged me tight before your colleagues took him away from me."

Dina broke down and buried her face in Sammy's chest.

"He shouldn't be proud of us. We're responsible for this nightmare. We ruined their lives! And for what?" she howled through her muffled tears while hammering her hands on Sammy's sternum.

"You have nothing to be ashamed of."

I couldn't think of anything else to say.

I wanted to comfort Dina but nothing profound came to mind. She was right, to some extent she and Sammy hadn't quite thought of the long-term implications of what they started. But then again, if you don't stand up for what you believe in, what kind of person does that make you? How does the world change if not for the small sacrifices brave men and woman make?

"I have a special, vacuum-sealed bag," I finally said as I pulled that item in question out of my jacket pocket.

"What's this for?" Sammy asked.

"We'll keep the photograph of the ultrasound in it and we'll have it cleaned and delivered to you on the other side," I said.

I wondered if Sammy had any idea what a lucky son-of-a-bitch he was to be married to the woman weeping on his chest. Dina was like a prototype of the perfect woman, the master mold from which all other females should have been manufactured if I had a say in the matter. Dark satiny hair, candle-white soft skin, sensual amber eyes, and a hand-crafted curvy figure so irresistible and delicious it could very well undo the noose off a death-row prisoner's neck if Dina so desired.

I stepped out of the room to give them a minute. Sammy hugged her tight and whispered in her ears until she composed herself.

Then it was time.

Dina and Sammy stood at the entrance of their apartment holding hands, with their backs to the door as they canvassed their living room.

What could be flowing through their heads at that very moment? They had been living in this apartment since they got married. This was the safe, nurturing nest to which they brought back their newborn children from the hospital. In this very home, long nights of mothering and nursing were had, rewarded with first smiles, coos, and the wondrous, organic connection to the life forms they created.

Now as they prepared to abandon their home for good, it was most likely the 'first times' that played back in their minds. Sitting up, crawling, walking, eating and talking. The first head bump. The debut fever. And the first official tantrum. The one year birthdays. Play dates. Sleepovers. Baking adventures.

Their nostalgia wouldn't just be about the past, but the

future their son and daughter will never have. The love-infused existence they had built was about to be switched off forever. Nothing but silence after that buzzing in the air. Even I found that haunting and unfair.

I sifted through their lone suitcase one last time for contraband, but found nothing. A few items of clothing for the next day. Dina's purple sweater and tight jeans, Sammy's folded white business shirt and brown corduroy pants, and an endless supply of underwear and socks.

I gave the suitcase back to Sammy and the three of us turned to face the door.

"This is it. We'll take the stairs and you'll stay ahead of me all the way down. The Lexus is parked right at the doorstep of your building. Don't look left, don't look right. Jump right in. We're flying you out on a private jet from the military airport in Almaza. Should get you to the tarmac in less than thirty minutes at this time of the night. Then you're done. They'll tell you on board what your first destination is. But it won't be your final one. You'll only be processed there for a few days. I wish you the best."

"Thank you for everything," Dina whispered.

"Wait—if all of our photographs have to be destroyed and they can't be cleaned, how will you be able to give us the ultrasound picture?" Sammy asked, about to turn to face me.

I pulled out a forty four caliber magnum with a pre-attached silencer and fired a rapid shot each at the base of their skulls.

Their brains exploded on impact, splattering over their recently painted walls.

Their bodies fluttered for a short while, before they fell on the floor, hands still entwined.

Thirty seconds later, they lay motionless on their perfectly polished marble floor, in an ever-expanding disc of blood that was quickly making its way to my expensive, leather shoes. They were made of slink. Picked them up in Milan only a few weeks ago.

I hopped over their blood and stood a few feet away until the ruby-red circle had stopped radiating from its epicenter that was their fused bodies.

I felt their necks for a pulse and when I was certain they had both perished, I spoke to Patel through the open mic attached to my sunglasses. He'd been listening all along.

"Targets successfully extracted."

"Masterful, Olson, as always. Surgeons are on their way up to you."

Two sets of warm organs. Now isn't that poetic justice?

"All clear for me to get out?"

"Good to go. You are a fucking legend."

"Thanks," I mumbled.

"Where the hell do you come up with this shit, anyway?"

"What shit?"

"Spray-on, nano robots with GPS capability. Bloody epic," he chuckled.

"Screw you, Patel."

"You seriously need to stop pulling stunts like this ultrasound crap though, Olson. You're killing them anyway, so what's the point?"

Some mercy, that's the point. That's how I liked to do it. I played the part until the very end. I'd like to think there's some compassion in keeping the killing last. A part of me hopes that they die quickly, not knowing what had really happened. If there is life after this one, maybe it's better they go there not knowing there are people like me in this world.

Patel hated my softer side, and always promised it would get me killed one day.

No matter what you see at the movies or read in crime books, not all of us who kill for a living have lost every tiny part of our soul.

It never gets easier.

I never accepted it as normal.

I derive no pleasure from the act of taking someone's life.

What I love about it, though, is the money.

It's just a job for me.

The only job I know how to do this well.

But I too have a heart.

I too have kids.

And I too have some moral choices I can exercise to feel somewhat...human.

I chose to kill Dina and Sammy, because it was either that or something even more heart-wrenching: To murder their children. You need a man like Patel for that kind of killing.

THE VIRGIN

It's blistering hot in Dubai on Miriam's last night as a virgin. She can't sleep.

It will hurt like hell when he enters me. That's the only thing she can think of. He'll pay little consideration to her fears when he takes her for the first time.

With little mercy, he will ride her for hours on end, with the sole purpose of satisfying his deep, primordial needs. Sure, he may rest for a while but he'll keep coming back at her. She's young and soft and fine smelling.

He will surely be decades older than her, she grimaced at the thought. They're always old and needy, the men who covet someone like her. Probably insatiable as well. He'll devour her, as if her youth could rekindle his. As if her innocence could render him less jaded, less cynical. And as if her virginity would ignite his virility.

It's all been prearranged by the men.

Other than her assumptions about his age, Miriam had no idea who her chosen man was or what he looked like. But she's conjured up many images in her mind. When she is euphoric and hopeful, she imagines him as a handsome, dark-haired Arabian prince with kohl around his eyes. A gentle soul who would break her in with compassion.

But when she is feeling trapped with nowhere to go, the image would be of a decrepit, hairy, ogre with lizard-like skin, yellow teeth and hazy eyes.

In the past, when other friends were taken, they'd come back for brief visits and recount some lore from the battlefield, while the men chitchatted and went about their business. Not once did Miriam hear of a painless first time. The range went from dreadful to inhuman.

"Eventually everything becomes bearable, Miriam. Sometimes even enjoyable. You will force yourself or figure out a way to love him," her friends would add, as if to soften the truth.

Force myself to love him?

Miriam tried hard to lull herself to sleep.

Her thoughts drifted to her life before being brought to the Middle East against her will. She misses the natural crisp air of a European morning touching her skin. The green landscapes and the natural terrains crafted by random acts of nature, rather than multimillion dollar architectural contracts.

Dubai was an inferno of concrete monstrosities on the outside, and an air-conditioned purgatory on the inside.

The sun cracked through the sky and the fateful day Miriam had been dreading arrived. She woke up drained from a night of tormenting thoughts.

Did I even sleep?

If she did, the nightmares were so vivid, she might as well have been awake. Like a cow at an abattoir or a death-row prisoner about to be hung, the nervous energy of the people around her, cognizant of what is about to transpire, buzzed on her skin. No one seemed able to look her in the eye.

The prepping began. They bathed and perfumed her, then dolled her up so she's mildly seductive but not vulgar. Still Miriam is obsessed with the pain, and how inevitable it would be.

She waited until he finally arrived.

Her heart started drumming at a frenetic pace.

The men gravitated around him, like he was a planet and they but subordinate moons. He's rich and he's powerful, and he needs this sort of attention.

There were too many people around him for her to get a full impression, but when the crowd finally thinned, she stole a few glimpses, and what she saw set her heart ablaze.

Horrific is an understatement.

Obese like a grizzly bear with long oily hair slicked back and tied in a ponytail. He wasn't just old, but certifiably ancient. The ponytail was an ominous sign, confirming he was desperate to stay youthful. Miriam made out whiffs of something truly stomach-churning coming from his direction. Not a terrible body odor, but the stench of a man who's sense of mercy and compassion have withered away a long time ago.

The thought of this savage inside her suddenly seemed equal to or worse than a tragic death.

With little thought, she made a snap decision. But she needed to act quickly and decisively. She had one chance, and one chance alone, to escape. If she died trying or perished in the journey that ensues, well at least she took matters in her own hands. Maybe she'll set an example for others to stand up against their inevitable bondage. Even start a revolution.

As the men continued with the symbolic niceties and final arrangements, Miriam made her move.

It was fast, it was drastic, and by God it worked!

She made a run for it on the hot asphalt of the Sheikh Zayed Road. Never before had she felt more alive. The essence of liberty pumped through her, powering her to accelerate faster.

Through her rear-view mirror, she caught one final image of the men she had freed herself from, the three brothers who own Dubai's premiere BMW dealership, surrounded by their army of staff and minders, and man who had come to take her. All gathered outside exposed to the million degrees of a scorching sun, their jaws almost touching the ground.

As her old life disappeared to a mere blur, Miriam was certain she'd given these jerks the show of their lives.

When again will these circle of idiots witness a brand new convertible BMW 3 series crashing through the showroom window and driving away, unmanned?

THE WRITER

Last night, I experienced every aspiring writer's wet dream. I was dining at a hot Thai restaurant in Hollywood called Jitlada.

Outside, a snaking line of ridiculously beautiful human beings waited for their turn to get in this tiny hole-in-the-wall culinary wonder.

I was one of the lucky ones inside, sitting across the table from my dinner date, a long-legged goddess from the Weinstein Film Company, with a powerful last name.

You are probably thinking, what would a rookie writer like me be doing in the company of Hollywood royalty? The truth is, I lucked out. Big time.

My chisel-faced companion perused the elaborate menu and flicked her perfect blond hair to one side. Every so often she would penetrate me with blinkless glares as she pouted her lips to sip on an ice-cold Singha beer with measured seduction.

She had invited me to dinner at her studio's behest to—get this—discuss 'optioning' my novel for a 'film adaptation.'

I had to keep pinching myself.

I looked around, and most everyone was young and beautiful. A mix of Hollywood's up and coming and a few heavyweights.

I spotted the bearded guy from the sitcom *Men at Work*, dining with my favorite television actress at the moment, Kerry Washington from the show *Scandal*.

Funny men Will Ferrell and Owen Wilson were sharing a quiet, business-like meal. It's true what they say about comedians being mostly withdrawn types in real life.

You would think any hungry writer would be laser-focused on every second of this improbable opportunity. To inhale deeply the oxygen molecules of success floating in the room. That I would want to do a fine job licking my dinner partner's ass to ensure that at the end of this night a deal was struck.

But I am a writer, you see. We are an odd strain with our own brand of madness forcing us to filter things differently, even against our will at times.

I wasn't dazzled by any of the A-listers or mesmerized by the beautiful woman who had come to make me the offer of a lifetime.

Instead, a bizarre, mismatched couple dining in silence at a nearby table had captured my attention, distracting me from the most important meeting of my writing career.

Something about the dynamic between these two people was just off. I wanted to do nothing all night but analyze them to try to understand it.

As a writer, I live off human connections and stories. My mind was desperate to stay focused on the studio lady, but all I could do was stare at that couple's body language, and feverishly try to unwrap their 'back story.'

I suppose I should tell you how I got here in the first place.

Last year I wrote a novel. A pretty damn good one. Not just by a first-time writer's standard, but by any standard really. At least that's what the Amazon readers who purchased it gushed in their reviews. My story was full of twists and turns. Laced with adrenaline-pumping, thinking man's action. Dotted with steamy erotic scenes, none of which was gratuitous. Sharp, realistic dialogue with the right amount of humor permissible in a thriller. I threw in some Middle Eastern terrorists in the mix, a burned-out FBI hostage negotiator brought back from the dead for one last case, and, of course, a corrupt senator for good measure.

Like any self-respecting new writer, I skipped the humiliation of trying to dance with an agent or a publisher only to end up in the slush pile over and over again until your heart felt like it had been run through an industrial shredder.

"The writing is on the wall," many of my peers and self-proclaimed publishing gurus announced on Twitter and other literary forums like Goodreads.

"Mainstream publishing is dying, if not dead. Self-publishing is the way of the future."

I am not sure if deep inside I believed that assessment to be entirely true, or if I saw it as the emerging writers' proverbial way to pat ourselves on the back. But it was a mind-set that provided a modicum of hope for the sprouting scribe, so I bought into it, wholesale.

I hired an editor, a proofreader, a designer and skillfully put together my debut novel to make it look, read and smell just like the real thing. I even had a small launch party for friends and family at my father-in-law's house in Calabasas.

One year later, my first royalty check came in from Amazon. Ninety-five dollars, and sixty-two cents in total. Enough money to take my wife out for dinner at our local Italian eatery. But not enough for the requisite valet parking or after-dinner drinks at a nearby bar.

We laughed about it all night.

You guessed it.

I didn't quit my dayjob as a development economist fighting hunger in Africa with complex statistical models. And I was okay with that.

Despite the dismal numbers, the fifty or so people who had bought the book and reviewed it had loved it. And every one of them was a genuine reader who had actually parted with their hard-earned cash to read my words. Not just my college buddies in London, or my aunts and uncles in Tuscany, or my neighbors in Toluca Lake. But real, honest men and women of the reading public.

Even though I wasn't making any serious money out of my craft, I was slowly building a semblance of a fan base. I didn't have the resources to pay for a proper marketing campaign, the likes of which mainstream publishers unleash to carve a market advantage for their thoroughbred writers. Instead, my only real shot at success was to bank on a slow-burning ascension to the upper echelons of literary heaven.

And I couldn't let the $95.62 'killing' I made go to my head. I started writing the sequel to my novel, unlike other writers who commit the foolish mistake of thinking they'll have a run-away success with their debut work. I had heeded the wisdom of the veterans who keep reminding noobs like me it's all about building a large body of work. That's how you earn your place, and eventually make a living in this cutthroat industry.

Yet, despite the classic odds being stacked against me, fate had for once intervened to my advantage.

Six months ago, my father-in-law went on a Caribbean cruise. He met a lovely younger widow called Anna Von Wiesenberger from Santa Barbara, now living in LA. She quickly became his girlfriend.

Back in Los Angeles, my father-in-law proudly shared a copy of my book with his new lady. Anna read it, fell in love with it enough to recommend it to her book club in the Pacific Palisades.

One of the other book club members passed it on to her sister, who passed it on to her girlfriend, who happened to be the French tutor of the youngest daughter of the ridiculously talented director Chris Nolan. The tutor passed the book on to Chris Nolan's wife, Emma, who then recommended it to the actor Aaron Eckhart, who was a family friend from the days he worked on her husband's debut installment of the Batman franchise.

In between his movie projects, Aaron Eckhart found the time to read my book and was apparently 'spellbound' by my writing, so he passed it on to Harvey Weinstein at a Thanksgiving party last November.

Four months later, when Harvey finally had a chance to read it, he passed it on to his contacts at the shingle he had cofounded and once owned, the Weinstein Film Company. Before long, the powers that be there tracked me down and dispatched a statuesque executive to appropriate my novel for a film adaptation. That's how I got here.

We ordered.

We nibbled.

She spoke.

And I listened. At least I pretended to. The man and woman

who had stolen my attention were sitting behind her, so I could stare at them and still appear vested and focused on my dinner partner. Or that's what I was hoping for.

The woman was Asian, probably of Japanese heritage. Early fifties I guessed. The man, who I assumed was her husband, could have been of an Iranian or Armenian persuasion. He was roughly around her age, but that's where the similarities between them ended.

Stubby, short and large like a bad Danny DeVito clone, just lacking the charming comedian's wicked sparkle and presence. Not short enough to be classified as a dwarf, but not tall enough to avoid going through life being defined by his height. His head was bald and had a bulging forehead like a flower-horn fish.

Jitlada was a pretentious restaurant but not a fancy one by any stretch of the imagination. Still, even by the restaurant's relatively relaxed vibe, this guy stood out in his cargo shorts, crumpled white polo and dirty sneakers. Who goes out on Friday night dressed like that? As if he had stepped out to pick up the mail or do a grocery run.

His wife or girlfriend had exerted effort to dress appropriately for a nice dinner. Effort that was not nearly matched by her man. Her knee-length skirt showcased her soft, candle-textured legs, while her expensive sandals revealed perfectly manicured and exciting feet. Arched like an elegant swan, her upscale grooming was evident in her posture.

I guessed she was fifty by the way her eyes exuded the sort of wisdom only acquired after you've kicked around the world for a while. Her body and face, however, were that of a much younger woman. She had a captivating, sensual aura that she must have possessed all throughout her womanhood.

Everything about her was soft and refined like an expensive art collectible. Clearly she hailed from relative material comfort. Two or three decades earlier, this woman must have been a showstopper. Even now she was still extremely attractive, despite a barren disposition, as if the joy of life had been slowly smoke-dried out of her, almost like a curse had befallen her when she accidentally kissed the frog sitting right across from her.

Why was this couple dining out when they had nothing to say to each other? They might as well have stayed home.

Their dinner arrived. Some fish cakes to start, and then a mountain of chili crab to share. She picked at her food with a pair of chopsticks and plenty of well-honed sophistication.

He, on the other hand, was an animal. As his wife nibbled with minimalist grace, he savaged through the best parts of the dish, leaving her all but nothing. This Neanderthal was here for the food, and the food alone. There was nothing gentlemanly about him and the only affection exuding from him was for the chow.

After about twenty minutes surreptitiously spying on them, they had barely exchanged a few words and neither of them cracked a smile. Not once did they compare notes on their take on the food or exchange side jokes or inside humor. No touching or doting eyes, and definitely no discernible chemistry. Just a long, cold, miserable silence that kept them glued at the table for whatever reason, I couldn't quite figure it out.

I was eager to appear interested and grateful as the representative of the almighty film industry dangled before my eyes the secret key to enter my wildest dreams. The platinum opportunity that every struggling writer alive would auction their soul for. I was being invited to jump years, even decades of waiting to make a name for myself as a novelist, without even having an agent representing me.

If I played my cards right, my first book would go straight to the silver screen. How many writers come by this sort of luck within a year of self-publishing their first book? I nodded politely and spoke in short spurts of gratitude, but my mind had already decided where it wanted to stay firmly focused on: the other table with the odd couple.

How did this delicate Asian princess meet this ghastly amphibian, I kept wondering. Women who look like her don't end up with guys like him unless there's a dark, chilling story behind it. It's hardly ever about true love. In this case, certainly not about sexual attraction either. I tried to imagine them making love, but the mechanics of it just didn't seem to come together. Even if I could conjure an image of them 'doing it' as younger versions of themselves, it still was far from pretty.

With little doubt, I concluded, the only reason she was with him was for self-interest or self-preservation. She had settled for him and paid a price to get something else in return. But what?

The studio lady probed me to find out if I had signed up with an agent or a publishing house since we spoke, five hours ago. Yeah right.

I was hard at work in my head coming up with a convincing theory about this odd couple, a back story to satisfy my own hunger for a plot.

It could have gone something like this: Maybe three decades ago, she was an exchange student at UCLA. Studying something quaint, but not at all practical. Let's say she was the daughter of a Japanese industrialist. I'll call the empire she hailed from something like Kitagawa Enterprises. Powerful. Mr. Kitagawa must have sent his daughter to America for some overseas exposure and grooming before she came back to join the family business empire.

After her year abroad was over, she had a change of heart. She decided to stay in America. The taste of freedom outside the controlled and highly scripted realm of how her life was supposed to play out in Tokyo was addictive.

She wanted an escape route away from her dreary and predictable destiny where she would have little say in anything. Mr. Kitagawa would have expected his daughter to get married to a top executive who reported to him, have a litter of kids and then transform into a docile, stay-at-home subservient wife.

Then something clicked inside her when she met this monster, probably around campus. I am guessing he was probably more hideous as a young man. At least now in his fifties, age had added some character. The lines on his forehead, the streaks of white in the little hair he had left. Time had imparted on him some unique visual interest that could detract from his disproportionate dimensions and awful appearance.

Thirty years ago when he was younger, being short as a tree stump and fat as a boulder would have singled him out for derision. The only thing he would have had going for him was money, probably a lot of it. I'll wager he was the son of an Iranian Westwood real estate mogul. The ugly duckling in a family of otherwise beautiful specimens.

The Asian princess would have seen a way out in this abysmal man. It wouldn't have taken a lot of effort on her part to seduce him all the way to the altar. He would have been her ticket to stay in the land of the free. Maybe she thought she could rough it out with him until her paperwork was done and then find her own way. But he would have been shrewd and calculative and realized quickly that a woman like her would be hard to come by again. His strategy would have been to knock her up quickly and repeatedly and shackle her with kids. Then shower her with affluence and comfort to make her entirely dependent on him, to never contemplate leaving.

Now, thirty years later, this miserable silent dinner is how their unholy union had shaped up to be. The empty, opportunistic infrastructure of their marriage had decimated their souls as they stared with empty eyes into bitter nothingness. The princess kissed the frog expecting eternal happiness and salvation from bondage, only to find she'd come under a different spell. The gray, barren wasteland of a loveless marriage.

Every so often, the studio lady would glance around to see what exactly I was looking at when my eyes would drift away. Whatever excitement I had felt at what this meeting represented was overshadowed by the very instinct I possessed to recognize a good story when I saw one. If they wanted a good writer, there I was at our preliminary meeting exercising my craft in its full glory. Not that she would have been able to know that, of course.

Finally, the odd couple paid their bill and got up to leave.

As I had expected, he went to the toilet first. The chili crabs and the exotic Thai spices must have played a number on his otherwise carb-primed guts.

The wife stepped outside the restaurant to free the table for the next group, from the legion of would-be diners waiting impatiently outside. That's when I saw my opportunity.

I stood up abruptly and said, "Do you mind if I step outside for a minute? I just spotted an old family friend I need to greet."

The studio lady nodded, her bewilderment at my bizarre behavior all night seeping through her eyes and body language.

I rushed outside to speak to the Asian swan before the frog had done his business in the toilet. I didn't want to scare her off or come across as flirtatious so I just smiled at first.

"Exquisite food, right?"

She smiled with her eyes and nodded politely.

"The chili crabs you guys had, it looked amazing. Was it too spicy?"

Another tiny grin, but no words.

"Look, I am sure you get this all the time, but you are a very beautiful woman. I really hope the gentleman with you appreciates how lucky he is. Your husband, right?"

Whatever politeness had lit up her face when I first approached her quickly faded away. I saw a glimpse of terror in her eyes. I turned back and the frog was making his way out of the restaurant.

I wasn't sure if he had spotted us, but judging by her reaction, I gathered it was probably wise for me to walk away. Still, a part of me heard a desperate cry of help coming from deep within her.

The smart thing to do was to let go of this whole affair, mind my own business, and go back inside to start the rest of my life as the successful writer who crossed over to Hollywood. My mind said go, but my heart exerted more influence on my legs so I stood there planted firmly like a Southern California oak tree. Too stubborn to yield to common sense.

"Please walk away now. The man I am with has a notorious temper and is very volatile. He's walking out now, and it would be safer for both of us if you leave." Her voice was as soft and velvety as I had imagined it to be, with no trace of an exotic accent. Even with its nervous undertones, it was still wistful and evocative. The sort of voice that can save a man from damnation.

"I'm sorry, I didn't mean to bother you. You caught my attention inside and I wanted to give you a sincere compliment."

"Thank you," she said, with a sigh suggesting it had been many years since she'd heard a compliment.

"You and your husband reminded me of my own parents. My father wasn't a very attentive man either."

"I never said he was my husband," she muttered.

Before I could say much more, he rolled out of the restaurant with glistening sweat on his brow. Must have been all the pushing and straining in the toilet. He looked like he would get out of breath just by reaching out for the toilet paper. Remarkably, he was even shorter than I thought he was. I stepped aside, pulled out my phone and pretended to be texting. But my eyes were firmly fixed on them.

As I expected, his car was a brand new luxury German sedan. He sank in the driver's seat like Goldilocks in Papa Bear's chair. Any glamour exuded by his stylish wheels evaporated with this guy in the driver's seat. The Asian princess, on the other hand, was the perfect accessory to the expensive car. Right before she stepped inside the passenger seat, she glanced at me and whispered something softly.

I didn't hear it but I tried to read her lips.

Later when I returned to my table to resume my dinner and salvage my writing career, I couldn't get over the possibility that maybe what she had said was, *help me.*

THE BUNKER

My father-in-law threatened to execute me, but I beat him to it by getting his daughter pregnant. My first child saved my life. How many men do you know who can make such a claim?

This may sound like conjecture on my part: Every father hates the man sleeping with his princess at some level, right? But this is not hyperbole, he told me so himself. Not directly, but through his agents, the men he sent to warn me five years ago.

I had just started a new job at the United Nations in Manhattan, and was cutting through Central Park to get back home. In broad daylight, three men of an imposing build jumped me, covered my head with a cloth bag that stunk of freshly excreted urine, then stuffed me in a van parked on the ninety-seventh street transverse. Just like a terrible mob movie, only it wasn't. Far from it.

We drove for close to two hours, with my heart thumping through my throat, my mouth parched like the Sahara, and the only image floating in my mind was of my live-in girlfriend, Jessica, reacting to the cops when they turn up at our doorstep in a few days to tell her they found my bullet-riddled body floating in the Hudson.

When we got to the final destination, they removed

the bag. I didn't find myself tied to a skeletal chair in some nondescript warehouse in Jersey. Instead, I was in the living room of a spectacular mansion overlooking what must have been a national park of sorts, with a purple sun plunging in a meadow, and free-roaming deer sauntering like they were the star attraction in a high-definition National Geographic program. The smell of opulence was mildly reassuring. Rich people don't usually kill on their grounds, I wanted to convince myself.

I glanced around. Cocaine-white carpets and minimalist leather furniture, the sort you admire but can't touch at museums of contemporary art and design. Pretentious graffiti paintings, by elusive street artists without a real name, were strung relentlessly on all walls.

And there he was, the centerpiece of this grand display of wealth, an impeccably dressed man who couldn't have been older than fifty, sitting right across from me smoking an electric cigarette.

Hardly an extra from the set of the Sopranos as I was certain I would find, based on my Central Park introduction to his subordinates. He struck me more like a sophisticated Eurozone politician, the likes of whom I walk past in the office corridors every day at the UN.

After staring me down while puffing intimidating but odorless smoke, he finally said, "Do you know why you're here?" in a refined northern Italian accent that further rendered his criminal actions incongruous.

I shook my head, not being exactly honest. A part of me was almost certain this shit-show had the fingerprints of my girlfriend Jessica's estranged father.

"Mr. Alemagne has asked me to deliver you a message."

Bingo.

"From this day forward, consider yourself a dead man walking. The only reason he's allowing you to live— for now—is for the sake of your unborn child planted inside his daughter's womb. That girl will need a father."

How did he know the gender of our unborn child? I didn't.

"Even if it's someone like you...a father is a father."

My head dropped and I stared at my feet. There was nothing I could say at that very juncture. One persistent thought, however, danced about my head: *What the hell did I get myself entangled in?*

"Within a week you will marry Jessica, and if you ever let her down or fail to take care of her and your future daughter, you will lose this immunity, at which point your head will come off. Trust me, sir, it's never attractive when that happens."

As he cut me loose, he punched me with all his might, smack in the center of my gut where it hurt the most. He was close enough for me to sniff his perfume and determine he had been with us in the car all along when his goons had abducted me.

"Why?" I managed to extrude, as I wrapped my hands tight around my belly and gasped for air on the soft carpet.

"Why?" he roared in my face, like I was an imbecile student, asking a redundant question in a class of otherwise gifted children.

I shuttered my mouth and bit hard on my lower lip to tamper the urge to puke.

"Look at you. Isn't it entirely obvious?"

I saw the reflection of my face in his shoes and it all made sense.

They dropped me back from where they had picked me up. I never mentioned to Jessica what happened to me that day.

Many years later, I find myself driving from Rome to the heart of Tuscany. I am about to finally meet the man who had promised to kill me if I didn't do right by his daughter what I was already intent on honoring, with or without his theatrics.

With me in the car is Jessica, now my wife, who hadn't seen her father since she escaped his tyranny ten years ago. He'd been watching us all along, keeping an eye on me to make sure I held up my end of the bargain. Our children, Zoe and Marcus, are in the backseat. Their small faces and sparkling eyes oblivious to the notion of grandparents, let alone that they were about to meet their very own. My own father and mother had perished in a plane crash over the Ngorongoro crater a few weeks after I had learned to walk.

If he was ill or dying, Jessica wasn't given any details by the very same Alemagne executive who had assaulted me five years ago. The man in the impeccable suit had shown up at our doorstop one Sunday morning, still sucking on an electric cigarette. Once again he came bearing a message, this time for Jessica, from her old man, summoning the four of us to Italy for a matter of "extreme urgency."

Jessica wasn't surprised he had found us, and didn't seem threatened or perturbed by him. There was a historic warmth floating between them, like he was an uncle or a trustworthy family friend.

If Jessica had any inkling why her old man was desperate to see us, she didn't tell me. I was adamant against it at first, given what he had done to me, but at no point did the option of not going seem remotely viable. I figured if she of all people was willing to make this pilgrimage with the three of us by her side, on what grounds could I object?

I considered coming clean to her about the manner by which her father had 'reached out to me' five years ago, but I knew this would be inconsequential to her decision, and if I am going to be truthful, I had my own self-serving reasons to agree to go. I owed Mr. Alemagne something. Decrepit old man or not, the shit-face was going to get it straight in the gut, even if it had to be in front of Jessica and the kids.

Jessica had spoken of her family only once shortly after we got together, and made it clear then that we would never broach the subject again. She had run away from home and escaped Italy when she was only eighteen. Life at the Alemagne estate was soaked in tears and drenched in pain, under what Jessica described as the iron-clad oppression of a detestable, megalomaniac father and a spineless mother cowering in his shadow.

Mr. Alemagne was an immensely wealthy industrialist, and a founding member of an ultra-right secessionist party. The kind of man who operated by micromanaging and terrorizing every molecule in his universe. Jessica believed the political movement he had founded was a thinly veiled vehicle for a blatantly racist paradigm that blamed everything wrong with Italy on immigrants and the 'lazy, unproductive' portion of the country south of Tuscany.

My wife was a wild child who began to challenge him from the moment she possessed the intellectual faculties to do so. Her younger sister wasn't quite as thick-skinned. She found salvation by sucking on her father's Beretta subcompact and taking her life in his study. Two days after the funeral, Jessica made her escape.

Accessing the Alemagne estate was like going through a maximum security military complex with multiple fortified gates, aggressive barbed wire wrapped around everything, and sniper towers and cameras covering the entire perimeter.

The residence was perched on a majestic, gently sloping hillside. As we approached it, we were sandwiched and escorted by two military-grade vehicles that seemed to materialize out of nowhere. The security shenanigans tried but failed to rob me of the breathtaking view of the stunning estate where my wife spent her formative years. A peculiar sense of familiarity that I had seen this place before came over me. Perhaps Jessica's vivid description of her life on that single occasion when she spoke of her family had implanted the imagery in my consciousness.

It seemed like every member of Jessica's extended family was there on the lawn, forming a loud and gregarious welcoming committee.

Except her father.

A few of the men my age and younger made me feel at ease with delicious Brunello di Montalcino, while the women formed a thick circle around Jessica and our kids. When all the tears had been cried, and Zoe and Marcus had been smothered with a lifetime supply of retroactive hugs and kisses, it was time to eat.

As we walked to a banquet table laid out by a large lake, once again the same man who had punched me in the gut emerged wearing an even more remarkable suit. If the blood between us hadn't been so tainted, I may have even asked him where he gets his suits tailored.

"Mr. Alemagne would like to see you," he said as he grabbed my arm a little tighter than was hospitable. I felt he had a personal, long-fermenting dislike for me.

For the second time in my life, I got into a car with this man, only on this occasion it was without the benefit of a suffocating urine-flavored cloth bag over my head. We drove away from the estate in a muscular Range Rover heading south for about ten minutes.

We parked at the foot of a small hill, and there he was, a towering figure of a man with ample shoulder-length white hair flapping in the wind. He stood motionless on top of the hill gazing in the opposite direction, like he was meditating or speaking to God, quietly ignoring us as we trekked on foot towards him.

When I was finally standing across from Jessica's father, the vow to punch him in the stomach in front of his goon was deliciously tempting. I had already tasted in my mind the softness of his belly against my hard knuckles only a thousand times leading up to this encounter. But as quickly as my desire to inflict a lot of pain on him had resurfaced, it started to fizzle, almost against my will.

All I could do was extend my hand to him in peace. In his eyes, his lips and his finer features, I saw the genetic ghost of the woman I loved and the children we made together. He was her father and their *nonno*. Whatever animosity I held in my heart wasn't nearly as strong as my inexplicable deflation of aggression in his presence.

The Alemagne patriarch didn't shake my hand, but turned to his centurion and dismissed him with a flick of a finger and a subtle nod. Still without acknowledging me, he marched away in some random direction, providing no verbal or body cues to suggest he wanted me to follow him. Seeing no other option, I followed him all the same like an abandoned puppy robbed of its bearings.

Never once looking behind to see if I was trailing, he descended from the other side of the hill and marched between geometrically perfect olive groves. Above us, the lilac sky was speckled with tufts of cottony clouds, floating like fluffy sheep on a leisurely schedule to graze an endless field. This is what it would feel like if one could step into a Raphael painting.

Right there between the trees, Alemagne and I were alone, possibly with only God as our witness. Far from civilization, I stood beholden to a man who had made it clear in the past my life was worth little to him. Nothing could stop him from pulling out the same gun his own daughter had used to escape his tyranny, and extend me the same fate.

Somehow, a wiser version of me whispered in my head that murder was not likely going to be on the menu today.

"What is this place?" I said.

We stood facing our images reflecting on a gray metallic structure, built into the face of another small hill, about three miles west of the olive grove. A door of some sort, but without handles or knobs to operate it.

My father-in-law glanced up to the heavens with a fatalistic sigh escaping his lips, as if he was observing something only he could perceive.

Finally, he croaked, "A war is coming," in unexpected neutral English. His was a battle-worn voice of a man consumed by a tragic life.

I said nothing.

"When it's time, I will be long gone, but you will know of this place and will bring my daughter and your children here. What I am about to show you will be the only safe haven to protect you from whatever hell will have broken out on the outside."

"Is this why you called us here?"

For the first time since we had met, he finally looked me straight in the eyes, and extended his arm, now willing to take my brown, African hand in his.

"Come, we don't have much time."

Franco Alemagne didn't take my hand to shake it warmly, but placed it on the cold metal door, which he wanted me to believe was the entry to a life-sustaining bunker in the heart of the Val d'Orcia region of Tuscany.

When my hand touched the metal surface, a small window slid open, revealing a rectangular glass tablet, like some sort of LCD screen.

"It's a secure entry system. It reads your genetic code from you skin cells. Only five other people in the world can access it."

That my father-in-law had somehow procured a 'part of me,' and used it to configure my genetic profile as one of the five people who could access this place, was chilling.

I could only guess that Jessica and the kids, and Mr. Alemagne himself, were the four others. Getting a hair follicle or some biological sample from Jessica was feasible, since she had lived with him for the first eighteen years of her life. But it was the thought of an Alemagne operative handling my children back in New York, to get a sample of their genetic source code, that left my ears on fire.

"Who are you?" I blurted. The same rage I had felt when I was abducted in New York bubbled up my chest.

He did not supply an answer, but removed my hand off the screen with surprising strength.

The outline of my palm was imprinted on the glass tablet and looked like the infrared rendition of a night vision device. As the system analyzed my profile, random numbers and cryptic figures blinked and danced around the screen, until everything dissolved out and the word *approvato* began to flash in amber, confirmed by a woman's voice. The screen slid up with a high-tech hum revealing yet a third surface beneath, in brushed aluminium and two glass spheres.

"Look inside these prisms."

"Why? What is it?" "

"It's a retinal scan. A secondary protocol."

I complied, and the glass tablet materialized again announcing once more I was who I needed to be. The words *inizia test di riconoscimento vocale* appeared on screen for five seconds, followed by a countdown from twenty, accompanied by unnerving beeps.

"When it reaches zero, say something—it's the third and final security protocol of this gate."

Livid at the thought that this man had gotten inside my head, and that of my wife and children to scan our retinas, all I could say to satiate the voice recognition system was, "*Vaffanculo*, Signor Alemagne."

And with these honest words, my life changed forever.

We crawled through the first gate into a dark chamber. Motion detectors activated faint pilot lights almost immediately. My naive assumptions that whatever Alemagne had summoned me to see was at hand were quickly laid to rest. It would take us another ninety minutes to reach our ultimate destination.

From the first entry point onward, we processed ourselves through no less than seven security access points by validating my genetic profile, my retina and my voice every single time. With each successive entry we were incrementally removed from a layer of human civilization, until I eventually lost count.

We crawled on all fours through tunnels, stripped naked and were sprayed by disinfectants in a decontamination zone, changed into HAZMAT suits then back into civilian garb, took elevators that traveled us deeper inside the earth, and rode high-tech electric cars the likes of which I had never seen on the streets above.

"We have arrived," he finally announced, after we emerged into a circular space roughly the size of a baseball field.

All around us, there was foliage and vegetation. Above us a sky, like an optical illusion, challenging everything I had learned about the physical world.

Beneath my bare feet, the softest grass I had ever walked on played an equally cruel cerebral hoax.

"Are we back up on the surface?" I asked, not because there was any possibility of that to be true, but because the only other thought to pass through my head was *The Truman Show*.

Franco Alemagne smiled for the first time of our mutual journey through his underworld, like an artist revealing his seminal work to a most discerning public.

"We are one thousand feet under the surface of the earth."

I raised my head up to the 'sky' and inhaled deeply the freshest, most sanitized air I had ever allowed through my lungs. My head was light, not from the purity of the oxygen, but the multiple distortions of reality battering my senses.

What kind of man has the resources to construct a synthetic atmosphere?

"What you are seeing here is the distillation of human

civilization and scientific achievement. We broke ground thirty years ago, using technology from decades in the future. It became fully operational two months ago. There are five other facilities like this on every continent, with one single purpose."

"What?"

"To preserve life for as long as possible while the world outside is scorched to the ground."

I must admit I didn't pay much attention to Alemagne's apocalyptic forecasts. My mind was wrapped around the perfect realism of the virtual sky above our heads. I gazed into it until I lost all sense of time. This wasn't a run-of-the-mill theater or studio-fake sky. This sky was moving, changing, evolving. The genius of its design meant one could never tell how high up it was or what it was made of. It was, for all intents and purposes, a sky. Deep inside the earth's crust.

"But...why?" I finally let out, although hardly expecting a satisfying response.

"You work in networks and computers at the United Nations, right?"

I wasn't expecting a redundant question, either.

"As if you don't know everything about me."

"In terms you are familiar with, we developed these six facilities as humanity's backup drives of life on earth."

"We?"

He ignored me.

"Who else is part of this?"

He didn't stop ignoring me. "Each facility has a genetic bank containing samples of all known living species on this planet. There is a digital library of every piece of information ever generated or created by a human being, constantly being updated.

"And that's not all. Every aspect of human life and culture is being captured in the vast learning archives of each of these facilities. Think of it like a camera taking continuous snapshots of our world. It will only stop when these facilities go into service."

"What do you mean?"

"The moment each of these facilities is activated, they will be entirely sealed from the outside world, like a Faraday cage on steroids. Nothing linking them to the earth that remains. Not a single sign of life that can escape to the outside."

Before I asked about air, he was ready with the answer.

"This is an entirely self-sufficient ecosystem. There is an air management matrix that mimics the composition of the atmosphere on land, and is programmed to introduce low-level seasonal pathogens to maintain the evolutionary edge of the human immune system.

"Carbon dioxide and other unwanted gases are extracted and stored in compartments embedded even deeper underground."

Once again he answered a question I was about to ask. "There is enough oxygen and fresh water to last fifty people for thirty years. But there's not going to be fifty people here when the time comes. Just you and your family."

"Where are we now?"

"The entire estate is about fifteen acres. This area here we call the sanctuary. The only part of the complex that serves no purpose but to remind you of what life above ground used to be. Because other than yourselves and the occasional synthetic cold viruses and pollen injected in the air, there's nothing else here that's alive. No plants, no animals and no insects. No flowing bodies of water or wind. No sun or moon."

I pointed to the foliage and trees around the sanctuary.

"Designed in Stockholm, assembled in Bratislava," he said as he walked away and disappeared in the artificial lush green.

Alemagne called the estate Eden.

I concede there's not much subtly or imagination with a name like that. I suppose when your life project is to build an underground Noah's arc to give humanity a fighting chance, being nuanced is at the very bottom of your priorities.

What I saw that day when I followed Alemagne beyond the artificial foliage of the sanctuary would remain vivid in my consciousness forever.

I know now that's exactly what he wanted. He was priming me. Revealing everything he had ever worked for, not just to educate me, but to hand over the keys and the responsibility to shepherd what he had built. Alemagne was dying.

He was right. Eden was a self-contained ecosystem, but one built to sustain four members of one single life form. The genetic bank of plant and animal life was not something we ever needed to worry about or interact with. It was there for after the apocalypse. He didn't tell me how or why on my maiden tour of Eden, but I would eventually find out.

Eden was built not just to support our lives, but to sustain and nurture our humanity. There was no house, because there was nothing we needed to shelter ourselves from. No elements, no predators and certainly no humans.

There were only five built structures.

First, a genetic repository was located at a far edge of the estate, out of our day-to-day scope of vision.

The second building was the central nerve of Eden, which he called the 'learning temple.' This place was a marvel of human ingenuity, powered by a talking, artificially intelligent being. Everything was conducted through speech and didn't require a computer interface to operate.

It wasn't just the automated classroom designed to educate children from preschool to postgraduate levels that amazed me, or the bountiful warehouse of learning, leisure and entertainment supplies. Let alone the infinite library of audiovisual instructional material on any human task imaginable, from how to make an origami crane, to a step-by-step guide to surgically remove a kidney stone.

What really blew my mind away most was the existence of two operational modes. The default was designed to be powered by adults, but if the system sensed that adult interaction suddenly went silent, it would switch to assume the primary operators where children. Just in case something ever happened to me or Jessica, Eden would continue to guide and educate Zoe and Marcus.

The third built structure was the largest. Alemagne called it the 'life core,' a spectacular automated food preparation system and warehouse of frozen, dehydrated and preserved food and potable water. Like a figment of Roald Dahl's wildest imagination, food storage, processing, and preparation were all conducted behind closed machinery.

There was a total fire ban on Eden, so cooked food was prepared by microwave and then dispensed for consumption.

I guess humanity had already lost its innate instincts to forage, hunt or grow its food long ago, so there was no point for Eden to account for sustaining that skill.

The fourth structure was an infirmary where we could extract teeth, or, indeed, perform outright surgery. Whatever we cared to train to do in the learning temple.

The last of the structures was the 'power and waste management hub,' at another far corner of the estate. I didn't ask, but only assumed that whatever was inside it, able to sustain our energy requirements for thirty years, had to be nuclear. Not that I wasn't intellectually curious about feces to inquire what happened with human bodily waste on Eden, but after everything I had seen, I trusted Alemagne to have figured out where to hide it.

Six hours later, Alemagne and I emerged and once again stood on top of the hill where I had first met him. We were both silent as we waited for our ride back to the mansion. I had forgotten about the present-day version of Jessica and the kids, engrossed instead with a future where we lived as survivors of some destructive global war, in this obscenely expensive, highly secretive, but technologically mind-boggling world my totally bonkers father-in-law had built.

"You wanted to kill me because I am black. Why do you want to save me now?" I said, shattering the silence.

"Is that what she told you?"

I inched closer to him. "No, that's what the mafioso sleazeball you sent to scare me said after he struck me in the gut. I was going to marry her anyway, with or without your bullshit."

My fist was clenched tight, the vow I had taken to repay the Alemagne debt once again overpowering me.

"He said those exact words?"

Wrath rumbled in my belly as I strode even closer to him. "When I asked him why you wanted to kill me, he said 'look at you, isn't it entirely obvious?' What else could he have meant?"

"Of all your attributes, why did you assume it was the color of your skin he was referring to?"

His question stopped me in my tracks. "Because of your political beliefs. The neofascist party you formed. I just assumed you were racist slime."

Alemagne smiled for only the second time since we met.

"Jessica is a smart girl, which means she's also... convincing. But—"

"What?"

"Don't get me wrong. I would have killed you. With my own hands if I had to."

That's a relief.

"But I didn't want to kill you because you were black and sleeping with my daughter. I wanted to kill you because I had my doubts you would stay with her and be a husband and a father. If you were just stringing her along, you would have been an obstacle to her making a family. Eden was designed to sustain a family. Not a single mother."

He left me with a new version of the truth and started trekking down the hill when he saw the Range Rover approaching.

"Wait!" I yelled at him. "Are you saying Jessica knows about this place? That she was in on it?"

He marched on, silently ignoring me.

"Yours is one fucked up family, Alemagne. You can take your doomsday bullshit and shove it up your ass. I am taking my kids and we're flying back tonight."

He stopped moving but didn't turn to face me.

"2:03 p.m., Friday, April 13, 2018," he said like he was dictating a grocery list. Like he had said it a million times before that, and it had lost any real significance or value.

"What is this date?" I said.

"The precise moment every living cell on this planet outside the sealed bunkers will be vaporized. The war will start forty-five days earlier. Then the first wave of destructive attacks will strike on April 7th. Massive wide-scale devastation of major urban centers on April 11th. Then..."

He turned to face me, eyes glistening with brewing tears.

"Then what?"

"Total annihilation on April 13."

I shook my head and rolled my eyes, adamant to be as dismissive as I could. I just couldn't be responsible for encouraging this nonsense any longer.

"Do you have any idea how absurd you sound? How deranged you come across? There's absolutely no way an intelligent man like you can seriously expect me to believe this."

"You must believe me, if you want to survive, and you must survive for my daughter and my grandchildren. For humanity."

"In your universe, perhaps. Down here on this humble planet, unless you can travel through time or foretell the future, typically, the way wars work, the way they've always started in history, is that they just fucking happen."

"History rarely happens, son. It's almost always agreed upon in advance."

"Now what the hell is that supposed to mean?"

"It means there is another way one can know in advance of an impending war."

He sighed deeply and finally the tears he'd been curbing

erupted from his glassy eyes. He reached out and placed his hand on mine. His skin was leathery, cold, repulsive and painfully human all at once.

"How?"

"If you are the one who is going to start it. Many decades ago I was involved in a series of terrible events beyond my control. Events I wish with every part of my being I could overturn. Events that will ultimately lead to the destruction of this planet."

"What events?"

"Don't wait until the war starts to get here. Social structures, telecommunication, services, transportation, governments and law enforcement will crash and fail a few months before the destruction. Save yourself. Save your family. I've shown you a glimpse of the future. It's up to you to grasp it. I am not asking you to believe me right now, just to remember what I showed you here today for when it's time."

I stood motionless, speechless, bereft of any desire to rubbish his sanity further.

"One more thing, son-in-law."

"Yes?"

"Get all your natural teeth removed and replaced before you come to Eden. There is nothing more painful than an infected nerve, with no one to care for it. There is a dentist we work with in Boston who uses our advanced technology."

We are on the plane flying back to New York. Jessica and I have only exchanged distrustful looks but we never spoke about what I knew, or what she was hiding.

I did not want to censure her, or to try to probe further. We had five years ahead of us to thrash it all out. I observed Zoe and Marcus both fast asleep now in the comfort of a flat bed in the sky. If and when this war comes, they will be ten and seven, and Eden will be the only life they will ever know after that.

Do I believe Alemagne? That's an impossible question to answer with what I know. Everything he told me sounds like the overstretched science fiction imagination of a stunted teen. But the technology and the resources I witnessed inside Eden point to a different sort of man. A villain perhaps, but one with terrifying resources, and maybe some twisted code of honor. For better or for worse, the sort of villain who kept his word.

It's been three weeks since I saw Eden and met Alemagne in Tuscany. I can't get either out of my mind. A question has been bugging me since. One upon which my trust of this man and the vision of the future he seemed so desperate to sell me could be contingent on. An inconsistency in his story.

When I first met him, he told me when the war will come, he will have been long gone. Yet Eden was accessible to five people, my family and me, and one other person, who I assumed was Alemagne himself. Why would he retain permanent access privileges even though he seemed certain he was departing well before the war? There was a stink of dishonesty I needed to probe.

I was indecently drunk as I sauntered out of a bar on Fifth Avenue, where my work colleagues and I usually gather on Friday night. I tried to hail a cab, but I was not doing it with much assertiveness. A black Range Rover drove by and I thought of Franco Alemagne. I dialed his cell number, not giving a damn about the time difference.

"Pronto?" He's unexpectedly civil and alert.

"You lied to me, you son-of-a-bitch."

Silence.

"You said you would be dead when the war comes, but yet you're one of the five people who can access Eden."

"Why did we use your hand, retina and voice every single time to access the various check points, and not mine?"

Even through my slurred thoughts, stunted logic and a judgment clouded by volatile rage, I picked up on the soundness of his reasoning.

"Who is it then? Who's the fifth person with access to Eden?"

"A scientist. Part of a team of six. You can think of them as humanity's litmus test. A group of people who have agreed to survive the war in smaller, research-centric bunkers near each of the six complexes, for five years after the war."

He explained that the six would emerge and see if they can survive for another five years in the aftermath of the destruction. No one knows how long after the annihilation earth will remain inhospitable. That's why the Eden complexes were stretched to support life up to thirty years because of the limitations of the supply of water and oxygen, and waste management. But it's a conservative guess. If at the ten-year anniversary each of these six individuals are still around, with no adverse reactions on their bodies, they will come to liberate the citizens of the six Edens scattered around a barren planet.

"Who wants to live underground forever, right?"

"Why are they in separate bunkers, Alemagne? Why not join us and have them leave after five years?

There was a lump of nothingness at the other end of the phone.

"Alemagne?"

More silence.

"Answer me!"

"Because once you are inside Eden, you can only leave every fifteen years. It's a one-way valve that opens for twenty-four hours, once, every decade-and-a-half."

Cold tingling dribbled down my spine.

"What you're not telling me then is that if we take refuge in Eden, and chance would have it that your war never happens, we will be forced to live underground for at least fifteen years. Right?"

Alemagne sighed from an archaic part of his soul, like I had stumbled on the fundamental moral dilemma of his proposal a lot sooner than he would have liked.

For the first time since Alemagne had seduced me with Eden, an unthinkable thought crossed my mind. Maybe, just maybe, when the time would come, I would choose to take the risk of staying on the outside with Jessica and the kids, possibly perishing with the rest of humanity, rather than be imprisoned underground like lab rats not knowing what really happened.

THE IRAQI NURSE

Jumana wasn't getting the damn job, she knew it even
before the silver-haired director of the maternity ward had
launched into his prologue.

Maybe it was the three lady doctors sitting at the mahogany
table beside him, avoiding the slightest eye contact with her.
Jumana's sensitivity to the stink of rejection had become acute
of late.

Barely had she made her way across the cavernous
boardroom to sit on the lone chair at the center, and any
hope that had tentacled in her chest was cruelly extinguished.
This wasn't going to be a second interview. She was in for a
crucifixion.

She had been through these motions before many times
since she and her family had sought political asylum in Sweden,
although never in person. Previous rejections had come in the
mail or over the phone. Still, the lead-up was the same.

Jumana had tasted all flavors of canned preambles ahead of
her heart being shredded. Some variation of the same bullshit
line about how her past work as a nurse at the Al Yarmouk
Hospital in the red zone of Baghdad humbled them.

Having been at the 'frontier of where humanity ends and
depravity began,' they'd tell her, her experience was awe-

inspiring and had humbled them, even though they were mighty doctors and she a lowly nurse. The harrowing stories she had recounted during her first interview would forever haunt them. Like the heart-stopping screams of the seven-year-old girl she helped pin down while doctors inserted an adult-size tube in her chest, without the mercy of anesthesia.

Jumana had reminded them why their profession was important, and for that they would be forever grateful.

When they were done patronizing her every other way, "regretfully," they would tell her, due to some obscure regulation or technicality, they were unable to hire her.

Today was no different.

"Ms. Rawy, as you know, the St. Görans is a private hospital," the male doctor said as speckles of unexpected tenderness escaped his eyes when he peered up from behind his wire-frame glasses.

"We abide to strict internal hiring regulations," he said, then flashed a stern glance to his three female colleagues.

Perhaps he had been the lone voice lobbying for her to get the job, while the women—one white, another of African heritage, and the third of some nondescript Mediterranean or Arab background—were vying for her neck.

When she had come in for the first interview four weeks ago, this rich tapestry of diversity had kindled hope in her heart. The numbers seemed to be in her favor.

Half of the panel was of immigrant backgrounds and three-quarters were women. Surely she would touch something in them, she had hoped. Sisters standing up for a fellow sister in need. Now with her head on the chopping board, and the lone man on the team exhibiting the only symptoms of a beating heart, the irony of her naivety wasn't lost on her.

Jumana fixed on his lips, struggling to throttle her tears. Latched to her breast and near comatose was her baby son Firas. No amount of noise could ever wake that child up when he was on high on milk. The only thing capable of jolting him screaming and terrified was when Jumana broke down and cried. The rest of the world was on mute as far as Firas was concerned. He was plugged into his mother's emotional core, crying when she did. When that happened, a small part of her withered away, and there wasn't much left.

Dragging her flesh-and-blood to every single job interview was hardly her choice, but this was Sweden where the external veneer of being a civilized society allowed for such indulgence. Let alone not having anyone to leave him with. Her husband Gaber worked impossible shifts at a *halal* butchery in the heart of the Rinkeby Torg market and was rarely home. The only other person in her household was her thirteen-year-old daughter Badreya, who attended school.

"Regretfully, we are unable to offer you the job of assistant nurse at the maternity ward."

Clear, concise and unambiguous words. No room for wiggling. Zero space for 'maybe.'

Jumana's head stooped until the image of Firas's tiny fingers resting on her heaving chest was the only thing in her field of blurred vision, her head heating up a few degrees. Dreading rejection was one thing but hearing it vocalized was quite another. One felt like the edge of a sharp knife merely brushing against her throat, and the other like a blade sawing deep through her flesh.

Firas massaged her breast with his tiny hands. Decades ago, his order brother Hadi would do the same when he nursed.

They were much alike, her two boys, addicted to the boob, unlike her girl who had practically weaned herself after starting solids.

Jumana tried hard to expel Hadi from her thoughts but her eldest son was the reason she could get down on all fours and kiss someone's feet for a job if it meant she would get it. His life hung in the balance, which meant dignity was not a luxury she could afford to flaunt.

In the last year, her heart had ceased to respond to most everything as it focused on one singeing emotion—the rage of a mother at risk of losing her child.

"Your experience is unquestionable, but your Iraqi credentials fail to meet our minimum qualifications," the male doctor continued, then raised his eyes to assess the damage.

"I came to your country as a refugee seeking shelter and protection. Aren't there any special considerations for my status?"

He turned to his three colleagues, challenging any of them to respond. They continued to nod their heads with their lips tight, not in the least bit vested in this encounter, all three visibly bored and eager to get it over and done with. To them, Jumana was just another file number they needed to process to get on with the rest of their day. To get back to their smooth-sailing lives, which didn't include the sight of a desperate Iraqi refugee impinging on their conscience.

The male doctor sighed and pressed on.

"I know what a terrible dilemma this is. I really do. It's one faced by all new immigrants, not just you, Ms. Rawy," he said, removing his glasses and biting on the tip of the frame temple.

He sounded repugnant, like he wanted to vent a blanket critique of the racial biases bubbling in his country.

A few renegade tears escaped her eyes but she wasn't quite ready to wipe them yet. "I thought I had performed well during the first interview. Isn't that why you called me back?"

The male doctor locked eyes with her briefly. It seemed he was silently echoing her sentiment. *Why the hell did we bring this lady in if we weren't going to hire her?*

"We were moved by your passion and commitment and thought we owed it to you to convey our decision in person. Out of respect and appreciation," the young, white female doctor spoke for the first time, but devoid of any palatable empathy. Empty words that meant nothing to anyone.

How very thoughtful of you.

"Doctor," Jumana said, directing her attention back to the man, now it was clear he was her sole benefactor. "I am willing to do absolutely anything. I don't have to be on the maternity ward. In fact, I don't even have to be a nurse. I'll wipe vomit off the floor, handle the biohazards, clean the geriatrics, you name it—"

Jumana paused briefly to determine how far she had burrowed through to the stone hearts of the three women listening to her desperate pleas. She had barely managed to scratch the surface.

"Give me the worst job at the ward, sir. I will get down on the floor and kiss your feet if it means you and your colleagues would reconsider your decision, I beg of you—"

"This is really unnecessary," he cut her off but still with no malice in his voice, like he wanted to protect her from the other people in the room, or perhaps from herself.

"We can provide you with valuable advice on how to navigate the local system. How to move forward and stand on your feet in this country."

"My only option is a salaried job, immediately," she whispered, struggling to keep back the waterfall welling in her eyes.

"You should consider going back to nursing school in Stockholm. There are certain scholarships for immigrants you can apply for. We'd be more than happy to write you any number of recommendation letters to boost your chances. We would, of course, reference your almost-successful application here, which is no small achievement."

Almost successful. The story of my life.

Jumana finally wiped her tears.

"I heard you've made exceptions in the past and allowed immigrant nurses to work while they qualified," she managed to counter with a quiver in her voice, despite a thick lump lodged in her throat.

That took all four of them by surprise.

They exchanged glances as if a murky secret they shared had somehow gotten out, and they were trying to determine who among them had squealed.

A long and awkward silence elapsed before the group huddled and muttered in monophonic Swedish for a bit. The women sounded livid, the man appeared indignant and Jumana didn't understand a fucking word. Not one.

Her Swedish was primitive. *Rinkebysvenska* was the derogatory term the white Swedes referred to her brand of the language, emanating from Rinkeby, the low-income and immigrant-infested neighborhood where she lived.

The most senior person on the panel, the black woman, eventually turned to address Jumana.

"We've only made some exceptions in the past, two or three at the most. In each of these cases the candidates had a perfect command of Swedish," she said as she started stuffing her documents in a dossier, implying the meeting was in its dying minutes.

"I am learning the language as fast as I can—"

"That's excellent!" the man screeched, then turned to face his peers like a child who had stumbled upon an adult-proof excuse to take back to his parents, hoping to justify precisely what they said he couldn't do.

"I am fluent in English and Arabic is my mother tongue. I also have a good grasp of Kurdish. I've trained alongside the British Royal Army Medical Corps in Iraq, working with some of the best physicians and nurses. Qualifications are what they are, but experience and other language skills must account for something, right?"

Cold silence emanated from the panel and slapped Jumana in the face. Her only cheerleader shrugged with helplessness now setting in his expression. He had seemed genuinely keen to help her but it was clear now he was castrated of any real firepower. Still, she soldiered on.

"Sweden is a multicultural society. I am certain many of your patients are also immigrants from all over the world. You need someone like me around who can speak their language and understand their needs."

"That's correct," he said, nodding repeatedly like an industrious woodpecker, hammering in search of hope.

"Doesn't that count for anything?"

The woman boss snapped back sharply, perhaps down to her last patience bar with Jumana.

"There's a huge line of other qualified people with similar or better skills. Don't waste everyone's time applying for jobs like this without qualifying first. That's what we're trying to tell you if you only stop and listen—"

The male doctor's eyes widened and he coughed a few times as if the deepest stab was yet to come.

"I also counsel you to be perfectly honest on your future applications. To be perfectly honest about your proficiency in Swedish. You said you had—" she paused to glance at Jumana's application, "…a working knowledge of our language. That's a rather exaggerated claim, wouldn't you say? Especially considering we had to conduct the entire interview in English for your benefit, and we continue to do so now at our second meeting, four weeks later."

Jumana snapped, she didn't know if the woman's unfiltered arrogance had triggered it or something else. All she could see was Hadi's severed head lying on the sand hemorrhaging as the heartless Baghdad sun baked down on it. The last seconds of his life feeling nothing but terror vibrating through his every cell. Not a warm smile or a gentle touch to bid him farewell from this world. His mother, father and two siblings thousands of miles away living in an affluent, safe cocoon, which his death had helped subsidize.

No parents must ever outlive their child.

She shot up to her feet, unlatched Firas and put him back in his stroller.

"Do any of you have children?" she howled, raising the stakes as far up as they could go.

Either the question was inappropriate or her elevated voice betrayed Jumana's intention to hold back nothing, but the minute she spoke, all three women started shuffling away like school bullies dispersing far from the scene of their crime.

"Don't walk away from me!" she screamed with a voice she didn't know she possessed. It curdled her own blood.

All the while she was glancing at Firas and back at her audience. He could sleep through even louder fighting matches between her and Gaber, but all it would take to wake him up was for her to do what she'd been avoiding all along. To break down in tears.

"You think I need this job so I can afford a new iPhone for my daughter? Or to buy better quality, hypoallergenic diapers for this baby? This job is a matter of life or death for my family. My eldest son will perish in Iraq if I don't get this job. Now do you understand?"

That didn't even solicit a pause.

The three women continued out of the door.

"Don't turn your back on me like I'm some insane woman under a bridge scrapping for pennies!"

The male doctor was the only remaining person seated at the table and seemed in shock at how quickly things had spiraled out of control. One minute it was a civil professional meeting between employers and a potential employee. The other, all hell broke loose and it was down to the most basic of human instincts and emotions.

"Look at you! You make me ashamed of being a woman," Jumana said, speaking to the back of the Mediterranean woman who was the last to leave.

"Someone must have extended a helping hand for you to get to where you are today. Why have you forgotten that? Why can't you do the same for me? Give me the one chance I am so desperate for—"

Jumana couldn't keep it inside any longer. She exploded

in acrid tears and collapsed on the floor wailing. Right on cue, Firas woke up screaming his lungs out, competing for airplay with his devastated mother.

The worst thing about an imminent death is how you and your loved ones die a little bit every day. No matter how many breaths you have left, knowing the expiration date robs everyone of the sweetness of life.

Death becomes your only constant and you exist by its arcane rules and under its dark mercy. You are no longer vested in life or able to enjoy its delicious smorgasbord of experiences, emotions and pleasures. Even the very slim chance you may be able to avoid this death is more cruel than comforting. On the one hand you want to believe in a happy ending but on the other, any light of hope you allow in stands the risk of scorching you if death does transpire.

These were the thoughts swimming wild through Jumana's mind as she sat on a lone bench at the Kronoberg park, a few blocks away from the hospital after her aspirations to get a job there had been dashed.

That was a total disaster.

The doctor she had thought was Greek or Turkish was in fact an Arab, most certainly a Jordanian judging by her accent.

When Jumana had broken down in tears with Firas screaming in the background, the Jordanian rushed back in the room, not to comfort her as Jumana had initially thought, but to chastise her for being an embarrassment to all Arabs. She threatened to call security if Jumana didn't leave immediately. Like pouring vinegar on an open wound is what it felt like.

Quietly, Jumana fed Firas lunch under the canopy of

giant trees. Cardamom-perfumed basmati rice and a mashed stew of peas, carrots and tender lamb. He was a smiley, low-maintenance baby, but he couldn't have come at a worst time of her life. Firas popped out a few months after a thirty-hour drive from Milan to Stockholm completed their horrific trek to escape Iraq.

With every successive child she and Gaber had, their fortunes and quality of life as a family plummeted to more treacherous depths.

Their eldest son Hadi was born in '89, well before Saddam's ruinous campaign in Kuwait. Still he had enjoyed a relatively uneventful childhood. Next up, their daughter Badreya arrived a few years shy of the fall of Iraq's tyrant. The civil hell that ensued in Baghdad had shaded her character darker. She was more fragile than Hadi, an emotionally complicated child. Despite that, Badreya was tethered to a homeland, no matter how chaotic, and for the most part had enjoyed a semblance of a normal life. In between the US smart bombs and the terrorist IEDs, life chugged along in Baghdad, interspersed with lulls of normalcy.

But what future lies for this sack of flesh here?

All over Rinkeby, young immigrant children born in Stockholm like Firas were caught in a warp, like cultural zombies. Stuck between the mores of the old worlds their parents had escaped, which these children could hardly relate to, and a new country that only pays lip service to fully embracing them, like a fake-faced stepmother. Unless you hail from money or prove to be brilliant in some capacity, you will always be an outsider in Sweden if your blood is not certified Nordic.

It didn't help her maternal conscience that the only thing

Jumana could give Firas was sustenance and basic care. Her heart and mind were back in Baghdad with Hadi. Not because she loved Firas or Badreya any less, but because Hadi was the one who needed her most.

Jumana had once asked her mother if she had a particular preference for any of her five children. Her answer had caught Jumana off guard and it was only in the last year that she had finally understood what it meant.

Yes, her mother told her, she did harbor certain preferences: she loved the young until they grew up, the sick until they healed and the travelers until they came back home.

Like her mother, Jumana was obsessed with her eldest son, convinced that whether he lives or dies rested entirely on her tired shoulders.

It's true. A future death kills you every day and plunders your ability to love and live. We might as well all be dead. God help you, my child.

A few hours after midday and the park was abandoned. Adults were at work being productive and children were at school being children. Jumana preferred it this desolate.

Although her skin was fair and she didn't stand out as particularly Middle Eastern, her generous curves and ample breasts made her somewhat noticeable in a city of skinny women. Most immigrants in Stockholm had a certain aura about them, she felt. Some invisible field hovering above their heads singling them out as anomalies and attracting undue attention, even if for fleeting seconds.

Exactly like the woman dressed in a black tunic with a veil covering her head, approaching Jumana. Pushing a twin pram, there was something tentative about the way she moved that screamed 'fresh arrival.' And that distinctive energy field around her shared by all immigrants, like she wasn't certain she was welcome to this party.

They exchanged smiles and a silent communication transpired between them, conveying more than words could ever achieve. Theirs was a mutual affinity made possible by the profound experience of being transposed from your roots.

Who knows what misery she's hiding inside, too?

A short while after the woman had vanished to a mere black dot in the horizon, a figure of a man in a business suit appeared in the opposite direction. When he approached closer, there was something familiar about him, too. His silver hair.

Kristian Nielsen stood a few feet away from Jumana biting his lips, with the guilty face of someone who had just run over a small animal. The compassion he had conveyed at the hospital seemed more organic now in the absence of his three female colleagues.

After a short silence, he clasped his hands to his lips apologetically and said, "I tried. I really tried."

Jumana wanted to smile but couldn't get herself to do it. There was an infinite supply of rage and bitterness at the very tip of her soul. She saw a rare opportunity to vent her anger at the unfairness of the systematic odds stacked against her in this country. An irrational part of her soul perceived the man standing before her as a mere symbol of every single rejection she had been handed down.

"You were right," he continued. "We could have made an exception for you, but they chose to play by the rules. I wish I knew why and I could tell you. I wish I was able to change their minds, but—"

"Doctor Nielson..."

"Call me Kristian, please."

He pointed to the empty space on the bench next to her, requesting permission to join her.

Jumana nodded and even though there was ample space, she shifted to the very edge of the bench until there was an honorable distance separating them.

Across the employer-job seeker divide, Kristian had seemed like a god who up until a few hours ago yielded infinite power over her entire universe. Sitting beside him now on a park bench like they were neighbors or work colleagues was bordering on surreal.

He sat close enough for her to actually notice what he looked like. Kind features, she thought, reflecting his character and disposition. Not the sort of handsome that would distract attention on the street, but he possessed an interesting, masculine look, which in the right hands could muster a small but hysterical fan base. Nothing about him suggested he had problems with the fairer sex.

His gray-blue eyes were his most captivating asset. Like an opaque gateway protecting him from the world peering inside his soul to find out exactly what sort of mettle he possessed.

Kristian wasn't nearly as old as she had previously thought. His silver hair was misleading from afar. Studying his face and eyes up close suggested his hair had lost its tint prematurely. Early fifties was her revised guess of his age.

Jumana was a big believer in signs. Perhaps there was some cosmic logic for them to cross paths again. The only one she could think of was a chance for her to repay his kindness by absolving him of the guilt he was clearly harboring. The anger she wanted to vent would not serve a purpose directed at him.

She began preparing a little speech in her head about how everything happens for a good reason, and although she was devastated she didn't get the job, she couldn't hold him personally responsible. It felt more true now that the wounded animal inside of her had scurried elsewhere.

Before she could articulate anything meaningful, Firas interrupted their shared silence with a spontaneous smile flashed at Kristian, the sort of tenderness only a pure, yet-to-be-corrupted soul is able to muster.

"Well hello, good man," Kristian beamed, reciprocating the warmth and reaching out to tug at Firas's tiny, extended fingers.

"You know, I've delivered thousands of babies," Kristian said, turning to look at Jumana, who had cracked an involuntary smile. "But I honestly have no idea what it's like to go back home with one of these. I hear things, of course, from friends and family. Exhausting I would imagine?"

"You're not married?" Jumana's eyes lasered to his ringless left hand, instantly regretting her impertinence. A wave of self-consciousness made her ears tingle.

He smiled as if he had seen it coming.

"I was once for a few years. She never wanted kids. Until she left me for another man. Now I hear she has two or three."

An awkward silence ensued at the unexpected intimate twist in the conversation.

"And you?" she asked.

"Never got around to it. You need to be with someone to have children. I am a bit old-fashioned like that."

Another chunk of silence ensued, but a little less awkward. Whatever disjointed thoughts of magnanimous forgiveness she had started to weave had now escaped her mind. Instead, she focused hard on what comes after the 'I was married, then divorced, and now childless' conversation with a man you hardly know?

Like any woman, a part of Jumana was innately curious why a perfectly good male specimen remained single. In another life, and if she was in a different frame of mind and was better acquainted with him, her matchmaking instinct would have churned up at least ten women she could have set him up with.

Then it struck her. This was her very first encounter as an equal partner in a conversation with a white Swede. At least not one dictated by a transactional need. Every other interaction in the past had been with people who wielded some kind of authority over her and her family.

From the immigration officials who processed their asylum application, to the school officials who enrolled Badreya, all the way to the string of landlords from whom they rented one dreadful apartment after the other.

On each of these occasions, she and Gaber would automatically assume the passive role of the fragile newcomers. It wasn't conscious or a cynical attempt to solicit sympathy, but just the survivalist mind-set of anyone uprooted from their home trying to keep up with a difficult language and entirely alien customs.

"What happened to your son in Baghdad?" Kristian said, finally breaking the silence. It seemed like he was giving her the chance to reciprocate some candor.

Firas was spitting rice away and giggling with his lips shuttered to ensure no more food was allowed in. He seemed besotted by Kristian and was putting on his cutest performance for his benefit.

Jumana's husband was a wonderful father, but these days he

was hardly ever at home as he worked to the bone to keep them afloat. She wondered if Firas's interest in Kristian reflected his hunger for a male figure in his life.

There was something about Kristian that made her feel at ease in his orbit. Still, she didn't know him well enough to divulge her innermost demons. Her allusions to Hadi a few hours ago at the hospital were nothing but an impulsive Hail Mary in a moment of desperation. Now with her faculties restored, Hadi's predicament was not a cheap social currency she could circulate every time someone asked.

"Sorry to pry. You don't need to tell me." Kristian must have inferred her reluctance.

He reached out and took the plastic food container and the spoon from Jumana to try his hand at feeding Firas. Sweet, spontaneous and unexpected.

He tilted his head away from the baby then suddenly looked back and meowed like a cat. Firas found this tentatively amusing and let out a monosyllabic chuckle. His thick eyebrows sprung up as he eyed the Swedish doctor with provisional intrigue.

Kristian played peekaboo a few times with Firas, punctuated with different farm animal sounds. Her baby son laughed louder each time and kicked his legs and waved his hands in excitement. When his mouth was open, Kristian introduced the few remaining spoonfuls, with an affection not typically ascribed to a man who's never fathered a child.

"Have you considered looking for another less regulated job?" Kristian said out of nowhere.

"Everything in Sweden is regulated, Dr. Nielsen," Jumana responded, as she handed him a wet wipe to clean Firas's blotched face.

"I have no problem working as a maid or a caretaker for the elderly, if that's what you're suggesting."

Kristian didn't confirm or deny this, but continued to listen.

"Even these jobs require the right paperwork," she continued. "Yes, before you say it, I know you can do it in the black market, but then the pay is dismal and the conditions potentially dangerous for a woman. I need to save twenty-thousand dollars within eleven months. That's about one-hundred-and-thirty-thousand krona by March next year."

Kristian nodded and then looked up to the sky as he massaged his chin.

"I don't know how to put this, but I would really like to help you."

"Thank you," she said. There was no point deluding herself this in any way meant there was still hope she could get a well-paying job at the hospital. But she was grateful for the sentiment.

The Swede seemed suddenly flustered and started coughing nervously as he looked in the opposite direction.

"Are you okay?" she said as she handed him a small bottle of water.

"That's very kind of you," he said. He slid his sunglasses from the crown of his head back on his face, then up again. Then down again, before springing to his feet unexpectedly. He pulled out a card from his jacket pocket and gave it to her.

"This has my private numbers and e-mail address. If all the doors are slammed shut in your face and you have no other option, come to me. But let me be your very last resort."

With these cryptic parting words, he touched Firas on the head and walked away, never once looking back.

The walk from the Rinkeby T-ban station to her apartment block on Sörbyplan was seven minutes tops and usually obstacle-free.

When she emerged from the station, it was dark out and the streets had thinned. An invisible hand clutched at her heart. This was the latest she'd ever been out on her own without Gaber.

After leaving the park, she had walked with no particular purpose for hours until Firas fell asleep. Her sense of time was distorted and she was dreading coming back home to Gaber and Badreya's expectant eyes, only to crush their hopes.

Rinkeby offered the most affordable housing across the city and was close to Badreya's school and Gaber's work at the butchery. But ever since they moved here, Jumana and her family had been all too aware what a dismal urban trash can they had ended up in.

Just a few months before they arrived, a young Bosnian college student was walking home from the station late one night when she was accosted by two men, dragged into an abandoned temporary construction shack, and raped with little mercy for more than two hours. Mugging, car jacking and home invasion were not uncommon either.

The authorities never said it at the risk of being accused of racism or ethnic generalization, but the citizens of Rinkeby knew it was the gangs of disenfranchised and oversexed North African men who were responsible for most of the neighborhood's well-earned reputation.

Most crimes went unreported to the police out of fear of even worse reprisals. Not to mention that the authorities generally didn't lift a hand anyway when the immigrants in Rinkeby chose to inflict misery upon one another.

She and Gaber had developed a strict routine to ensure their safety. Gaber would drop Badreya to school and pick her up every day. If Jumana was ever out on her own or with Firas, she had to be back home well before sundown. This was the first time she had broken that rule.

As she stood by the relative safety of the station, Jumana contemplated calling Gaber to come and get them. Then she thought of Badreya who was probably in bed by now. He couldn't leave her alone at home.

She glanced quickly at her cellphone but found no missed calls from her husband. That's unlike him, she thought. Despite the sense of doom brewing stronger in her chest, she had no other option but to risk it, vowing if she made it back in one piece she would never again be so stupid.

The few commuters who had exited the station with her had all disappeared by the time she hooked a left on Rinkebystråket. More like a ravine, she loathed this part of the street even in broad daylight. It was uphill and lacked a conventional sidewalk. Just pathways lining the buildings with a footbridge to connect both sides. At least being close to the low-rise apartment blocks would allow her to scream for help, and be heard. Then again, the danger she feared could very well be lurking within the buildings themselves.

It would take less than a minute for an assailant to drag her inside a ground floor apartment and have his way with her, with her infant son as witness.

Her stomach tightened and her pulse raced. The nurse in her recognized the effects of the adrenaline flooding her system. Cortisol would kick in a few minutes later, because things were just about to get worse.

When she had penetrated deep in the residential part of the street, never before had such complete silence haunted her. Still, she kept her momentum and moved forward. Then, as if monsters only materialize to those who dread them most, a long shadow fluttered behind her, but with no discernible footsteps.

Someone was trailing her and they were treading lightly to avoid detection.

Only her shallow breath and drumming heart resonating through her head were audible now. Her face was cold, almost paralyzed, with pins and needles prickling from her neck to her scalp.

She clasped her phone tight in one hand and detested herself for failing to remember the emergency number in Sweden. All she could think of was 911 imprinted on her consciousness from all the American films she had seen. There was no point trying to remember the damned number or berate herself for the lapse. She toggled frantically to Gaber's number instead with her finger prepared to fire if things got gruesome quickly.

Right before the Bredbygången intersection, the surface became flat again and she came across a bus stop on the corner.

The shadow was still trailing her.

Jumana's legs refused to propel her further, like they had developed a fearful heart of their own.

She stopped under the canopy of the bus stop.

Firas was still fast asleep, protected in his cocoon from the fear slowly infusing nausea in Jumana's gut.

At the corner of her eye, she spied a shadow approaching,

a towering figure of a man in a red hoodie walking diagonally across the street towards her.

Slow, purposeful moves of someone who knew what they were doing and relishing in a ritual.

The faces of all the rape victims she had treated in Baghdad came back to haunt her. No two were the same.

The one thing they had all seemed to agree upon with searing conviction was how their attackers had fed off their fear. The more visibly terrified they had been, the more their rapists were intoxicated by the pleasure of the hunt.

Be brave and fight with every last calorie of energy within you, they had told her, as if foreshadowing a day when she too would come under the body of a man about to take her against her will.

After it's done, it's the memory of having resisted to the very end that kept them sane, and in some rare cases, putting up a fight to the death had helped them escape.

"Did I scare you?" the figure approaching said.

The voice was familiar but the face still indiscernible behind the hoodie, bathed in the faint salmon hue of the street lights.

"Who are you?" Jumana asked, her sweaty finger microns away from squeezing the call button, and her lungs fully prepared to scream for dear life.

To be continued.